The Dark Warrior
The Heart of Seras: Book Four

Joe Evener

Dedication

I want to dedicate this book to all of those who have supported me and encouraged me over the years, and led me to where I am today. Bronwen, thanks for always being the loving, supporting, and caring wife you are, and for that person I can always count on.

Five are the Elders with their gifts born in the black of night.
Five are the Elders' gifts hidden to set Seras right.
Five Elders pitted beneath an angry sun.
Blood will flow. Flesh and blade become one.
The blood is given to ease time;
The breath known to free men's minds;
The bones to merge distance and space;
The body a destined warrior, the Solia Custor, out of place,
forged in battle with one true oath –
protect Tolth's final gift, the Heart of Seras, our final hope.
~ Ancient Seras Prophecy

Chapter One
Earth - Julie

"Julie, please!" The words Mr. Campbell said rang through Julie's head.

She had just seen her mentor, her teacher, her friend change into a monster, the one from her dreams five years ago. That was the same night her dad's car almost ran over the naked man who appeared out of nowhere. *Now it makes sense. The naked man was Mr. Campbell when he first came to Earth, and I dreamed of that monster because he was...no, he is the monster who killed a priest. Oh my God!*

She had to leave Allon to catch her breath. The thought of screaming at the top of her lungs pierced her soul. When she exited the portal, she couldn't contain herself any longer. "No-o-o-o-o-o!" she wailed into the darkness of Mr. Campbell's basement.

Julie stormed up the stairs, she didn't pause to acknowledge Shakespeare, Marcus's pet cat.

Tears streamed down her face all the way home. She sat in her car, the Purple Jellybean, in her parents' driveway trying to compose herself. Then the last words the immortal, Redderick Bobo, said came back to her. "I am saying, the reason Ostram let Marcus kill him was because he saw you in his eyes, not the demon." What did that mean? Was Julie a demon too? Did Ostram see Julie through Marcus's eyes? How was that even possible? Julie left Seras in a panic.

Julie walked up her front porch. She paused. The door reminded her of the first time Mr. Campbell...Marcus came to her home to have dinner with her and her family. The house welcomed her with its warm patterns of blue and brown in the main living room. She removed her shoes at the door and shuffled down the dark wooden hallway to the kitchen. She brushed her hand across the table. He had sat there and loved her mother's meatloaf. *What the hell?* She opened the refrigerator and took out the pitcher of her mom's ice tea and poured a glass. She gulped down the first glass; it cooled her throat, then poured a second. "Mom, Dad, I'm home!"

"We're upstairs," her mother, Michelle, yelled.

Julie moved to the staircase, and used the thin wooden banister as a crutch to make her way up to her room. "I'm going to my room." The last thing she wanted to do was see her parents.

"Wait, come here," her mother requested before Julie could escape.

Her mother, Michelle, had her brown hair pulled up into a bun. With her hair pulled in a bun, her brown eyes, skin tone, and round face Julie looked so much like her mother. She was sitting on the edge of the bed going through a box of papers.

Her father, Phillip, was lying in bed with a laptop opened. He had his glasses resting atop his thinning blond hair, rubbing his tired eyes. He looked up. "Hi sweetie."

"What are you two doing?" Julie asked.

"Your father is paying bills," Michelle said. He grumped. "I'm organizing my genealogy files. I think I'm going to write a book about…our ancestors."

"You mean me, don't you?" Her voice was tense.

Her father peered at her with a knowing agitation.

"Well, I think it's interesting. Besides, the ladies at the library said it would make a fascinating read. The first girl born in several generations…that's a gold mine."

"Seriously?" Julie exhaled deeply. "I don't want to be a gold mine. I want to be left alone." She spun around, storming away from her parents' room, leaving them stunned and confused in her wake. She slammed her bedroom door and collapsed on her bed no longer able to fight back the tears.

Julie was unsure how much time had passed before she heard the faint sound of soft rapping on her door. She slowly opened her eyes, taken back by the darkness that had surrounded her. Another slightly louder knock was followed by her father's whisper, "Hey."

"Thank goodness it wasn't mom," she thought. "Yeah?"

"Hey sport, can I come in?" her father asked, while cracking the door just enough to be heard.

Julie sighed. "Sure."

Phillip Ayers opened the door to enter. He flipped on the lights. The brightness made Julie squint as she adjusted to the brightness. "Can I sit down?"

Julie nodded and slid up to a sitting position. Her father sat on the edge of the bed. The mattress sank slightly.

"Listen, you have to understand your mother. She doesn't want you to be mad at her, she's proud of you, and she wants to tell everyone how special you are."

"Dad!" Julie rubbed her eyes. Phillip brushed the tangled strands of hair from her face.

"I know. I get frustrated too, sometimes. But let her have this. She can research her family history, my family history, all the things she wants, and put it together. It won't change anything. It will just be the end of this hobby for her."

Julie pursed her lips. "Okay." She sighed. "I just hate being a hobby or a project."

He patted her leg. "I know." He got up. "The faster she writes the book, the faster everything gets back to normal." He walked across the room to leave. "Lights on or off?"

"Off." She fell back into her bed.

He flipped the switch off. "Good night."

"Good night, Dad."

"Love you."

"Love you too."

He closed the door, and in the quiet of the night Julie sobbed into her pillow. How could her day have been any worse, Marcus…no, Mr. Campbell was a demon. *"I killed a person for the second time…even though he wasn't really a human,"* she argued with herself. *"And I did it to keep from dying. Does that make it better?"* Her mother wanting to make her unusual birth circumstance into a book was just an annoyance.

~ * ~

3

The alarm woke her up. "No, no, no!" she screamed. "I'm not ready for another day!"

She pounded the alarm button on her phone, and sat up. Her eyes were nearly matted shut from the tears the night before. *I should take the day off. I really don't want to go to school today. And I really don't want to see him.*

Julie forced herself to stand and get ready for school. After a quick shower she pulled her hair back into a ponytail. It didn't take long to get ready. She slunk down the stairs, fortunate neither her mom nor dad were downstairs. Julie tried to cheer herself up by placing a piece of chocolate cake in a bowl, filled the bowl with cereal, poured milk on top, and ate her favorite breakfast creation.

A little more than an hour later she walked through the glass doors of Cedar Creek High School. "God, I don't want to be here," Julie said aloud to herself.

Her anxiety was worse than it had been after the story broke three months ago that the school's biology teacher and girls' basketball coach, Mr. Trotter, had tried to rape her in the coach's office after practice. She was fortunate all of her training with Mr. Campbell gave her the ability to fight him off, and Mr. Campbell had "sensed" something wrong with her and came to the rescue. Even four months after the fact, and through all the testimonies, Julie sometimes felt the eyes of the student population on her. It made her uncomfortable; the rumors, the side stares, the constant disbelief she hadn't played a bigger role in the attack, or even some thinking she may have deserved it. If that wasn't the most absurd thing she had heard. The idea of switching schools never crossed her mind. She would not let that man win a victory over her by chasing her out of the school she loved. Plus, Mr. Frye, along with the rest of the administration and the teaching staff had been so supportive. It helped bridge the pain of those who doubted her.

And, now I have to deal with Mr. Campbell. That's just great. Julie quietly made her way to her locker, put away her book bag, and got her binder and laptop out for the first two periods of the day.

Why did he have to be a teacher? She knew the answer to the question, of course. Marcus was sent from the dimension, Seras, to find her and train her to fight Queen Pallanex. He having this strange connection with her was alarming in its own way. It was how he tracked her to the school, and with the help of the Gifts of the Elders he became a teacher. *But it doesn't make sense. He is a demon, worse, he is a Skorei demon.* Everything she had heard about the Skorei was horrible. *They destroyed Callista's people. They destroyed Seren's people. They destroyed Jayna's people. All three of them loved him. Did they know? I'm so confused...*

"Hey Jules, what's up with the face?" Julie's best friend, Claire, interrupted her thoughts as she appeared in front of her in the hallway.

"Hey." She jerked in surprise.

"What's wrong?" Claire asked.

Claire Bennett was all smiles. Her brown hair was also pulled back in a ponytail. She was holding hands with her boyfriend, Jimmy Warner. Over the past three years Claire and Jimmy's relation had grown, making them the clichéd popular couple; football star dating the cheerleader/track star. Julie wasn't mad at their happiness, maybe just a bit jealous. *When was the last time I went out with a guy?*

"Nothing, just thinking." She forced a smile while giving Claire a hug.

"Hi," Jimmy said with a wave.

"Hi Jimmy." She hugged him, too.

Julie felt sorry for him in a way; whenever they were together, he became a third wheel.

"Did you have a good weekend?" Claire asked as the three friends began walking to their first class. "I tried calling, but you never answered."

Julie paused to think for a moment. "Eh, I got grounded. So, I had to just stay around the house. No phone. My parents played board games the whole time, and I stayed in my room and did homework."

"Grounded? What happened?" Claire asked as the bell to first period rang.

Julie's mind scrambled to find an answer to her lie. "My mother. She didn't like the way I reacted to the news she was writing a book about me."

Claire grimaced. "Got pretty bad, huh?"

"You have no idea what I've been through," Julie told her.

"We'll talk more at lunch," her friend said.

The two hugged again, then she and Jimmy walked away, still holding hands.

"I need a life."

Julie made her way through the monotony of her morning classes, all with the dread of seeing Mr. Campbell. Luckily that wouldn't happen until after the first three class periods and lunch.

Julie's morning classes were some of her favorites. First, she had Mrs. Larson for Math. Mrs. Larson, formerly Miss Slovarsky, made math fun. Something Julie had never experienced when she was in elementary and middle school. The students could always tell when the weather got nice just by the amount of freckles appearing on Mrs. Larson's face. The math teacher with long straight black hair and small frame was also the school's newspaper advisor. In class, Mrs. Larson had the students break into groups and work on video presentations to solve different equations.

Second period was Mr. Langston. He taught History, and was the Head Coach of the Track and Field teams. He had been trying for two and a half years to get Julie to run track for him. Mr. Langston was in his mid-fifties with silver hair, mustache, and glasses. He reminded Julie of the actor Tom Hanks: likeable, non-threatening, and very good at what he does.

He took a drink of his sweet tea, or 'liquid candy' as he called it. "Good morning, Julie," he said. He pretended to look out the window. "Gorgeous day for running."

"I'm sure it is," she answered with a smile.

He patted his chest just above the emblazoned Ohio State symbol. *He almost always wore something Ohio State.* "Sure, would do this old ticker of mine some good to have you on the team. Mr. Schultz and your buddy, Claire, always tell me how fast you were in gym."

"We'll see," Julie said, and took her seat before he began teaching about China's Taiping Rebellion from 1850 to 1864.

Julie had Spanish class third period with Señor Vincent or

Professor Evil, as the students called him. Some even began calling him the "Spanish Nazi." Julie loved Spanish even though most of her friends had switched to French or German just to avoid the short, dark and seriously intimidating teacher. *"Buenos días estudiantes. Quiero que todos se pongan de pie y reciten Neruda's* la *quincuagésimo sexto soneto,"* Señor Vincent said loudly, clapping his hands to get their attention. *"Levántense, Levántense!"*

Julie joined when he had the students stand to recite the famous poem Soneto LVXI by Pablo Neruda; she emphasized the line *"te odio sin fin"* while thinking about Mr. Campbell. *I hate you without end.*

At lunch Julie sat with Claire. She ate her salad before digging into her Panini sandwich.

"So, what happened with your mom?" Claire asked.

Julie could always count on her best friend since second grade to get right to the point of a conversation.

Julie tried to remember what she had told Claire earlier. "Oh…so she has decided she wants to write a book about my life, and the fact that I'm the first girl in my dad's family line since, heck, I don't know, forever I guess," Julie said. "I got so mad at her I couldn't help myself. So, she grounded me."

"A book about your life? No offense, but that would be pretty boring. You don't even have a life," Claire said with a slight giggle.

"Ouch! In what universe isn't that offensive?" Julie grimaced, knowing her friend was teasing but also aware she was right in regards to her life on Earth.

"And you so need a life," Claire continued, dragging out the word so.

"I was just thinking the same thing," Julie responded.

Their lunch conversation was interrupted by Jimmy's arrival.

"Dude, where's Mr. C. today?" Jimmy asked as he sat down with Julie and Claire.

Julie looked over to the table where he normally sat with Mr. Langston and Mrs. Larson. The two teachers were eating with Mr. Schultz, who preferred being called Schultz, but Mr. Campbell was nowhere in the room.

"That's weird. He never misses school, does he?" Jimmy asked. He nabbed a French fry from his girlfriend's tray.

"Hey." Claire playfully slapped at him.

He winked.

Sure enough, as Julie and Claire entered Mr. Campbell's class the next period a substitute teacher was sitting at his desk. It looked weird having someone other than Mr. Campbell sitting in his chair.

The substitute teacher had the students take their seats. "Hello, I'm Mrs. Kim. I apologize for the lack of planning, but apparently an emergency kept Mr. Campbell from making lesson plans."

"I hope everything's okay," Claire said. "I would hate to have something happen to him."

"I'm sure your little crush is just fine," Julie answered.

Claire gave her a look. "Like you have any room to talk," she said.

"He's your crush, not mine," Julie argued.

The substitute teacher continued, "The only notes I could find were you learning about early Gothic literature. I found this online. Please hit the lights."

"Whatever gets you through the night," Claire said, then added, "Do you know what happened?"

"I have no idea," she answered with a shrug. *Good, I hope I don't have to deal with him... ever again.*

Chapter Two
Earth - Julie

A different substitute took over Mr. Campbell's duties in the classroom until a permanent one was found nearly a month after the strange disappearance of Mr. Campbell.

Julie felt great relief. She had no desire to see him and it seemed he was content with not seeing her. By then Julie began to feel normal, life was going on. She was forgetting the horror of seeing him as a monster.

By the end of the fifth week, she received a text in class from Claire which she had to hide from Mrs. Eisenstein, the biology teacher nicknamed Einstein or Frankenstein depending on the students' moods. Luckily the old, prudish woman walked around the classroom with her bouffant hairdo and angular face ignoring what Julie was doing. "Hey, why don't you come to the track meeting after school?"

Julie met Claire at their locker after school. "Are you going to come?" her friend asked.

"I might," she answered. Claire had tried the past two years to convince her to join the team along with Mr. Langston. "Basketball is over for me, so it wouldn't hurt."

She had also always been too busy with her frequent trips to Seras to commit to anything else and that was now over. *I can't say that aloud.*

Mr. Langston led the meeting and discussed the ins and outs of joining the track and field team. "An individual sport with team goals," he finished.

"So, what do you think?" Claire asked as the two stood up to leave.

"I think I'm going to put my name on the list," Julie answered.

Claire clapped. They stopped at the table, and signed their names on the yellow pad.

Mr. Langston couldn't stop grinning. "Well, well, well, Miss

Ayers. You don't know how happy this makes me." He turned his attention to Claire. "I knew between the two of us we would win her over."

"I know, right. I've been trying to convince her since seventh grade," Claire said, then looked at Julie. "You're going to love it."

"I hope so," Julie said.

She wasn't sure what she was getting herself into, but without ever wanting or, hopefully, needing to go to Seras again Julie should have time to do what she wanted.

Julie couldn't wait to go home and tell her parents. She gave Claire a hug. "I'll call you soon, okay."

"Okay."

Julie pulled into her driveway. The sun was out, but she was still surprised to see her father with his car out of the garage giving it a bath. *Ugh, I hate that car, but nothing is going to screw up my day.* She pulled next to the blue Chevy Nova Super Sport. The same car she was riding in when the sky crackled and a naked man, who she learned was Marcus Campbell, appeared out of nowhere. Julie also knew why he arrived naked, a big hindrance of traveling through the portal to and from Seras.

"Hey sweetie," her father called out.

His shirt was soaked from spraying the car. The car he liked to compare to Magnum P.I.'s Ferrari, Bo and Luke Duke's General Lee, or Sam and Dean Winchester's 1967 Chevy Impala, 'Baby.'

"What are you doing?"

"I wanted to get'er out and hose her off a little. I might take her out for a spin. You wanna ride with me?"

Julie knew how much the car meant to her father, sometimes in moments of pure weakness she wondered if it meant more to him than she did, which she knew it didn't. "Maybe later," she said faking a smile. "Guess what I did?" she asked, then answered before he could. "I joined the track team!"

"Jules, that's great! What made you decide that?"

"Mr. Langston has been trying for years, and Claire has been trying since we were in middle school. Now that I don't have basketball, I wanted to give it a try," she said while looking up at the basketball hoop her dad had attached above the garage. She had avoided coming out and shooting baskets since her 'incident' with Mr. Trotter. "I'm going to go tell the news to Mom." She bounded up the white railed porch and past the small brown porch swing. She slid off her shoes at the door and shuffled across the hardwood floors to the kitchen. "Hey, Mom!" She gave her mother a kiss on the cheek.

"Hi honey, why are you in such a good mood?" her mother asked.

Julie hadn't forgotten how angry she was with her mother deciding to write a book about her life, however, there was no sense arguing, just accept it. *Heck, I probably know more about it than she does thanks to Redderick Bobo.* She shuddered thinking about the immortal man on Seras, someone she hadn't thought about in over a week. "Guess what I did? I joined the track team."

"Really? Wow, that's surprising. Are you sure you're ready for another sport?" her mother asked.

"Yes, why?"

"Well, it's only been a few months since…you know?"

Julie knew full well what her mother was talking about, neither wanted to discuss it. "Yes, Mom. Mr. Langston is no Trotter. Everybody knew he was a perv, but nobody knew how bad it was. Track will be totally different."

"I hope so. Thank God Mr. Campbell was there in time, and saved you from that horrible man."

"Yeah," Julie said with apprehension, "thank goodness for him."

Her mother was right, Mr. Campbell did show up in time to rescue her from the psychotic science teacher and basketball coach, thanks to their strange connection. The same connection which led him to find her on Earth to begin with; and when she accidently got drunk drinking spiked punch and passed out at a New Year's party. She didn't want to think about him helping her, or their link to one another. "I'm going upstairs, I have homework."

Julie walked into her room. She looked around at all of the trophies, team pictures and individual poses from her years of playing anything from tee ball, soccer, and basketball when she was as young as young as five years old. All of the pictures of her playing sports had her wearing the number forty-four. The number helped convince Mr. Campbell she was the 'Heart.' "Time to clean this room up."

Her room was a wreck. Her clothes were scattered about, hair products on her make-up table, three different sizes of curling irons and two blow dryers. She got two boxes out of her closet and loaded all of the trophies and pictures in them. The clothes went into a laundry basket. She cleaned off her makeup table, dusted, and wiped down her entire room. Julie collapsed on the bed and began to cry. "Stop thinking about him. Stop!"

~ * ~

A week later, Julie dressed in the warmest clothes she could pack for the first day of track practice. "I can see my breath."

The seniors led the two-lap warm-up about a half hour after school. Afterward, the girls made a giant circle on the high jump apron for stretching and conditioning. Mr. Langston...Coach Langston walked around and spoke to all of the girls. He made it a point to say something to each of them, introducing himself to the freshmen girls he didn't know. "Hi, Julie. Are you ready for today?"

"I hope so," she said.

It was odd for her to not know her place. As a cheerleader she was an experienced upperclassman far from the timid freshman she was three years ago. Her basketball career was cut short, but she was confident in her ability outside thinking she wasn't going to make the team at first. In Seras she was the Savior, people looked up to her and respected her. Heck they worshipped her. Here she was starting all over.

After the team completed the required stretching, conditioning, and bounding drills they gathered around Coach Langston and sat on the track. "Hi ladies, welcome to the first day of track practice." He went on to remind them about physicals, the schedule, and pay-to-play, then had the groups' breakdown into their specializations. "Throwers, go throw, hurdlers go hurdle, sprinters go sprint, jumpers go jump, vaulters go vault, distance you're stuck with me." The girls separated to go with their event coaches.

"Coach Langston, where do you want me?" she asked standing alongside seven other new girls who did not know which events to try.

Coach Langston sent two of the girls to the jumps' coach to try high jump and long jump. He sent one girl to the hurdles, and two other girls to the sprint coach. He turned to Julie. "I want you and you," he pointed to Julie and the final girl, "you two I want you to go with the distance team." Then he gathered the distance runners, eleven girls in all. "Okay ladies, today we are going to run the 'Tour of Sunset'."

The experienced returners groaned.

"I know, I know, now get out of here." He waved his arm at them dismissively. "And don't lose the newbies," he shouted as they started to jog away.

"What's the 'Tour of Sunset'?" Julie asked Claire as the girls headed out of the stadium.

"It's pretty much running around the entire town of Sunset."

Julie's eyes grew big.

"It's only about a five-mile run. We do it about once a week," Claire explained. "Pretty sure he is making us do this to thin out the herd."

Julie gave a confused look. "Huh?"

"That's what he calls it when he gives us a workout to see who wants to stick with it, and who quits…thinning out the herd." The girls got to the road. "Do we want to go left or right?" Claire asked one of the seniors.

"I say left," a senior girl with fiery red hair said. "We can run across the bridge."

Julie looked left. She knew just around the bend was the small cement bridge which crosses over Cedar Creek; the same bridge Marcus first appeared to her almost four years ago. She hoped they didn't choose that route. "Can we go right?" she asked. "I really don't want to cross over the bridge. I mean, it has dead mice and all kinds of other dead things on it."

Her comment started to pay off. "Yuck, yes, let's go right," another one of the seniors agreed.

"We'll have to cross it to come back," the red head argued.

"True. Shoot," the other senior said. "I guess it doesn't matter."

They went left. No such luck for Julie.

The girls crossed over the bridge, much to Julie's chagrin. Flashbacks of Marcus's first appearance popped into her head. She did her best to squelch it. They traveled down the road, made a right into one of the older neighborhoods and continued through the town, past Fritz's garage where Marcus fought the Death walker named Rinna, until they arrived at the square in the middle of town. The brick lined streets made their foot strikes uneven. Even in the chilly temperature, the large fountain on the south lawn looked inviting. "I wish we could jump in the fountain," Julie said.

"Oh no, Coach Langston would kill us," Claire told her. "Besides, it's empty for winter."

"Oh yeah," Julie smiled.

They continued past the three competing pizza parlors, four insurance companies, endless antique shops and flea markets, the flower shop, the Sunset Grill, a tavern, two banks, a Chinese restaurant, and the local newspaper, 'The Sunset Gazette.'

The girls stopped at the square's white gazebo across from the police station to get a drink. Trees were lined every ten or fifteen meters across the plush green grass which gave the tired girls shade from the sun. The corner across from the gazebo was a veteran of war memorial. An American flag was centered between the flag of the state of Ohio and the flag that recognized Prisoners of War. A white marble slab listed the names of former residents lost to wars gone by.

"Come on, we need to get going," a girl said.

The group started running once more. Julie felt good about her decision to join the track team. They ran by the large colonial building which stood in the heart of the square. It once served as the town's public library until city council and the mayor, a friend of Julie's father, decided to build a new one. "We have one quick stop."

The girls stopped at Doyle's Hardware. "It's tradition," another girl said.

"What?" Julie asked.

"You'll see." Claire winked.

They walked into the store. Mr. Rupert Doyle was at the cash register. Julie remembered seeing him when she went with Marcus to get wood to make their fake swords. She remembered how good the owner, Rupert Doyle was to him, giving him a job, and giving him a place to live in an apartment over the warehouse. The co-worker, Sam, was stocking shelves. Both gave the girls serious looks. "What can I do for you, ladies?" Mr. Doyle asked.

"I think you know," a senior said.

"Of course, I do," Mr. Doyle's serious face turned to a smile. "I wouldn't have it any other way." He reached under his counter and pulled out a wicker basket of lollipops.

"Thank you, grandpa!" the senior said, giving him a hug.

"Love you, girl." He passed the basket to each of them. "I've been doing this since my daughter ran track. Any time you gals run by my store, you stop on in, and I'll take care of you."

After receiving their treats from Mr. Doyle, the girls headed back to the school. Julie couldn't help smiling. It was the first time since she entered the portal in Mr. Campbell's basement during her freshman year, she actually felt normal and felt as if she belonged.

Chapter Three
Earth - Marcus

Marcus sat in the quiet of his apartment, his head in his hands. It had been a month since he called in sick from school. He couldn't face Julie after what she had seen.

"How could I have been so stupid to show up like that in front of her? I've ruined everything," he had told the immortal Redderick Bobo thinking of what happened when he returned to Seras.

His plan was to sneak off to confront William and kill him, then find Pallanex and put an end to all of what has caused Julie so much pain. Redderick had caught up to him inside the stables and stopped him.

"You need to go after her, Marcus," Redderick Bobo had said.

"She won't listen. She now knows the truth about me. I am a monster." Marcus dropped his head in shame.

"No, you are not a monster. You only think you are a monster. You were raised as a warrior and you forgot who you were to become a monster. But I know that is not who you are," Redderick spoke in an almost fatherly manner.

"How do you know?"

"Because Ostram saw the goodness in you."

"There is no goodness in me."

"I disagree. I would say the Evandells you saved would say there is. I would say Griffus, Pertheus, and their men who you saved from Bellor would say there was. The Greagons would agree with me. And I know Julie would say there is once she gets past the fact you happen to have a demon side in which you have done very well to control."

"Julie will never forget this, or forgive me."

"Perhaps you are right, perhaps you are wrong, but my point remains. You have the qualities Tolth and Ostram wanted. Pallanex, or should I say Eryx, wanted William to find Ostram to become the Solia

Custor, but it would have never worked. Ostram would have never relinquished his power to William as easy as he did to you. William would have never been found worthy. And just imagine what he would have done to Earth and Julie when he got there? He would have killed her without a thought of remorse. You, my friend, are good. You are the one the Elders wanted. You were recognized at an early age as the one they wanted. Why do you think you do not bare the mark of the Skorei?"

Marcus reached absently to his right shoulder blade. A reminder of the emblazoned mark all Skorei warriors had branded on them except him.

"And the two of you are what the Elders waited for to fix their mistakes," Redderick said before Marcus could finish processing what he had said and knew. "Now, go back to Earth, and remind Julie of who you really are and why she should be here by your side."

Shakespeare jumped up next to him on the couch, begging to be petted, bring Marcus back to the present. "Okay, okay." He stroked the cat's pure white fur. The cat purred like a motor. He stood up, knocking Shakespeare from his lap. "I'll be back." Marcus grabbed his keys and headed out the door toward his car.

Fifteen minutes later, he pulled into the old Civil War cemetery less than a mile from Julie's house. It was where he parked whenever he wanted to make sure she was okay without her knowing it. He had parked there a dozen times over the past month, hiding in the woods behind her house.

During his visits, he had watched her play basketball with her father in the driveway. He could see she still loved the sport even though she no longer wanted to play on the school's team. The bastard, Trotter, stole that from her. When the weather was nice, she joined her parents on the back patio as they grilled out. Sometimes she joined them in playing a game of Yahtzee or challenged her father in a game of chess. Other times, he watched as she went out for long runs down her road. He wished he could watch her compete on the track team. But his decision not to go back to school to pretend to be a teacher was for the best. He grew tired of the lies. Every time he walked into the building, said hello to the staff and teachers, he was lying to himself and to her. She knew who he was now. She knew he wasn't a teacher. She knew she was the Heart of Tolth. She knew there was another dimension, Seras, and it was her duty to protect it from Pallanex who was becoming more powerful in her own right. Now, she knew he wasn't just a warrior from Seras charged with finding her, taking her back to Seras and training her. He wasn't just the Solia Custor. He was a demon, a Skorei demon. The kind of demon others had told her were the worst of the worst, and Marcus knew he wasn't just a Skorei demon. He was the leader of the Skorei, and it was his fault the people of Seras feared them because he ordered the deaths of their families and friends. Julie knew all that now, and him pretending to be a normal teacher was just another lie he could not put her through.

Marcus moved from the tree line behind her house. He could tell Julie was alone. He ventured closer. She was kneeling in her mother's flower bed planting flowers and moving mulch around the plants and bushes. She was singing along with the song playing on her phone.

"Julie," he whispered, hoping not to frighten her. Either she couldn't hear him or she was ignoring him. "Julie," he said a little louder. She still didn't acknowledge his presence. "Julie!"

She jumped, startled at first, then when she realized it was him standing there, she was obviously infuriated. "What are you doing here?" She hopped up with hand trowel in one hand and a garden fork in the other. She was ready to attack him.

"I had to come talk to you, and apologize," he started.

"Well, don't! Go away! I never want to see you again," she screamed.

"Julie, please let me explain," he begged, moving closer to her. She had dirt on her face, and sweat beaded on her forehead.

"No! Stay where you are. I don't want to hear any more of your lies. I don't want to hear anything from you. I don't want to see you," she said. She pointed the trowel at him, the garden fork reared back to claw him.

"Jul--" he leaned toward her.

"I said stop! Go away Marcus, I mean it!" She tensed up.

"Okay, I'm sorry. I'll go," he said, backing away. "I'm sorry, Julie."

"Shut up, shut up!"

Marcus continued to take steps away from her as tears began to stream down her cheeks. He stopped.

She sneered. "No!"

"I'm sorry." He backed away, then disappeared into the woods.

He left the crying girl with one thing on his mind.

Chapter Four
Earth - Julie

Two weeks later, Julie, Claire, and Jimmy sat in the lunch room. "I can't believe it's been two months since Mr. C has been gone," Jimmy commented as he watched the frumpy substitute teacher who took the teacher's place walking through the cafeteria.

"You really have no idea where he is?" Claire asked Julie between bites of her sandwich.

"No, I really don't. I haven't seen him or heard from him just as long as you," Julie answered, lying about their encounter during spring break.

"I thought you two were pretty close? I mean, he helped you in the weight room, and he went to your house for dinner and stuff," Claire continued.

"Yeah, and luckily, he was there to help you when Trotter tried to…well, you know?" Jimmy added.

"Yes, I know, I know we were close, and my parents had him over for dinner and all that, but I have no idea where he is, or why he left," Julie responded, desperate to make them stop. "Can we change the subject, now, please?" her voice raised slightly to make them stop.

"Yeah, sure, sorry," Jimmy said with a shrug. "I didn't mean anything by it."

"I know, I just don't want to think about Trotter," Julie said, hiding the truth from her friends. Though it was true she didn't want to think about Trotter and the night he tried to molest her. She often wondered what would have happened if she wasn't who she was, and if Mr. Campbell hadn't crashed the door in time to witness his attack and rescue her. Three other former students who were on the basketball team came forward eventually to accuse the perverted science teacher and basketball coach of assaulting them, a half dozen others testified that he

20

made advances toward them. Mr. Trotter got locked away for what should be the rest of his life. There was a tinge of sadness she felt for the basketball team and the players. After it happened, Julie no longer wanted to play on the team, and many other players quit. The girls who played didn't have the concentration to handle the distractions, and a team that should have been good suffered through a miserable season. "Please," Julie begged.

"Sure," Claire said giving her a hug. "No problem." Claire followed Julie's advice, and turned to Jimmy. "How did your research paper turn out?" she asked.

"I got an 'A' on it. She really liked my paper."

"What was it about?" Julie asked, guilty she probably should have known.

"It's about how schools should move foreign languages like Spanish to the elementary schools when our minds can retrain more, then learning them would be easier than it is in high school," Jimmy said with a big smile on his face.

"You just wrote that because you're terrible at Spanish," Julie joked. She and Claire laughed.

Jimmy shrugged and nodded in agreement. "You're not lying," he said with more laughter. "But, it's true. Think about it, if schools started teaching kids in kindergarten or first grade how to speak different languages, they would be able to speak, I don't know, four or five languages by the time they graduate high school," Jimmy explained. "My dad told me about one time when he was in youth group in church, and there was a foreign exchange student from Germany staying with a girl he dated before my mom, and she was helping another girl with her French homework. So, she was speaking at least three languages: English, German, and French, and probably more as a junior in high school," he said, then asked Julie, "What did you get on your paper?"

"An 'A,' duh," Julie said.

She was relieved that the three of them could have conversations that did not involve Mr. Campbell.

"She liked your paper, too?" Jimmy asked, mildly shocked. "Its title was way too long."

"What's not to like? 'The Fallacy of the Single Sport High School Athlete' has a nice little ring to it." Julie took a drink. "Plus, it was really well written." She smiled.

"If you say so yourself," Claire added with a joke.

"Exactly," Julie bobbed her head, and winked at her best friend. "Well, it's true. I'm sick of all these so-called coaches forcing their athletes to only do their sport year-round. I mean, come on! Research has proven it's not good for athletes; colleges are looking for well-rounded athletes, meaning ones that play more than one sport, and it just became a thing for these club sponsors to make a lot of money."

"Don't look at me. I agree with you," Jimmy said. "I think club sports and private coaching is stupid."

"Good. Plus, they used to play two, three sports clear through the nineties. If they could do it, I know we can."

"I do. I play football and run track," Jimmy added.

"I know. I'm not talking about you. It doesn't seem to affect boys as much as girls. Soccer and volleyball particularly. Those coaches are the worst. Look at the girls here who play those two sports…how many of them do anything else?" Julie waited for one of her friends to answer, when they didn't, she added. "None."

The bell to signal the end of the lunch period chimed.

"I'm pretty sure Coach Langston is rubbing off on you," Claire said.

"Yeah, or his head would explode with excitement if you let him read your paper," Jimmy said.

"I might do that." Julie smiled. She and Jimmy made their way to their Speech class. One of the few they didn't share with Claire, who headed to French class.

Their Speech teacher was the cranky Ms. Newman. She was widely known as one of the 'old bitties.' She disliked Halloween dress up day, Homecoming events, and anything that distracted the students from learning. Her room was decorated with posters from old plays and musicals. "Okay Miss Ayers, I hope you have your poem ready," Ms. Newman said.

"I do," Julie answered.

"Good, take your place at the lectern."

She slid out of her chair hesitantly, and stood behind the wooden stand. Ms. Newman would have a fit if she called it a podium. *A podium is what you stand on, a lectern is what you stand behind,* her teacher would constantly remind them. Julie cleared her throat. The part she hated most about Speech was indeed giving speeches, but reading poetry she wrote was even worse. Poetry was always so personal. Luckily, Mr. Campbell had her and the rest of his students in Freshmen English to read and recite poetry to prepare them for moments like these. She cleared her throat, took a deep breath to calm herself, and begun…

"The Easiest Lie" by Julie Ayers.
"The easiest lie might be
to say it's not important (when it is to me)
Or, I don't need him (but I do)
I don't love him (though it's true)
It wasn't my fault, whatever it was
I can't let go of the past because…
I would be happy if I only had
My life is the worst and it makes me sad
I could stop or start at any time
Everyone's life is better than mine
If only I had more (this list could be endless)
'It doesn't matter' is a worn-out mess
Saying 'I don't have a choice' isn't very wise
What we tell ourselves are the easiest lies."

Julie finished, the students applauded and she took her seat. She could feel the warmth radiating from her face. She was sure her cheeks were beet red.

"I'm impressed, Ms. Ayers. Make sure you fill out the exit slip and turn it in with the poem," Ms. Newman said. She made a few notes on her scorecard.

"I will."

"Hey, that was pretty good," Jimmy whispered. "Where did that come from?"

"I don't know. I was just playing around at home," she answered.

"Geesh, I wish mine was that good."

The next student was called up and Ms. Newman said, "Let's give Chris your undivided attention."

~ * ~

After school, Julie headed to track practice. Coach Langston read the line up for the first meet, "Tomorrow, you need to be here by four o'clock to warm up," he started. "The meet starts at five." He then began reading off the events. "In the four by eight hundred relay: Mel, Jess, Julie, and Claire." Julie was surprised to hear her name called.

"Jules, you made the relay team," Claire said, slapping Julie's leg as the girls sat cross legged on the black track listening to their coach.

"In the four by one, Mel, Jess, Julie, and Stephanie."

"You're not in that relay," Julie whispered.

"No, I'm in the open eight hundred. It's my best event. Well, that and the four-by-four relay."

Coach Langston read off other events, then listed the girls running in the last relay. The four by four hundred relay, he read, "Team one: Miranda, Jess, Julie, and Claire."

Claire clapped loudly. "Oh my gosh! We get to run together. You'll love the four by four, it's the best."

Julie left practice an hour later. She went straight home to tell her parents the exciting news.

"Mom, Dad!" Julie called through the living room.

"We're upstairs!" her parents yelled in unison. Julie hopped up the stairs three at a time. Her mom and dad were in their bedroom. Her father, Phillip, was sitting on the edge of their bed watching her mother, Michelle, brush her hair in the large mirror of the makeup desk Phillip's grandmother had given to her before she passed away ten years ago.

"Hi, honey," Phillip said. "How was your day?" he asked as Julie kissed him on the cheek.

She hugged her mother from behind, and Michelle patted her arm lovingly. "Hi, baby."

"My day was great. Got an A on my paper, got an A on my poem, track was hard but good. I made the starting lineup in three races."

"That's my girl," Phillip said. "What three?"

Julie listed off the three relays Coach Langston put her in, then she noticed passports on the bed in front of her father. "What's going on?"

"We're planning a trip," her mother said. "How would you like to go to London this summer?"

Julie paused for a second. *What about Marcus...wait, he's not here.* "Yes! Heck yes I want to go," she said. "When?"

"It's for Patrick's graduation, so I'm hoping right after school ends, say, early June," her mother answered. "Do you think you can get away?"

She nodded yes as fast as she could. *The hell with Marcus.* "That's a great graduation present."

"Great, I'll order the tickets in the morning, and make the itinerary."

Julie hugged her parents. "I can't believe I'm going to England!" She started out the door, then stopped. "Don't forget my meet starts at five tomorrow."

"You got it. Three events, huh?" her father asked.

"Wow, you're going to be busy," Michelle said.

"Yep." Julie smiled. "I'm going to do some homework and go to bed."

"Don't you want something to eat," Michelle asked, starting to get up from her little work space on the bed.

"Nah, I got something on the way home. I'm good."

"Okay, if you're sure," Michelle added.

"Yep." Julie turned to leave the room.

"Night, love you," both parents said simultaneously.

"Love you too," Julie answered back.

~ * ~

Julie stood on her mark on the track. "Is this where I stand?" she asked the official standing nearby with a stick with a yellow flag on one end and a white flag on the other.

25

She kept looking into the stands toward her mom and dad, but secretly hoping or at least expecting to see Marcus as she had during every home football game she cheered, and every home basketball she played. Julie's teammate came around the corner with the baton in her hand. She could tell how tired she was, two laps around the track at nearly full speed could take a lot out of a person. The other team's runner was right beside her.

"Okay Julie, just like we practiced," Coach Langston was yelling.

Claire stood beside him. She would have to run the next leg as the anchor. Coach Langston had put Julie third probably hoping the first two girls would have run strong enough legs of the relay race to give her a lead of some type to take the pressure off, no luck.

When the incoming runner made it to the mark about ten meters away, Julie took off as they did ten times the day before at practice. "One, two, three, turn and look," she said as she followed the tempo of receiving a handoff. She got the baton and started her eight-hundred-meter leg of the race. The first one hundred meters she went out hard like Coach Langston told her, then she settled into a rhythm. Julie passed by Claire after her first lap, Claire was screaming encouraging things like, "Great job! You're doing great! Keep it up!" Julie's legs were on fire, but she felt good.

"I can go faster," she said to herself. Julie started going faster.

Coach Langston was on the backstretch.

"Relax, relax, save it 'til the last turn," he screamed. Julie listened. She heard the girl breathing behind her. When the two girls got to the final curve Julie started picking up the pace. "Open your strides!" Her opponent tried to keep up. "Pump your arms! Pump your arms!" Coach Langston appeared again at the start of the home stretch. *He's a quick one.* She remembered him telling the girls at practice more than once that the faster they pump their arms the faster their legs move. Julie concentrated on her arms. Julie heard her father yelling from the stands. She could see Claire waiting for her, ready for their exchange. Julie hit her mark, Claire took off, and they completed the handoff. Two and half minutes later Claire crossed the finish line well ahead of the other team. The four girls on the relay team hugged each other.

Coach Langston came over to them and read off their splits. "Mel, 2:41; Jess, 2:45; Julie, 2:31; and Claire, you ran a 2:26. Great job ladies!" He left to coach the next event and check on the field events. The four teammates continued celebrating.

"Jules, you ran a 2:31 without knowing what you're doing. You're going to help the team a lot," Claire said as they walked to get their warm-up pants and tops.

"My legs feel like jelly," Julie said.

"Wait until after the four by four," Claire laughed.

~ * ~

Two hours later the team was meeting in the center of the field. Julie, Claire, and their four by four-hundred-meter relay team had just helped the team win their first meet of the year. Claire was right. Her legs felt even worse than before. "Four hundreds are brutal," she said after the race.

Claire smiled between gasps of air. "Told you." They hugged.

"You were great," Julie said.

"So were you," Claire answered.

"It hurt like crazy, but it was so much fun. I loved the way the team gathered and cheered us on the final curve," Julie said.

"I told you." Claire bent forward to stretch as Coach Langston gave them the score.

"For the girls, Littleton, sixty-seven; Cedar Creek, seventy." The girls cheered loudly. "Boys, Littleton, fifty-six; Cedar Creek, eighty-one." The boys erupted. "Great job both teams! Get a cheer and go home! See you tomorrow."

The two teams joined together, and the seniors led them. "One, two, three, Cedar Creek!"

Julie started walking to her parents who were waiting patiently at the fence by the finish line. "Honey, that was so exciting!" her mother exclaimed.

"You did great kiddo," her father said.

She gave both of them a tired hug.

"That was so much fun," she said. "I'm so tired."

"I bet. You ran a lot. You ran on all three winning relays," her father said.

"I'm so proud of you," her mother said.

"I was so scared, mom. If we would have lost that last race, we would have lost the meet. That's a lot of pressure."

Claire joined the little family.

"Claire, you did so good," Michelle said, hugging her.

"You're pretty fast, girl," Phillip added. He gave Claire a high five.

Jimmy joined his girlfriend, and gave her a nudge with his shoulder. "Not bad for a girl."

"This girl is going to kick your butt." Claire nudged him back.

Julie saw Claire look around. Her family wasn't there. They were never at any of her games, and now absent from track meets. Julie knew Claire would just make an excuse, but she could see how much it bothered her friend.

Coach Langston approached Julie and her family. He patted Claire on the back. "Claire, you did so great!" Claire smiled shyly. He shook hands with Julie's father. "Hi, I'm Norm Langston."

"Phillip Ayers," her father introduced himself. "This is my wife, Michelle."

Coach Langston shook her hand. "You've got quite a little runner here."

"She is full of surprises," Michelle said, rubbing Julie's back.

"I was impressed. I would really like to have her run at the invitational this weekend." He looked at Julie. "I hope you don't have any plans?"

Julie looked at her parents, then back to the coach. "Nope, I have nothing going on."

"Good. I think I might try you in an open race to see how you do," he said.

Julie smiled. "Sweet!"

"I'll see you at practice tomorrow." He shook her parents' hands again. "Very nice meeting you. I'm sure we will be seeing a lot of each other." With that, Coach Langston excused himself and went on to talk to his coaching staff.

Jimmy took Claire by the hand, and they excused themselves.

"Hey," Claire said, turning to Julie. "We always go to Sullivan's for pizza after a dual meet. You wanna join?"

Julie looked at her parents for their approval. Her mom and dad looked at each other and nodded yes. "Don't be too late," Phillip said.

She hugged them. "I won't. Thank you!"

She rushed to the locker room, grabbed her belongs, and ran to her car, Jellybean, as quick as she could. The town of Sunset had seven pizza places within a ten-mile radius. Sullivan's was a little place southeast of town. It used to be a one-story house in the middle of nowhere, but when Lewis Sullivan bought it thirty years ago, he had a vision of creating the best pizza for the folks who lived further out of Sunset. He succeeded. His pizza was often voted as the best in Sunset. Students liked to go there after sporting events because it was a way from the other more populated pizza places, and being a little further out in the country it was a great pit stop before heading to a bonfire or party in the peace of county living.

Most of the juniors and seniors on Cedar Creek's boys' and girls' track teams were there. Mr. Sullivan, Sully, an older gentleman in his late sixties or early seventies, was behind the counter taking orders from the students. His staff busy making pizzas, delivering drinks to the tables, and talking to the athletes, many who went to school with them. Mr. Sullivan's wife went by the nickname, Mama S. She walked around visiting the different tables of students and made sure everyone was having a wonderful time.

Julie sat with Claire, Jimmy, and a mix of girls and boys. They ordered two pizzas, seven orders of hot wings, subs, and water. "Coach Langston would kill us if we drank pop."

"True," Julie said. "Not sure pizza is on his list either."

"Oh gosh, no!" Claire laughed. "You'll get used to his little sayings, and his attacks on pop, junk food, and everything else."

"Spring break," Jimmy added.

"Yep, we heard that one already, and I think we even heard part of that in his class during my freshman year," Julie said. Mama S brought the food to their table.

"It never gets old," Jimmy laughed and shook his head.

The group at her table began, "Spring break is out of control. It was meant for the farming community, so the kids could help out during the planting season..." their voices trailed off into laughter. Coach Langston's tirade on spring breaks and the unnecessary social status of parents trying to outdo each other year after year has become legendary.

The team get together at Sullivan's was successful. Julie got back in Jellybean and headed home. In her heart she felt conflicted. There was something missing. Marcus wasn't there to celebrate her victory with. *I want to tell him so bad?*

~ * ~

The next morning Julie woke to the sounds of her mother and father scrambling downstairs. *They're in a good mood...and loud.* She got out of bed, pulled her hair into a ponytail, and threw on some clothes. Her parents were in the kitchen starting to make breakfast.

"What are you two doing?" she asked, rubbing her eyes.

"Hi honey, we just wanted surprise you with your favorite breakfast," Michelle said.

"Second favorite, I guess, outside of a bowl of cereal and cake," Phillip added with a playful grin. Julie couldn't argue. Her dad was right; a bowl of cereal poured over a piece of cake was her favorite breakfast. Phillip handed Michelle a skillet. "Do you want a little olive oil?"

"Yes, please," Michelle answered.

"Oh Popeye," her dad said in a high-pitched voice, placing his hands on his hips and striking a pose familiar to the old 1960s cartoon.

Both Julie and her mom looked at him. "Oh Dad, please don't."

"That was my impression of..."

"We know what it was," Michelle said, swatting at him with the spatula.

The three of them began to laugh. It was the first time Julie could remember laughing that hard in a long time.

Nine hours later she and the rest of the distance team returned to the school from their three-mile run at practice, they saw Mr. Frye talking to Mr. Langston…or Coach Langston as she had started calling him.

"Have you heard from Marcus?" the school's principal asked.

The two men moved away from earshot. That didn't stop Julie from snooping. She positioned herself around the corner, far enough not to be noticed, close enough to hear what they had to say, and pretended to stretch.

"I haven't heard from him, but we really don't talk outside of school," Coach Langston said.

"That's what Schultz and Amy said, too," Mr. Frye told him, mentioning Mr. Schultz the Gym teacher, and Amy Larson, Julie's math teacher and the school's newspaper advisor. "It seems that no one knows him very well."

"Are you worried?" Langston asked.

"Yes, he hasn't called the school in over a month. No one is answering the phone. I wanted to check with you before I called the police. Now I have no choice. I'll have the police stop by his place to check on him."

"I think that's a good idea. Probably the sooner the better," Langston said.

Oh no, no no, what if he's not there? I can't let the police see the stuff in the basement. The anger she felt about the lying and him being a demon changed to fear of the police finding out everything. *I can't let them find the Elder's mark.*

Julie rushed up to Coach Langston. "Hi Mr. Frye. Hey Coach, is practice over?"

"It sure is. Get outta here. Make sure you stretch a little before bed, ice anything that hurts, and drink lots of water."

"You got it."

She said her goodbyes before hurrying to her car, and rushed to Marcus' apartment. She knocked on the door with no answer. She called his cell phone, no answer. She walked to the small enclosed back patio. "What are you doing here?" she asked as she saw Shakespeare sitting on the six-foot wooden fence. The pure white cat meowed happily to see her. She noticed a large troth of water and an overturned bag of food sitting on the cement pavement by the door. "Where is he?" She checked the handle, it was unlocked. Julie took a deep breath. The white cat entered the doggy…cat door first as Julie opened the door.

"Mr. C!" she called out. "Mr. C! Marcus!" she yelled a little louder and with a hint of panic or was it anger.

The apartment was empty. She ran down the stairs to the basement. Her face plowed into the strands of a spider's web. "Yuck! I hate spiders!" She wiped the webbing from her face. The bag that held the gifts of the Elders was still resting on the wooden shelf. "*Everything is in place.*" Julie ran up the stairs and continued to the second floor. She had never been up there. His bedroom was untouched. Clean, except the dust that had settled throughout the apartment. The spare bedroom was completely empty. "I shouldn't be surprised. What would he put in there any way?" she said aloud.

Julie sat on the edge of his bed. "Wait a minute…" She went back to the basement. "That's what I thought. There's no clothes on the floor. Was he even planning on coming back? He had to." She pretended to talk to Shakespeare; it felt better than talking to herself. "He had to, right? He let you out. I'm so confused."

A knock on the door interrupted her lonely conversation. "What the heck?" Julie rushed upstairs to the living room, making sure to close the basement door. She looked through the peek hole, and saw a Sunset police officer standing on the front step. She paused, and rubbed her hands over her face.

"Hi," Julie said as she opened the door.

The officer looked surprised. There was another officer sitting in the car. "Hi, um, is this where Marcus Campbell lives?" He checked his notes.

"Yep!" Julie forced herself to sound peppy.

"Is he home?" the officer asked.

"No, I'm sorry, is there a problem?"

"No, we just got a report that he has been missing from his job."

"Oh, yes, I'm sorry, I told him to call, but he got a call from his…sister, family emergency. He must have forgotten."

"Okay, and you are?" the officer asked. He flipped his small notebook to a new page and began taking notes.

"Julie." Her voice shook. *"Get a grip, Julie."*

"Julie?" the officer wrote her name down, and waited for her to give him her last name.

"Oh, I'm sorry…Ayers."

"And what is your relationship to Mr. Campbell?"

"Relationship?" her nose wrinkled.

"How do you know him?" the officer explained.

"Oh, I'm one of his students. He asked me to…" Shakespeare slinked around her ankles. "Take care of his cat." She picked up Shakespeare.

"I see." He jotted down more information. "Do you know where his sister lives?"

"I'm sorry, I don't. He was in such a hurry. I'm sure he meant to call but probably forgot."

"I'm sure he did. Did he leave his contact information?" he asked.

"He did," her voice reached a higher pitch than intended. She gave the officer his cell phone number.

The officer tapped out the digits, and the phone rang. Then, they heard Mr. Campbell's phone chime.

Julie could feel her heart thumping in her chest. She followed the sound to the small kitchen, and retrieved it. "I told you he was in a hurry. I mean seriously, who leaves and forgets to take their phone?" She hid her hand deep in Shakespeare's fur to keep the officer from seeing it quiver.

The police officer looked skeptical. "Can I have your parents' names and contact information?"

"Sure." Julie gave him what he needed.

"Please wait here." He walked back to the squad car, and gave the information to his partner. The partner held up a radio and spoke into it.

The two men looked at her. Julie wondered if the incident with Mr. Trotter popped up on their screen. The officer returned to her with his partner. "Thank you, would you mind if we come in and look around?"

The request caught Julie off guard. "Uh, um, yeah, sure," she sputtered out not confident in what she should say. She stepped aside and let the officer step inside. He was short and stocky with cropped dark hair. The bulletproof vest he wore made his chest look like a barrel.

"Would you mind if we checked upstairs?" he asked. The second officer was a little taller, and a little thinner, but had the same short cropped hair. He went upstairs.

"Sure, go ahead."

The first officer walked through the living room into his kitchen and dining room. Three board games were stacked on the small dining room table.

"Does he play a lot of board games?" he asked.

Julie shrugged. "Yeah, I guess." She was trying hard to control her breathing along with her emotions.

"I used to play this game with my grandpa." He picked up Risk. "It lasts forever. Who does he play with?"

Julie knew she couldn't say herself. "Beats me. I'm just here to pick up his mail and feed his cat."

He hesitated at the basement door. "What's in here?"

"That's the basement." Luckily, she was relaxed about the upstairs question and it carried over about the basement, otherwise she would have panicked.

The officer must have been reading her reactions to his questions, and felt satisfied with her responses. He didn't bother opening the basement door. "Everything checks out, Miss Ayers. Well, if he checks in, please have him call the school. They are very worried about him."

"I sure will," she kept her cheerful façade. "I am too. I thought he would be back by now."

"Maybe you should try to call his sister," the officer said. "He needs to contact the school, and he shouldn't leave a kid in charge for this long." The officer nodded. He walked to the front door. "Have a good day."

"You too." Julie smiled.

She closed the door and put Shakespeare on the floor. She understood how they never found the man in the woods or the person who broke Jimmy's bedroom window with a rock when they were in middle school. After blowing out a deep breath, she whispered. "Okay, where is he?"

Chapter Five
Seras - Marcus

Marcus sat atop of a beautiful black stallion. He looked over the valley leading toward his destination. *"I'm coming for you, my friend,"* was his only thought. The same thought he had when he left Julie alone in her flower bed a month earlier. He spurred his horse forward. The sun was beginning to sink behind the tall, green highlands of the Lobello Mountains. He felt he had no choice but to leave the natural fortification of Allon with its lush forests, high mountainous ranges, rocky terraces and vast water crossings; the landscape of the northern mountains was breathtaking. He wished he had spent more time appreciating its beauty, but that was not to be.

After Julie saw him in his true, monstrous form when he battled the Skorei Malcolm to the death, he had little chance to explain the truth to her. She left him and headed back to Earth. She wouldn't talk to him. She would hardly look at him. He had no choice. The last time he walked away from her he whispered to himself, "I can't."

He went to his apartment. He couldn't blame Julie. He had been lying to her since the moment he met her. How could he explain to her that he was really a Skorei warrior? She had already heard the stories about how horrible they were and much of the evil things they…and he had done. He did the only thing that made sense. Marcus made sure the cat would be okay without him. Then he returned to Allon, picked the finest horse from the stable, and rode out of the fortress in the cover of darkness, making sure Redderick Bobo would not stop him this time, not telling anyone, not his friends or his sister goodbye. His plan was simple. *I must find William, and end this once and for all.*

The path he chose kept him out of sight from the outposts of Allon. It was going to take longer to travel, but he couldn't risk being spotted. *"This is my mission. No one else needs to get hurt, especially Julie. I have hurt her enough.*" He crossed a field of rolling hills. "Julie, I wish you could see the beauty of Seras." Their relationship was a tumultuous one to say the least. From the moment she stepped in his classroom, after he discovered the approximate age of the Heart was fourteen to fifteen years old, and used the Breath of Ostram to relieve Waldo Christian from his thoughts, to take his place as a high school teacher, she had something special about her; something that pulled the two together. Now he knew it was the connection between the Heart and the Solia Custor, Tolth's Savior of Seras, and the Protector of the Heart. He fought the idea that Julie was the Heart. It didn't make sense to have someone so young burdened with such a daunting task. He remembered the day she first asked him to help her in the weight room.

It was at the conclusion of one of his classes when Julie stopped by his desk as he was placing some papers into an old worn-out briefcase, he had found in Mr. Christian's house once he began taking care of the invalid man after the consequence of the Breath of Ostram nearly killed him. "Mr. C. can I ask you something," she had started, her voice and movements were strange to him but he learned it was her way of acting cute to get her way.

"Is it about class?" he answered giving her a look of to warn her it should be about school, knowing that it wasn't.

"No, but...it's not about the cafeteria thing...or, or the sword thingy, either."

"Okay?" he gave in, something he did a lot from that point forward.

"Well, I heard you talking to Schultz...Mr. Schultz about working out in the weight room after school and I was wondering if I could ask you a favor?"

"I'll try."

"I want you to help me," she announced quickly.

"Help you what?"

"Get stronger...in the weight room."

"Why would you want me to help you?"

She paused then gave a small sigh. "Because being short, nobody takes me seriously, and I need to get stronger for basketball season."

"I thought you were a cheerleader?" He remembered being confused about why she was a cheerleader and a basketball player.

"Oh, I am. I'm a cheerleader in the fall for football season, but I play basketball...or at least I want to in the winter," she had tried to explain.

She clarified that most guys didn't think girls belong in the weight room.

"Well, they're wrong. I know firsthand the strength of women," he had said thinking about Callista, Freya, Otta, Seren, and Alainas among others he had witnessed before surrendering to her. *"Okay, okay, I will."*

"Thank you, thank you, thank you," she chanted, hopping up and down in excitement.

Shortly after that interaction, and visits to Seras to talk to Freya, he had begun to get suspicious of Julie. *"There was something about her. A connection we shared."* So much so that he began following her. Once to a concert her father had taken her to with her best friend, Claire. They were easy to follow since her father was driving his blue Chevy Nova. He wasn't sure what to do, regardless, his plan was thwarted by the pouring rain and her father meeting them at the concert venue's front door. Marcus was again following them to her home, where he parked at the small cemetery plot from the 1800s, and walked the half mile through the woods behind her house to watch through the kitchen window as Julie and Claire made a late-night snack of ice cream. He knew he couldn't get close enough to her, so he waited until the day he finally had enough faith there was no doubt she was the one he was looking for, and she had gained enough trust in him to convince her to go with him to his apartment where he revealed his plan to take her through the portal to Seras.

He made camp for the night. There were ruins which made a perfect resting place. They were scars from ancient wars, relics unattended for decades, maybe centuries the once proud outpost laid in decay.

He rubbed his face, rough from the beard that had begun to grow. It had been a long time since he had spent so many nights out in the open, away from the comforts of his apartment on Earth or his cabin in Allon.

Once he made a campfire and caught a wondering rabbit, he cooked the small meal, conceding the food on Earth tasted better than here, then got settled down to fall asleep. He looked up at the stars overhead and remembered the words he was told were spoken on the night of his birth; his father had taken him into a field and held him up to the sky, *"You, Marcus, the first son born to Canis of Cauleta, were formed in the image of your father. You will be forged in the fire of battle. You will not fear man or death. Men will learn to fear your name."*

"Canis, if you are looking down on me, I'm sure this is not what you had planned for me."

Chapter Six
Earth - Julie

"Hey, whatchya drawing?" Claire asked, looking over Julie's shoulder. "What in the world is that thing?"

She was sitting in the cafeteria doing homework as she waited for the start of track practice.

Julie tried to cover up her paper. "Nothing." She stuffed it in the middle of a textbook and closed it quickly.

"Don't try to hide it, let me see," Claire said. She held out her hand and smirked.

"Okay." Julie got it out of the book. "It's stupid, just something I was doodling." She handed it to her best friend.

Claire took it and looked it over. "It's hideous...I mean, it's a good drawing, just a hideous picture. What is it?"

"Nothing," Julie protested. It was a picture of Marcus the way he looked as a Skorei demon.

"You know what? It reminds me of that dream you had a couple of years ago. Remember?"

"Yeah," Julie answered. *How did she remember that?* "I was just...how did you even remember that?"

"Because it was such a big deal for you...duh."

"What's duh?" Jimmy asked as he walked into the cafeteria.

"Julie's drawing," Claire said. She showed Jimmy.

"That's pretty out there, Jules."

"It reminds me of her dream," Claire repeated her earlier statement to her boyfriend.

"What dream?" he asked, sitting beside her, still looking at the picture.

"You know the one she had..."

"Okay, enough about me," Julie said. She reached for her picture.

"You're a pretty good artist," Jimmy said. "Did you purposely draw Mr. Campbell as a monster because you're so mad he's bailed?"

"What, I didn't draw Mr. Campbell?"

"Oh, my goodness, you did," Claire exclaimed. "I see it now."

"No, you don't, because I didn't draw him," Julie said. She starts packing her school bag. "It's time for practice." She caught Jimmy and Claire sharing a look. "I didn't," she said with a huff.

~ * ~

Julie was sitting legs crisscrossed on her bed, laptop opened, but she was busy staring at the drawing she made earlier. After track practice she had made her way to Mr. Christian's home. She took to visiting the old man shortly after she discovered Mr. Campbell wasn't coming back. She made sure he was doing okay. Julie had visited Mr. Christian several times with Mr. Campbell, so the former teacher was used to seeing her. Julie made his iced tea, and checked in with him a couple of times a week to make sure the nurses assigned to him were taking care of him. He sat in his rocking chair, mumbled a couple of things, then continued to look out the front window. Julie felt sorry for him knowing that Mr. Campbell did this to him all in his search to find her. She thought about how Mr. Campbell had poisoned the man's brain with his Breath of Ostram; and used it on Principal Frye, Mr. Doyle from the hardware store, a poor man named Lukas who died, Fritz the auto mechanic, and some lady named Claire. Those were just the ones she knew of, there were probably more. "He's a terrible person. He's a monster. Literally," she said aloud as she looked at the drawing. Her phone pinged.

"What ya doin'?" Claire texted.

"Sitting in my room doin' hw. Why?" she responded, hiding the picture as if Claire could see what she was doing over the phone.

Claire sent another message. "I just got asked about you."

"By who?"

"Alex...what should I tell him?"

Julie rubbed her eyes. "I don't know," she texted back.

Her phone rang. It was Claire.

"What's wrong with Alex, he's cute?"

"Yeah, but, I…"

"You've got to stop," Claire said. "I love you, but you have become a hermit. What's going on?"

"Nothing. I just don't have luck with dating, and the last time I went to a party I got drunk and had to lock myself in a bedroom to keep from getting molested…not to mention the whole Trotter thing," she explained.

"Okay, okay, I get it. You've been through a lot this year. I'm sorry. I just worry about you. Plus, you know prom's coming up. I want you to go with us."

"I will. Tell Alex sure, I'm interested. I need to get out of the house a little."

"Yay! Maybe we can catch a movie this weekend?"

"You already knew I was going to say yes, didn't you?"

"I'm not answering that. I'll see you tomorrow," Claire said. "Bye."

"Bye."

The two girls hung up. Julie picked up the picture of Marcus. "Damnit! Where are you?"

~ * ~

Julie entered Doyle's Hardware. "Hi Mr. Doyle." The old man was working behind the counter, wiping off a display case of odds and ends, and tools.

"Hey there, Julie, right?" He stopped what he was doing, and dusted off his hands.

"Yep." It was probably a bad thing she had been in the hardware store so often with her teammates that he knew her name. "Mr. Doyle, can I ask you something?

"I think you just did," he laughed, too hard for the comment. It turned into a cough.

Julie chuckled to appease the old man. "I did, didn't I?" she continued, "Have you seen Mr. Campbell?"

"Seen who? Mr. Campbell?" he asked, then paused. "Marcus? My, my, my, now I remember you." He stroked the black and gray stubbles on his wrinkly face. "You came in with Marcus quite a while back. I knew you looked familiar."

"Yep." Julie smiled. "He helped me build a history project," she told him.

It was a lie, of course, he had used the wood to fashion practice swords to train on Earth until he felt she was ready to advance to dull metal swords, then eventually the real ones. Which she preferred.

"Yes, that's right. Bought some wood, didn't ya?"

"Yes sir. Have you seen him?" she asked again.

"How'd ya do on your little project?" he asked. "That Marcus, he's a good one."

"I, um, I got an A on it." Julie shrugged. "Yes, yes he is." *I guess.* "He's missing, do you have any ideas where he would be?"

"Missing?" The old man rubbed the stubble on his chin. "That don't sound like Marcus."

"I'm sorry, I was just hoping, I guess, that he might have stopped in here," Julie said.

"Sorry, girl. I haven't seen him since he came in that day. I didn't know he was gone?"

"It's okay. He's been gone for a couple of months," Julie said.

"A couple months?" he rubbed his chin again. "That's not like him at all. He's not at work?"

"No."

"Have the police been called?"

"Yes sir, I talked to them once," she answered.

"Well, let me tell ya. If that boy ain't working, there must be something mighty important keeping him away. He never missed a day's work for me. Heck, he worked all day for me, then took classes at night I didn't know 'bout to become a teacher. He was bound and determined to be a teacher…like it was his destiny."

His destiny. I'm his destiny. He went to the school to find me. What can be more important than that? "Thank you, Mr. Doyle. I'm sure he's fine. Probably went to visit family and forgot to tell anyone."

Julie left the store more confused than when she went in. She rubbed her hands across her face. *Yes, I'm mad at him. Yes, he lied to me from the very start, and yes, he is a Skorei demon. They are the worst of the worst from what I've been told. But he did come for me, trained me, and comforted me when I needed him. He never did anything to make me feel afraid of him...well, except that whole creepy basement thing.*

She drove toward home. When she passed by the cemetery she slowed down, came to a complete stop, backed up, and pulled into the dirt parking spot in the cemetery Marcus had told her he left his car when he walked to her house. *Maybe he's injured in the woods. She knew it was a long shot. First, who could possibly hurt him? Second, his car was still in the driveway at his apartment...Wait, if his car is still in the driveway, he must still be in Seras. Here I am worrying like crazy, and he just gave up.* "Well screw you Marcus!" she screamed at the worn and dirty headstones. "I'm done worrying about you! I didn't want to worry about you anyway...you lied to me! You are a monster!" she collapsed against one of the graves. "You. Are. A. Monster!" Tears streaked her face, and her voice graveled. "You are a monster and a coward!" Julie wrapped her arms tight against her chest. "Where are you?" she sobbed.

Chapter Seven
Seras - Freya

"It has been too long," Freya said.

She stood in front of the council. Everyone was there except Marcus and Julie. Freya's clothing reflected her mood, instead of light colorful frocks and scarves, she wore dark hues with an angry red sash around her waist. She turned to Redderick. "Why hasn't he returned with her?"

"My dear Freya," Redderick Bobo sat as he spoke. "When the Heart left, she was in a state of shock. It will take some time to restore that trust back."

"I am afraid we are at a loss Lady Freya," Lord Marek, the elder of the Hawkmir tribe began. He used his cane, and the shoulder of his guide to stand. "Why did the Heart and the Solia Custor leave in the first place? What shocked her so much she fled Allon?" he asked. His voice was slow and shrill.

Lord Avery, Marek's guide, asked, "Where did they go?"

Freya looked around the room. She was at a loss. Argos, Griffus, and Pertheus returned her stare. They had purposely left the people of Hawkmir in the dark, knowing their hatred of the Skorei, which was deservingly so, as the Skorei under William, had destroyed a large portion of their people and Lord Marek lost most of his sight in battle.

"Lord Marek," Griffus started. "There is much we have not explained to you, as it may sound peculiar, but I assure you we have everything under control."

"Then you may begin to explain it to us," Lord Marek said. "We are not slow minded people, Lord Griffus. We understand there are powers at work beyond our knowledge. We just want to understand."

"What are you hiding?" the third representative of the Hawkmir, Lord Atrow asked. He was more demanding than the other two.

"Lord Atrow, know your place," Lord Avery, the taller, reddish-blond haired man admonished the shorter, thicker Lord Atrow. "We are guests here, and they deserve our respect."

"Lord Atrow is correct," Redderick said. The two men stopped their bickering and focused on him. "There are unexplainable events in place." Freya, Griffus, Argos, Otta, Seren, Pertheus, and Argos's two living sons, Julius and Jakob, looked at the immortal with held breath.

"Redderick, do you think it wise to bore them about things we have no control over?" Freya asked, trying to stop him.

"I think we have put it off too long. They deserve to know," he said, then finished, "everything."

"Lord Marek, Lord Avery, Lord Atrow." Freya nodded at the three. "Julie, the Heart, is from a place called Earth. On Earth she is just a normal girl. She lives with her parents, has normal friends, and goes to school," she paused briefly to explain, "school is a place where children learn. That is where Marcus found her. He pretended to be a teacher, one who helps children learn, teaches, at the school Julie attended. He had to convince her to trust him enough to bring her through the Elders' portal from Earth to Seras. The Bones of Azahleah help make the portal work." She stopped. Redderick nodded to urge her to continue. With the blessing of the immortal, she did. "You know of the five gifts of the Elders?"

"I do," Lord Marek said. "The Bones to merge distance and time."

"Yes, the Bones allow Marcus and Julie to move back and forth between Seras and Earth."

"I understand," Lord Marek said. "But why? Why would she want to leave here, she is the Heart?"

"She doesn't want to leave her family and friends as of yet. She is young, much younger than we knew, and Marcus did not feel it was right or time to rip her from her family. It had to be her choice."

"I see. Marcus is wise to believe this," Marek said. He patted his two companions on their legs. They agreed.

"Yes, Marcus is a good man. A special man. A man destined to be the Solia Custor."

"Yes, yes, go on," Marek said with a bit of impatience.

"The Gifts of the Elders were each dependent on themselves. The

Bones, the Breath, the Blood were objects to support finding and helping the Solia Custor and the Heart. The Heart is the gift Tolth hid from others, and only the Solia Custor could find it…her, and he did."

"What are you hiding?" Lord Atrow demanded again, standing in anger. "Get on with it. It sounds like you are hiding something."

"Lord Atrow, sit down," both Marek and Avery commanded.

"He is right. We hid the truth from the Heart, and we hid the truth from you. The Solia Custor, the gift given by Eryx, was never given at all. Eryx had no part in giving her the gift. The warrior the prophesy talks about, *the Body a destined warrior, the Solia Custor, out of place, is about Marcus, how he had to travel to Earth, a place we knew nothing about, and find her and bring Julie to us, Marcus had to be a creation of Eryx, so the remaining Elders without Eryx knowledge or permission forged a bound between Tolth's creation, the Heart, Julie, and a creation of Eryx, Marcus, a demon, a S--"*

"Skorei demon," Lord Marek finished. "Marcus is a cursed demon, one of the Skorei who destroyed our cities, and killed our people."

"Yes, Marcus has done a lot of bad things, but he was not part of that. He was in the north. And he has paid dearly for his mistakes," Griffus defended his old friend.

"That is absurd! How could the Elders have done such a thing?" Lord Avery screamed. "The Skorei killed our families, my mother, my father."

"The Elders made their mistakes, and they tried to fix them," Redderick Bobo stood up. "I was there. Freya explained it as well as she could." He bowed his head to her. "What she says is the truth. Marcus is a Skorei demon, cursed son of Canis. He is also blessed by the Elder Ostram as being the Solia Custor, and found worthy by none other than Bhjuda Heilshorn, my immortal brother. I pledge to you Marcus is the Solia Custor and despite his early faults, he is the man we need to defeat Eryx, Queen Pallanex, and his former friend, William." The room fell silent. "Now, it has been a long day. I say we let the Solia Custor do his job, and convince Julie, the Heart," he directed his comment to the Hawkmir men. "To come back to us as soon as he regains her trust, so we can get back to the plan of the Elders."

Chapter Eight
Earth - Julie

"Let me take a look at you," Julie's mother said.

She stood back to soak in the hair, the dress, the makeup, everything Julie fretted over the past two hours – prom night. It started a month ago when Claire and Jimmy kidnapped her. Claire had set Julie up a couple of times with Alex. They went to a movie. He liked superhero movies – one test passed. They went to Julie's favorite fast-food place to eat. He liked Cincinnati-styled chili – second test passed. He like Japanese food, he played baseball, got good grades, didn't do anything stupid like smoke, drink, or worse. All the boxes were checked. Julie couldn't find a reason to dump him or avoid him. He was a nice distraction from everything else going on. When Claire and Jimmy picked her up from her house, they had her put a blindfold over her eyes and drive her about ten minutes to the high school when she knew what was about to happen. Julie could tell where they were since she's made the drive from her house to the school nearly every day for three years.

They led her up the bleachers, when she took her blindfold off, Alex was standing on the track with members of the track team holding up two large signs.

You're attractive & this thought has been RUNNING through my mind...wanna RUN to PROM?

Julie acted thrilled; she didn't like prom proposals, but she kept her mouth shut and said, "Yes!"

Here she was dressed in a sequenced blue gown standing in front of her mom, dad, and Grandma Franklin.

Thirty minutes later, Julie, Alex, her date, Claire, Jimmy, other members of the girls' track team, their dates, and all of their parents were at a former industrial park now turned into a scenic park with walking trails, sculptures, and ruins of buildings turned into event spaces.

The girls greeted each other with lots of hugging.

"I've never seen you with make up on," one girl said. "You look so pretty."

"*Is that a compliment?*" Julie thought. She ignored the snarky comment; nothing was going to mess up the day, even if she was reluctant to go in the first place.

The girls took pictures with each other. The boys took pictures with each other. The girls took pictures with their dates. They moved from place-to-place changing positions, more pictures, and repeated from spiraling tower to the glass waterfall to the brick ruins.

After the pictures, Julie, Claire, Jimmy, and Alex jumped in a limo paid for by Alex's parents. Julie thought it was over the top, but she played along.

"This is so cool," she said. Julie and Claire giggled as they opened a couple bottles of water.

"Water?" Alex questioned. He opened a can of pop.

"We're in season," both girls said at the same time. Julie followed it up with a "duh!"

Jimmy reached for a pop, but Claire glared at him, and he grabbed a water.

"Looks like I'm outnumbered," Alex said. He took a sip.

"Well, if you hang around these two for a while, you'll see you get out numbered a lot," Jimmy said.

"We made it to the State meet yesterday, and so did you," Claire chided him. "You aren't going to waste a chance to win the state by drinking pop."

"Coach Langston would have your head if he saw you drinking a pop," Julie added.

"See what I mean?" Jimmy turned to Alex, and shrugged.

"I'm sorry I missed your races yesterday. Going to the state meet is a huge deal," Alex said, first to Julie, then to the other two. "When do you run next week?"

"Friday, and hopefully Saturday," Julie answered.

"Friday and Saturday," Claire corrected her. "We are going to make it to the finals."

Julie smiled warmly.

"And Jimmy will too."

The ride ended when the limo pulled up to the Italian restaurant in Columbus where Cedar Creek High School always held their prom. The driver pulled the long black car under the awning. Parents dressed in green and yellow tuxedo tee shirts opened the car door, letting the four students out. Two more parents opened the large wooden doors. They entered into the foyer with a beautiful fountain. Balloons in school colors floated in the pool. Students were already posing for pictures. Julie and her friends said "Hi" to Mr. Frye, Mrs. Larson, and other teachers who greeted them.

They walked through a second set of doors made up of glass framed by dark wood into the main dining room. The dining room had black and white marble tiles like a chessboard. The tables had white linen clothes, and an arrangement of flowers for center pieces.

"Everything is so pretty," Julie said. She saw a spot for a picture under the star shaped balloons with a banner, "The Stars in Our Eyes" the theme for the prom. She handed Alex her phone. "Here, take our picture," she said, as she and Claire posed under the sign.

"See, I told you," Jimmy said. "Wait, I bet that's the photographer." He pointed and waved to a woman with two cameras wrapped around her neck. The lady came over to them.

"Hold on, you girls look so cute together," she said. She snapped a couple of pictures, then shooed the boys into the picture for a couple more. "Now each couple." She took more photographs. A line formed behind them.

"Thank you," the group said, leaving to find their table. Each table sat eight around, Julie and Claire sat beside each other separating Jimmy and Alex. Two other girls and their dates sat with them.

"I'll have a sweet tea, please," Julie said.

The waiter dressed in light blue tops and dark blue pants filled the glass then served salads to the table. The dinner consisted of a choice between chicken parmesan, beef stroganoff, or a vegetarian meal with seasoned potatoes and crispy green beans. Julie had a piece of chocolate cake to finish.

The music started, and the dance floor filled quickly. Julie and

Claire grabbed their dates by their hands. "Come on." The two boys followed.

"*It feels good to be normal,*" Julie thought when the music slowed down.

She and Alex remained on the floor, as did Claire and Jimmy. She let herself relax and enjoyed the moment. Julie felt his breath on her face. She kissed him, he kissed her back. It was the first time she had kissed a boy in two years. Her heart pounded. Her cheeks flushed. "Normal," she whispered.

"Huh?" Alex said.

"Nothing, I'm sorry." She pulled back. "I'm so sorry." She left the dance floor, grabbed her things from the table, and hurried away from the banquet hall.

"Julie, is everything okay?" Mr. Frye said as she rushed by him.

"Yes, I forgot something at home, I have to go," she answered, pushing one of the big wooden doors open.

"How did you get here?" he asked.

"Shoot! I rode in the limo with Claire, Alex, and Jimmy." She stood in the entry way under the awning surrounded by parent chaperones. Claire, Jimmy, and Alex caught up with her as did Mrs. Larson and Coach Langston. Her eyes stung as tears began to stream down her face.

"What happened?" Claire asked Alex.

"Nothing, we just kissed," he said. His face was pale. "I swear I didn't do anything."

"He didn't," Julie forced out through deep breaths. "It's me, not him."

"Okay, honey, do you want me to call your parents?" Mrs. Larson asked.

"We've got this," Mr. Frye told Claire, Jimmy, and Alex. "Go back in and enjoy the rest of the evening." He ushered them back. "She's in good hands."

"You okay, kiddo?" Coach Langston asked.

"Yeah, I just freaked out a little bit," she said. She wiped her eyes.

"Do you want a water?" Coach Langston asked, reaching out a bottle to her.

"Thank you." Julie accepted the water, and took a drink. It felt good on her dry throat. "I think I'm okay. I'm sorry. I didn't mean to…"

"No, you're fine. You've had a quite a year," Mr. Frye said. "Are you sure you're, okay?"

"Yes." She nodded her head, and took another sip. "I'm much better now."

"Alright, I'm going to head back in. I hope I see you in there soon," Mr. Frye said. With that, he went back inside.

Coach Langston patted her on the head, and left Julie with Mrs. Larson.

"What happened?" Mrs. Larson asked.

"I don't know. One minute we were dancing, having great time, then we started slow dancing, and I felt good, I felt normal, and we kissed." Julie paused. "I felt normal for the first time in a long time. I felt like myself, then I freaked out." She took a drink to keep herself from crying again. "I don't know what happened. It just didn't feel right."

"You know, after all you have been through, the thing with Trotter, Mr. Campbell disappearing, you're allowed to freak out a little." Mrs. Larson rubbed her on the back.

"I know. I'm sorry. I feel like a drama queen," Julie said. She rubbed her eyes, and wiped her nose.

"You're not a drama queen. You've been through a lot. Give yourself a break."

"Okay, I'm okay. I'm gonna go back in and get cleaned up," Julie said.

"Are you sure? I can call your parents to come get you," Mrs. Larson said.

"No, I'm good. Thank you." Julie left Mrs. Larson, walked into the restaurant, and made her way to the restroom. It was crowded with girls fixing their makeup, so she hid in a stall until she could clean her face. Ten minutes later, she rejoined her table.

Claire stood up and gave her a hug.

Julie apologized to everyone. "I don't know what happened. Alex, I'm so sorry!"

"It's okay," Alex said. "I thought we were…"

"No, it was my fault. We were. I did. I wanted to," she struggled to explain.

"Hey, they've already crowned the king and queen, ya wanna head to the after prom?" Jimmy asked.

He gritted his teeth, obviously trying to break the tension. Claire and Alex gave him incredulous looks.

"No, he's right. I'm okay. I just had a panic attack. We should go," Julie said. "I didn't want to ruin the night. Let's go have some fun. We need it."

They left the prom, jumped in the limo, and headed to a nearby athletic complex where the school and parent chaperones had set up activities for students to enjoy themselves safely.

"What do you want to do first?" Claire asked. "We can swim, or play a few games, eat or just hang out and chill."

"I wanna get out of this dress," Julie said. "And, I'm starving." The girls separated from the boys to change.

"You're okay, right?" Claire asked as they got out of their prom dresses, and into their jeans and tee shirts they had packed, and brought with them for the night.

"Yeah, I don't know. When Alex kissed me, I didn't know what to do. I barely remember the last time I kissed someone, and I just got overwhelmed."

"You freaked us out."

"I know, I'm sorry." The two hugged, then joined the boys where parents were serving sub sandwiches, chips, and bottles of water and pop.

"Hi guys," Michelle Ayers said as she served her daughter and friends a plate. "How was prom?"

"It was good," Julie answered. Embarrassed her parents were among the chaperones, as were Jimmy's parents.

"Where's my parents?" Jimmy asked.

"I think they have pool duty right now, sweetheart," Michelle answered.

"Cool." They found a table for four and sat down. "I guess the pool is out until their shift is over," he whispered to his friends.

Claire sat quietly.

"We'll have to check when mine are there, too," Julie said.

"When we're where?" Michelle asked, bringing the table a large box of pizza and enough waters to go around.

"No where," Julie lied.

"So, you all have to come to the house on Tuesday," Michelle said. "We're having just a small party."

"Mom," Julie said.

"I know, I know," Michelle responded.

"Of course, we're going to be there, Mrs. Ayers. Your best friend only turns eighteen once," Claire said.

"It's nothing big, but we wanted to do something," Michelle added.

"Thank you, Mom," Julie said.

Michelle kissed her on the top of the head. "Love you."

"Love you, too."

The after-prom tradition was born several years ago to keep students from going out and having parties of their own with the potential of drinking and reckless behavior. The parent committee spent a lot of time and effort earning money to rent the facility, buy food, and pay for the activities and entertainment. A DJ played music while the students relaxed, ate, and joked around.

They spent the night playing games, sumo wrestling in giant inflatable suits, jumping onto a Velcro wall, pummeling, and swimming. The facility had an Olympic size pool, a hot tub, a steam room, and sauna.

"This is the way to relax," Alex said as they sat in the hot tub.

"I don't know about you guys, but I'm getting sleepy," Julie said. "What time is it?"

They looked around the room for a clock. "Six," Jimmy said.

"Yeah, it's about time to call it a night...or a day," Julie said.

"I think it ends at seven," Claire said. "Jimmy's parents are taking us home."

"Mine are taking me home," Julie said.

"I'm going to be in the limo by myself all the way home?" Alex asked, his voice trailed off in disappointment.

"Sorry pal." Jimmy said.

Julie started getting out of the hot tub. "Speaking of, I'm going to jump in the shower and get dressed." Claire joined her.

Minutes later they met up, Claire rested her head on Jimmy's shoulder as they sat listening to the DJ play his final songs.

Julie walked Alex out to the limo, the sun starting to rise making the sky light up with orange and blue colors. "I know I've said this a thousand times, but I'm so sorry about what happened earlier. It wasn't you. I really had a great time."

"I had a great time with you, too," he answered. "I hope we can do this again soon. I mean, not prom or anything, but maybe go out?"

"I would like that," she said. "Hopefully we can. You know how everything goes so fast? We have the state meet next week. In two weeks, school will be out, then summer break. I'm supposed to go to England with my family."

"I know, but I really like you," he said.

"I like you, too." Julie leaned in, closed her eyes, and kissed him. It was short. They were interrupted by the driver opening the door.

"Don't mind me," the man said, but it was too late. The moment was gone. Alex climbed in, the driver closed the door, and the limo pulled away.

Julie touched her lips, then started to wipe them off. "I can't go one night not wondering where you are," she said looking around hoping no one heard her or saw what she did. "I just wanted one night to be normal. What is wrong with me?"

~ * ~

The following weekend, Julie tried to steady her breathing as she lined up for the final of the four by four hundred relay. The heat of the late May sun beat down on her. It had already been a banner week and meet for her and the team. Five days ago, she celebrated her eighteenth birthday. A quiet event with just her family and friends. They wanted to save the real celebration for after the state track and field meet, and her parents wanted to save money for their trip to London. Neither bothered Julie. She and Alex kissed again. This time she didn't freak out. The day before, her team won the four by eight hundred relay and stood on top of the podium in front of a crowd of thirteen thousand. On top of that, Julie had made the finals of the four-hundred-meter dash, as did her four by four-hundred-meter relay team.

After the first dual meet, Coach Langston played around with the line up until he settled on having Julie run the four by eight-hundred-meter relay, the open four-hundred-meter dash, and the four by four-hundred-meter relay. It had worked well all season. Julie won most of the races she had been involved in, as had Claire in the eight-hundred-meter run; and their two relays were nearly unbeatable from the conference meet, through the district and regional meets, and here they were running in the state finals.

Julie placed third in the four-hundred-meter dash, though she thought she could have won if she would have run smarter. With twenty-four points, Cedar Creek was in the hunt for at least a second-place finish. If the team from Bannister High School fell below fourth place, and Julie and her teammates could win the last event of the day, Cedar Creek would win the state meet title.

Coach Langston put Julie in the second spot, and Claire as anchor. Kristy started in the blocks. She was the slowest of the four girls, but as a senior, she was the best coming out of blocks and didn't mind the pressure.

Julie rocked back and forth in a crouched position inside her handoff zone. *Breathe in, breathe out.* She listened to the gun go off. Kristy exploded from the blocks. Julie had less than a minute until she got the baton. She listened to the roar of the crowd. The four by four, as it's more popularly called, was the most exciting race on the track, buoyed by the fact it was the last race, and more often than not determined the winner of close meets. *Which team had the four best horses? We do!* Coach Langston would often say.

She could hear Coach Langston over all of the sea of people. His voice carried beyond thirteen thousand others, not to be drowned out. Julie knew her parents were in there somewhere. She knew Marcus was not. She suppressed those feelings, turn it into anger and focus.

She looked at Claire. Her friend was hopping up and down,

chomping at the bit to get her chance to run. Julie was happy Claire and Coach Langston convinced her to try track and field. *"This is way better than basketball,"* she thought.

Claire placed second in the eight-hundred-meter run. Julie was so proud of her friend. It had been a tough spring for Claire; her parents were filing for divorce, and Claire's mother admitted to already be dating again. But through it all, she stayed focused, and used her pain to create a season to remember. Julie could hope to do the same.

When Kristy came around the curve it was a tight race. Six teams got the baton practically at the same time.

Julie listened to Coach Langston screaming for her to run smart. After her final in the four-hundred-meter dash, he took her aside and told her to get out hard, but save some energy for the final one hundred. She stayed pace with the girls in the race, cut to the inside after passing the orange cones on the backstretch. Julie's team was right behind the team from Crawley, and she couldn't see the girl from Bannister. *I have to get in front, I have to get in front.* She pumped her arms as fast as she could, trying to remember everything her coach told her leading up to this race, and opened her stride.

She passed the team in front of her on the final turn in front of the stand. The crowd at Jesse Owens' Stadium roared as she lengthened the lead. Julie handed off to her friend Amy. Amy ran her best time, and the team only slipped from first back to third. She gave the baton to Claire, and the race was on.

Claire and the girls from Crawley and Bannister were in a three-way battle. Claire fell back at the two hundred mark, but made a surge with one hundred meters to go. She crossed the finish line in first. Julie and her teammates celebrated the big win, and the possibility of the team winning the entire meet. The foursome made their way to the top of the podium. Unfortunately, Bannister placed third, and it was just enough to edge the team out as state team champions.

A few minutes later they received the trophy for being state runner-ups for the meet. "The highest finish in Cedar Creek's history," according to Coach Langston.

Julie could see her parents and Coach Langston snapping pictures.

"I wonder?" she thought. She panned the stadium knowing it was a long shot with thirteen thousand people watching. "He's not here." She felt her chest tighten, and her throat closed. She wiped her eyes. Her coach, her teammates, and her parents probably thought they were tears of happiness, but she knew better.

Chapter Nine
Seras - Pallanex

Queen Pallanex stood on the deck of the *Sea Tiger*. The ship rocked softly through the waves, much less stressful than their initial voyage. Her trip across the Stormont Sea proved fruitful. Lord Moran had fulfilled his mission to supply her with more men. The men were in poor shape, but their condition was of no conscience. *"Soon they will be part of my army, my army to put an end to this world, and the other."*

"Is everything to your satisfaction, my Queen?" Captain Javan asked.

He stood with his hands behind his back, puffing out his chest in his dull, blood red suit, and chest plate with three circling sharks. He had two ribbons adorning his beard, and two more matching ribbons in his ponytail which tightened around his receding hairline.

"It is indeed, Lord Javan. I could not be more pleased." Queen Pallanex stroked his shoulder with her long fingers. Thin, gold rings wrapped the length of each of her fingers.

"Then, may I ask, what happened to Lord Moran?" Javan asked.

"I am afraid we will not be dealing with Lord Moran any further," she answered.

Queen Pallanex recalled the moments after she and Lord Moran shared their final drink together following the performance of the Prey of Vinkara, and Moran showing her the condition of the men he had obtained for her to take back. They were in dismal shape, skin and bones, starved and scarred from beatings. She had withdrawn to visit the neon green statue of Eryx when Moran entered the room. "I was hoping for something better," Pallanex had said, closing the door from the lord. "They will do, however, as my plan only needs bodies, no matter the condition. Have them loaded to my ships," she ordered, "then join me for a drink, my dear Lord Moran." Pallanex handed him a drink. He didn't

59

think twice about swallowing its contents. "I want to thank you, Lord Moran, for your services, and for being such a wonderful host. Your loyalty has not gone unnoticed; however, you are no longer needed."

Lord Moran began to protest, "My Queen," he choked and spit.

Blood appeared on his hand as he wiped his mouth. The rest of his words were unrecognizable as he slipped into paralysis.

"By now you have realized you will be dead before long. I was impressed with what you have done here, but I expected more and I now understand you are not the man to lead Karros. The city is in shambles and you pilfer all the goods for yourself. The men you have given me, and I am taking back with me, are of the lowest quality yet. I need to have someone in place that will do my bidding and restore Karros to its once brilliant standing."

Lord Moran stood silent. His body frozen. His eyes blood shot, welled with tears. Queen Pallanex called for guards. Two men barraged into the room, they were dressed in Karros's dark green colors with the sigil of Vinkara, a golden, open winged eagle on their chest. They stopped at the sight of Lord Moran. The men looked from him to Pallanex and back. "Moran is no longer Lord of Karros. Remove him from my sight and find a suitable place for him in the swamps."

The two did not move, their breathing was forced and hard. "I said, Go!" Pallanex ordered. "When you return a new Lord will be named. You will serve him as you served Moran, and serve me."

"Yes, my Queen," one of the guards finally said. He grabbed the other by the arm and they picked up Moran, and as they took him away Pallanex whispered in his ear.

"As your final act of service to me, please know you chose your replacement, or as you said 'you handpicked him yourself,'" she teased. Once they left the room, she called out for the actor who portrayed Moran in the play entered.

He looked at the stiff body of Moran being escorted out. "My Queen." He bowed. "I received your letter. I waited as you said until the guards entered, then left.

"Yes, Lord Madeus, come in. Your timing was perfect."

"My Queen, I am no lord," the actor said, obviously confused.

"I disagree. I saw how you presented yourself, and I must say, I was impressed." Pallanex moved gracefully around the man, her fingers grazing across his chest. "I have a gift for you, Lord Madeus." She walked to a chair and lifted a cloak with an open winged eagle, the sigil of Vinkara embroidered on its backside.

Madeus cocked his head. "My Queen?"

"I want you to take Moran's place. He was ineffective, and I need someone I can trust, and know will serve me well," she said. "I have laid out instructions for what I expect from you. I want you to be the new Lord of Karros, and bring Karros back to prominence." She placed the cloak on his back, and fastened the brooch around the front of his neck. "Can you do this for me, Lord Madeus?"

The young actor looked at Pallanex. "Oh yes, my Queen, I can do all that is required of me."

"Good," she cooed moving him to the edge of the bed. "Then let us begin."

Captain Javan stood quietly as Pallanex finished her story before asking, "My Queen, are you sure you can trust a young actor you have never met before now to do your bidding?"

"Oh yes, he will play his role, and once I finish dealing with Tolth's little whore, I will be in position to rule this world and beyond."

"Beyond, my Queen?"

"Yes, Seras is only the beginning."

Chapter Ten
Earth - Julie

Phillip Ayers stood on the steps of the large brick building on the square. The August sun was coming up. "Hey Jules, go get your mother, I think we're done," he said.

Julie stopped decorating. She and her family, along with a few others on the committee for the summer festival her dad created for the town of Sunset, Ohio, worked most of the night and returned to start again before dawn broke. "Okay."

She looked around. Her mother was wrapping streamers around the gazebo. Julie hopped from the ladder she was on and jogged to her mom. "Mom! Dad said we could stop," she called out.

"Almost finished," Michelle answered. She made a final staple to secure the colorful flags. They walked back to Phillip, who was talking to the helpers cleaning the lawn, sweeping the sidewalks and chalking lines for vendors to park their trailers.

"It looks great, Dad," Julie said.

"Thanks, sweetie." When her dad started the Coffee Festival three years ago, it wasn't well attended, and the town council came close to canceling the idea for the second year. Luckily, that year more people showed up and it became a highlight of the growing town. Now, year three, budget and expectations were at a high. Plus, the mayor and council convinced him a summer date and extended time would be better. It would take place the week before school began and last four days, Wednesday through Saturday.

"I think we're ready," Phil said. "Thank you for all your help."

Soon the streets would fill up with townspeople as the summertime festival got underway. The square became the focal point for games, bounce houses, food, and crafts. A giant stage was brought in for the performing bands and local soloists.

"Hey, do you mind if I go take a nap?" Julie asked her father. "I'll be back in plenty of time--"

"Go, go, you worked hard. I'll see you soon," Phillip said before she could finish. "Your mom and I are going to eat some breakfast at the Grill."

Julie kissed him on the cheek. "Thanks, love you!"

"Be back before they crown Miss Sunset," Michelle added.

Julie watched the two of them walk away hand in hand across the lawn to cross the street. Her heart melted seeing how much they loved each other. She headed to her car and took off toward home. Waking up so early to help her parents with the decorating was rewarding, but exhausting.

The Ayers had a busy summer. Shortly after school ended in late May, they took a two-week trip to England. First, they flew to New York, then to Iceland, before landing in London. The trip was everything Julie had thought it would be. They walked miles upon miles daily, taking in all of the sites. Her favorite was the Tower of London and the history that went along with it. It did remind her a little of Seras, but only in the idea of being medieval times. They watched Shakespeare's Hamlet at the Globe Theater. They walked across the top of the Tower Bridge, which she had mistaken as the London Bridge. They visited Westminster Abbey. Her mom did some research as they traveled across the countryside. Her dad wanted to visit Oxford to visit the burial site of his literary hero, J.R.R. Tolkien. Then they took the ten-hour train ride from Oxford to Edinburgh, Scotland where her mother took her advice about where Phillip's side of the family came from. Michelle had learned about the Royal Highlanders, and Duncan Ayre. While the family was in Scotland, Michelle learned the history of Duncan's father Malcolm; his grandfather, Connor; and great grandfather, Kontar. Julie hinted at Kontar's Roman name Arian, and Michelle found the rest about the Roman soldier who abandoned his position for the daughter of a sheepherder.

"This is so much fun," Michelle had exclaimed. And that satisfied her curiosity.

Michelle loved the romance of the story, and the history of Phillip being a descendant of a Roman soldier. She would never know Kontar's story of being born to Eshe, servant to a Roman commander who took her in after she claimed to have been impregnated by a mysterious figure at the bottom of a well…Tolth who named Eshe, the Sword Bearer for her role in carrying the male seed as part of Tolth's plan to create the Heart.

Michelle had everything she could have asked for, and couldn't wait to get back home and start on her book.

Once they returned home, Phillip began plans for the Coffee Festival. And that brought Julie to this point. Instead of driving all the way home, she drove to Mr. Campbell's apartment. "It's close, empty, and I'm too tired to go all the way home."

Julie texted Claire. "Hey, what are you doing? Wanna hang out?"

Claire responded, "I'm getting ready for the Miss Sunset announcement."

"That's right. I'll be cheering for you."

She opened the door to be greeted by Shakespeare. "Hello, my pretty boy." She got a glass of water, and went upstairs. "Still no sign of him, huh?" she asked the cat.

Julie laid down in his bed. The pillow and sheets smelled like him.

She slept. She slept too well. When she woke up the official announcement of the start of the festival was going to begin in a half hour. "Thank goodness I stayed here. I can make it back," she said, unsettling Shakespeare as she hopped out of bed.

She arrived in the center of town as her father took the stage. A large crowd had gathered and Julie squeezed her way through.

"Thank you all for coming," Phillip spoke into the microphone. "Thank you, Mayor Thomas, and council members. Thank you, Sunset for supporting this venture. I hope you all have a wonderful time!"

The audience clapped.

"Now, let me introduce a person I could not have done this without, my partner in crime, my wife, Michelle Ayers."

The audience clapped again.

Julie's mom took her place beside her dad. Michelle introduced Mayor Thomas once more. He had an envelope in his hand.

"It is my pleasure," Mayor Thomas began, "to announce this year's Miss Coffee Festival Queen. This year, we had seventy-five candidates enter applications based on grades, public service and outstanding contributions to Cedar Creek and Sunset. It is with great honor to introduce your new queen." He opened the envelope. Looked at the Ayers with a smile, and said, "Julie Ayers!"

Julie couldn't believe her ears. "What?"

The crowd awkwardly clapped as they parted to let her on stage. She moved slowly up the steps to the stage. The former queen gave her a hug, a crown, a sash, and bouquet of roses. Julie moved closer.

The mayor shook her hand. "Congratulations, young lady."

Her dad gave her a hug. "I'm so proud of you, honey," he said with a bit of hesitation.

Her mom gushed. "Oh, Julie, this is wonderful." She wrapped her arms around her daughter.

"Mom, I didn't apply."

"I know." Michelle pulled back. "I knew you wouldn't, so I did it for you." She hugged her daughter again. "I convinced the judges to let you enter, and gave them your resume."

She was completely caught off guard, wearing jeans and Cedar Creek Penguin tee shirt. She looked at the other girls on stage wearing beautiful gowns, Claire among them. Julie started to cry. "I'm so sorry," she mouthed to an astonished Claire as tears of frustration rolled down her cheeks.

Chapter Eleven
Seras - Marcus

Marcus wiped the rain from his eyes. The sudden deluge didn't help his travel. *I need to find a shelter quick.* The unfortunate combination of darkness and pouring rain left him and his horse wandering in unfamiliar territory. It didn't help the horse flinched and whinnied with every flash of lightning. "Easy girl, easy." He patted the horse's side. Its coat soaked, but it didn't matter, everything was wet and miserable.

With a crackle of lightning too close for comfort the horse took off in full gallop. Marcus strained to control the spooked animal. Low hanging branches ripped at his arms and face. He ducked and weaved to avoid being thrown. Marcus tried to spit out the gritty taste of mud caked around his mouth as it was kicked up from the racing horse.

The horse made an unexpected turn and slammed into a tree. A sharp pain pierced his leg as it was trapped between the two. Marcus pulled with all his might at the reins. The horse reared up, and he lost balance as did the horse. It stumbled, and its leg buckled from underneath. Both Marcus and the animal tumbled to the ground.

Marcus looked down at his leg. A large gash opened, revealing bone. Blood drenched his pant leg. The horse whimpered, and tried to stand. Marcus slid toward the frightened beast. He pulled himself closer with the help of the rein still wrapped around his hand. He started to remove the bridle. "There, there, girl. It's okay." The horse struggled, and pulled away, not wanting to give up the fight for life. "I know, I know. You did great. It's okay." The horse jerked and bucked on the ground, then with one final jolt it pulled itself up and away from Marcus, stretching his arm caught in the leather rein. As the horse began to collapse again, it toppled backward, losing its balance and sliding down an embankment. "No!" Marcus commanded to no avail. He clutched desperately, trying to keep the horse from falling over. He whipped around, grasping for his sword to cut himself free. "Damn it!"

He wrestled the sword free, and chopped the strap tethering him to the plummeting horse. Unfortunately, it was too late. Marcus couldn't regain his position, and began sliding down the muddy edge. The rain had made it impossible. He scrambled and clawed, but couldn't find a grip or footing to keep from falling.

Marcus watched as the edge he had just been on blur from his sight. He felt tree limbs crack under his weight, stabbing, poking, and shredding his body as he tumbled to the ground before everything went black.

~ * ~

Marcus heard sounds, muffled sounds. Was it an animal or man? He couldn't move. He didn't know how long he had been out. The rain had stopped and daylight had arrived, shafts of sunlight broke through the tree line causing him to squint. He tried again to move his arm. "No." He spit out thick mucus of his own blood mixed with the grit of caked mud. It made him cough, and everything hurt when his body convulsed.

"Look, I told you he was alive," a voice from just above him said.

"By the ghost of Canis," another voice said, "nobody can survive that kind of fall. Look at him. His body is mangled and broken."

"He just coughed. Dead men do not cough," the first man argued.

"Fine. We will take him. Throw him in the wagon with the rest," the second man said. "I am going to cut up this horse. No sense wasting good meat." Marcus could feel cloth being wrapped around his legs, torso, and arms.

"Are you sure he is alive?" a third man asked. Marcus could feel one of them drag their fingers across his face to pull mud from it. They picked him up and carried him a few feet. "Get out of the way you maggots!" the third man shouted. Marcus could hear the squeaking of a metal door and the grumblings of other voices.

"From what I know, he does not care what condition they are in," the second man said.

"I doubt he wants them dead," the third man joked. They tossed his body onto the wooden surface of the cart and slammed the door shut. "Go help Atan with the horse. I need to visit a tree."

Marcus lay still, unable to move. It was some comfort knowing he had feeling in his body. "I will heal soon enough," he thought, then groaned as someone either kicked him or hit him in the ribs.

"Great. Bad 'nuf we stuck in this wagon, now we got to share it with a corpse," a voice shouted, gruff and rougher than the three who found him and put him in the cart.

"He not dead. Look at 'im," another spoke. "He breathin'."

"They gonna eat that horse. I say we eat 'im," the gruff one said.

"With no fire?" the second one questioned. His voice sounded young, almost innocent. "I not gonna eat no meat without cookin' it."

"I not see no fire in this cart, do you?"

"Both of you stop that nonsense," a new voice called out. "Nobody eatin' nobody in this cart. We all stuck here together."

"Thank you," Marcus mumbled.

He heard the sound of shuffling.

"See, he alive. He said somethin'." The sensible voice said. "Now leave 'im alone, and let me rest."

The wagon creaked and jarred. The driver must have hit every rut in the road. Without the fear of being eaten, Marcus could rest and let his body continue its healing process. There was no doubt every bone was broken, and the wrappings must have closed the wounds enough to let them fuse together again. It was going to take a while for him to be at full strength. "How much time do I have," he wondered.

The ride came to a stop for the night. The three men took the others in the wagon with Marcus out one at a time to relieve themselves. Once everyone had their turn, they tossed in chunks of meat for them to fight over. It ended when the smartest of the group stopped the arguing and had the meat divided equally. Then they would sleep until the break of daylight, one more round of a restroom break and back in the cart for a day of travel.

On the fourth day of travel the wagon came to an unexpected stop. The men jumped from their seats in the front, and when they returned, they had another prisoner to add to the cart.

"We not have room for another person," the chatter began in a broken language.

"You maggots have no choice," one of the guards said. "You think this is hard, wait until William gets a hold of you."

"William," Marcus whispered.

The guard laughed and walked away.

"Have you heard of William?" the smart one asked.

Marcus tried to nod his head. It was painful, but he did, slightly. "Water?"

"No, I not givin' dead man water," one voice said.

"Shut up. Give 'im water."

A hand guided a rag to Marcus's mouth, and wrung the water out. He breathed out, and opened his eyes for the first time since he fell. His eyes stung, and everything was blurry. He still couldn't move, but he felt alive with just this small victory.

"Welcome, my friend. So, you 'ave heard of William. We are his prisoners," the smart one told him. "The men that picked you up are his men. They are called Collectors. We are going to die or worse according to them."

"Worse?"

"We are dead men walkin'." The smart one washed his face, especially his eyes, then rinsed the rag into a bowl of water, and squeezed it into Marcus's mouth.

He choked and coughed. Everything tensed, and sharp pains attacked his body. Marcus moved his head to the left. It cracked and popped. He could see five ragged looking men huddled away from him, leaning against metal bars. He was in a prison wagon. He moved his head to the right. He saw the one who had been serving him dirty water, along with three other men. One was severely beaten. "He must be the one they caught today," he thought.

He moved his head just enough to see the one who had been doing most of the talking. "Why does he need all of these men?" His voice was barely above a whisper, and hoarse. It hurt to speak.

"We not know. He has been capturing men, and takin' them to his fort."

"This is not how I wanted to face William," Marcus thought. His body tingled with the same feeling as if his arm had fallen asleep. It was going to be a long process. *"He is going to kill me before I can move a muscle."*

Chapter Twelve
Earth - Julie

Julie was thankful school started soon. She had spent the week of the Coffee Festival mortified her mother had set her up as the queen. "How could you do something like this to me?" she had argued with her father.

"I didn't know," he said. "I will talk to her."

"It's too late. I never want to talk to her again!"

"Jules, honey," he pleaded.

That was two weeks ago. Julie hadn't talked to her mother since. She had spent most nights sleeping at Mr. Campbell's empty apartment. It was a nice escape and she could cuddle up with Shakespeare. Eventually school activities began as summer started to wind down.

"Have you talked to your mom, yet?" Claire asked during the beginning of cheer practice.

"No," Julie said sharply. "I can't believe she did that."

Claire looked down.

"You deserved to win," Julie continued. "That was totally unfair of her to do."

"I get it, but your mom has apologized a billon times. Plus, she didn't rig it for you to win, she only entered your name."

"Can you be sure about that?" Julie asked. She placed her hands on her hips.

"Come on, you won it fair and square. Besides, senior year is going to be a blast. Don't you want to share it with your parents?"

"How can you be so forgiving?" Julie asked.

Claire smiled. "Look. My parents have been absent from everything I've done since middle school. Your parents just want the best for you. They screw up, but it's better than not trying. My dad's thinking about moving to Florida. My mom is dating a third guy since Easter. You have to accept facts. Life sucks, but I mean, this is our last first cheer practice, tomorrow we'll have our last first day of school, then in a couple of weeks we'll have our last first football game, and then…"

"Okay, okay, I get it. I'll have to forgive her."

The two joined the other girls for practice under the hot August sun.

When she got home, she found her mother cooking dinner as her dad was grilling steaks on the patio.

"Hi, Mom," Julie said as she walked in the door. Michelle froze. Julie kissed her on the cheek. "I'm going to jump in the shower."

She bounded up the stairs, grabbed a towel, and closed the bathroom door.

A minute or two later there was a gentle rapping on the door. "Jules, you, okay?"

"Yep, let's not make a big deal out of it. You made a mistake, I overreacted, it's over," Julie said from behind the curtain.

"Can we talk about it?"

"I would prefer we didn't," Julie answered.

Her mom closed the door. Julie finished her shower, got dressed, and went down stairs to eat. They sat at the table.

Michelle turned to her daughter as she handed her the broccoli with cheese. "Honey, I'm so sorry about…"

"Mom, I said it's over. Can we drop it?"

"We haven't talked in two weeks. I think it's something we should discuss," Michelle argued. She started cutting into her steak.

Julie stared at her. She took a bite, refusing to engage her mother on the topic.

"I made a mistake. I should have never sent your name in without asking you, but I know you would have said no," Michelle said.

"Hey," Phillip tried to intervene. He touched his wife's hand. "Let it go."

Michelle shot him a disappointed look. "Okay, I'm sorry. Let's start over," she said. "Are you excited about tomorrow?"

Julie made a big sigh of relief. "Nervous, but yes, pretty excited," she answered. They ate the rest of dinner talking and laughing as if nothing happened. After dinner, they helped each other clean up, then Julie headed upstairs to play on her laptop before falling asleep.

~ * ~

The next morning Julie woke to the sound of her parents making noise in their room. "Shh, you'll wake her," her mom said.

"Oh God," Julie thought, "Aren't they too old for that?" She crammed her head between two pillows. Seconds later a knock came at her door.

"Jules, hey, sweetie, time to rise and shine," her dad said from the other side of the door.

"What?" she answered in a whine, rubbing the sleep from her eyes.

"It'll be fun," he said. She could hear the smile in his voice.

Julie crawled out of bed. She opened the door to a rainbow of balloons. They had signs about senior year, congratulating her for making it this far, streamers in Cedar Creek's green, gold, and white, and her dad was tossing confetti in the air. Her mom turned on the graduation song, "Pomp and Circumstance."

"There's our little senior!" Michelle squealed. "Aren't you so excited?"

"Yes, Mom!" Julie could see how much work they had put into her first day of school. They escorted her downstairs. Her dad went to the kitchen. Balloons lined the banister. Pictures blown up to three by four feet were arranged on easels in the living room. "Oh my gosh, I can't believe you did all of this." Her mom started snapping pictures of her reactions.

"Is someone hungry?" Phillip came in the room waving a spatula. "I have your favorite!"

"You guys," Julie protested. "This is too much."

"Nonsense, nothing is too much for our little senior," Phillip said. "Come into the kitchen." Julie and her mother followed him. He had everything laid out perfectly. Michelle continued to take pictures. "Sit, sit, eat."

They sat down, and ate.

"Oh, my goodness," Julie said after a bite of French toast.

"What?" her parents asked at the same time.

"When I heard you shush dad because he was going to wake me, I thought…"

They laughed, and shared a knowing look.

"Oh gross!"

They finished their breakfast, Julie ran upstairs to change, and they continued chasing after her as she got in her car, and drove off.

~ * ~

She met Claire and Jimmy in the school's parking lot. "Here it is," Julie said. "Our last first day of school."

"Do you remember when we were on the bus riding up the driveway?" Claire asked Julie.

"The school looked like a big fortress on a hill," Julie said. "Remember how scared and excited we were?"

"Oh my gosh, yes," Claire said.

They walked up the staircase from the senior parking lot to the front of the building.

"Let's make it an epic year," Jimmy said.

He took Claire by the hand. She took Julie by the hand and they walked through the glass doors of Cedar Creek.

In the main foyer Mr. Frye greets them.

"Mr. Frye!" Julie squealed, then gave him a big hug even though he tried to give her a side hug.

"Hi, Julie." He patted her on the back. "I'm going to miss you, too, but we have one hundred and eighty days of school before that happens."

"Oh gosh, you mean we have to actually learn this year, I thought senior year was just for having fun before you're kicked out into the real world or college?"

"Yes, I hate to break the bad news to you, but your teachers have a full school year of learning for you." He smiled, gave Claire and Jimmy high fives and continued greeting students as they walked into the building.

That was how the day went. Each class was her last first day. She hugged Mrs. Larson, and was happy she had become used to calling her 'Larson' instead of Slovarsky. She hugged Coach Langston, her favorite track coach and history teacher; and she hugged grumpy old Mr. Schultz, who still hated to be called "Mr." Even though Julie no longer had to take gym class, she liked him, and still talked to him every time she was in the weight room.

After school, she and Claire went to cheer practice, made sure Shakespeare had enough food and water, then off to visit Mr. Christian, before settling in for the night to do homework.

At Mr. Christian's, "How was he today?" Julie asked making small talk with the nurse who was just finishing her shift before an attendant would stop by later that night to get the old man to bed.

"Oh, not good. You would think he knew today was the first day of school. He still misses it, you know?"

Julie reached out to pat his hand. "I wish I would have had you as a teacher, Mr. Christian."

When their hands touched, the old man straightened up. His eyes blazed. "Marcus needs you," he said. "He is in trouble."

Julie pulled her hand back. The nurse looked at Julie, then to Mr. Christian. Julie wrung her hands together.

"What did you do?" the nurse asked.

"I didn't do anything, I-I just patted his hand."

"Who was he talking about, who is Marcus?"

"I don't know," Julie lied.

"Marcus needs you. He is in trouble," Mr. Christian shouted, his voice was frail and gravely, but his message was clear.

"I've got to go," Julie said. She ran out the door, jumped in her car, and burst into tears.

Chapter Thirteen
Earth – Julie

Julie avoided going back to Mr. Christian's home for three weeks. The outburst scared her. She waited until she could settle into the new school year; cheering, studying, and hanging out with Claire and Jimmy took most of her time. Finally, on a Saturday night with nothing to do, she was ready to go back to see the former teacher.

Mr. Christian seemed fine. Everything was as it had been before his revelation that Marcus was in trouble. Julie summoned up the courage to hand him a cup of warm tea. "Okay, Mr. Christian, here's your tea."

She purposely let her hand graze across his. Once again, he went stiff. His eyes rolled in the back of his head revealing cloudy white orbs.

"I see Marcus on a black horse. He's looking for somebody."

"Is he looking for me?"

"No, he's looking for somebody he hates. He's angry and looking for somebody to take his anger out on."

Julie pulled away. "Yeah, yeah, I gotta go. Bye Mr. Christian."

She was going to drive home, but stopped at Mr. Campbell's apartment. She let Shakespeare out, gave him food and water and when the cat returned, instead of heading home, she texted her mom and dad, "I'm going to spend the night with Claire, okay?"

Her mom responded with, "Yep."

She made herself a quick dinner, then went upstairs, and collapsed on his bed. "It's kinda nice having a secret get-away," she told the white cat that joined her. "You miss him, too, don't you?"

She dreamt of Redderick Bobo. "Not you again," she said as he walked up to her, wearing his robe opened to display his round gut, and gnarled belly-button.

"Julie, Julie." He took her by her shoulders, and looked her up and down. "So, this is how you look on Earth? Hm, well, I say the attire on

76

Seras suits you better."

She looked at her wardrobe. She was wearing the same thing she had on as she did before falling asleep; jean shorts, green hoodie, and running shoes. "What are you doing in my dream now? I'm not going back."

"My dear, you have no idea." He took her by the arm. "You're upset because Marcus lied to you. You're upset because he is a demon, a Skorei demon. You're upset Callista didn't tell you the truth."

"Yes, yes, and yes!" They walked into a corridor. "Where are we? I've seen this place before." She saw the priest from her dreams four years ago. Then she saw Marcus in demon form approach him from a staircase. "No!" she screamed. Neither heard her. She flinched as she watched the exchange between them before Marcus rammed his sword into the Priest of Ostram. "Why are you showing me this?"

"This is all you know of Marcus before you met him. You know nothing else about him except this vision, and what you have heard."

"I know he killed Callista's people. I know he slaughtered Seren's tribe, among a whole lot of others."

"He does have his weaknesses." The temple started to shake, and the floor was engulfed in flames. "As you will see." They watched as he ushered the women to safety in the courtyard, then as he avoided detection from the warriors there as they burned the bodies of the fallen. "Come there is more."

They reappeared in a field about a quarter of a mile from the fortress. Marcus was on horseback as were three other men. She recognized two of them. "Those are the two demons who wanted to kill me and Marcus."

"Indeed, and the third is his brother, Darius."

"He told me his brother's dead," Julie said.

"No, no, not yet."

They watched Marcus argue with the three men, then both armies gathered around them. A fourth warrior stepped up. "That is William. He and Marcus were best friends up until this day." The arguing continued, it worsened after they saw the priestesses escaped from the fortress and run into the woods. "Needless to say, this doesn't end well for the two."

"What happens?"

"Let's go see."

On the hilltop, Julie and Redderick listened as Thomen abandoned Marcus and his comrades. They watched as Thomen was stabbed by William and left for dead as William's men began marching toward the six warriors.

"They are going to take on the entire army?" Julie asked. Her voice cracked. "Where are the rest of his men? Where's Griffus and Pertheus?"

"You'll see," Redderick said.

"He's going to get killed!" she screamed.

They watched as the fighting intensified. Then Marcus's army, and the rest of William's army, spilled out from the woods. She caught herself weeping as one by one Marcus's men fell to the overwhelming forces. When she saw Marcus get struck by an arrow, then another, and another, four in total.

Julie began running to him. She panicked at the sight of Marcus dying.

"Where are you going?" Redderick asked.

"We have to help him," she said, not understanding why the immortal wasn't trying to help her.

"Julie, this has already happened. He lives through this."

Wha...yes, of course he does." She stopped. "How?"

"Look for yourself." The pale warrior threw his sword into the archer, stopping the arrowed attack on Marcus. Then Bones was struck down by William.

"He died for Marcus, all five of them did." Griffus and Pertheus grabbed Marcus's body, and strapped him to his horse. As they did, William retreated, leaving his men to die. "Griffus and Pertheus saved him."

"Indeed. They understand." Redderick Bobo nodded.

"Understand what?"

"What you need to understand. What happens when you discover all you have known your entire life is wrong? Do you fix it, or do you continue in your ways?"

"I don't get it?"

"I know." They walked through a clouded veil to a clearing by a swamp.

"Where are we now?"

Then Julie saw a horse carrying Marcus. His body limp as four Greagons creatures ran toward him. "The Greagons."

"Yes." The horse, lowered its head, exhausted, and collapsed next to Marcus. "That was Wolfblood, Marcus's horse."

The Greagons removed the arrows from Marcus, buried his horse, and loaded him onto their boat. "They brought Marcus into their camp." As she walked with Redderick they moved from the site to when Ter-Ra, the chief Greagon, spoke to the rest.

"Of course, I's did. How else could I's be sure that we's would see the prophecy when he's arrived?" Ter-Ra asked those standing around him.

"Master, may I's care for him's until he's is at full strength?" the creature known as U-Wea asked.

"U-Wea, I's insist you's and Kam-Lem care for the human, and when he's is well, bring him's to my's hut."

"Marcus lived with them, hunted with them, played with the Greagon children," Redderick continued, and the two of them walked through images of the Skorei warrior interacting with his hosts.

"A horse of death bearing a gift - comes from the east 'fore the setting sun. Treat him well for the Elders would tell - he's is the one," Ter-Ra sang as he sat on the floor of his hut across from Marcus.

"I keep hearing that, the children…sing it wherever I go," Marcus said.

Julie watched as the Greagon spoke to Marcus. "It is an old song. One written about you's."

"I's…I doubt that very much."

"He doesn't believe the prophesy any more than I did," Julie said.

"No, you both are a lot alike. What do you call it…stubborn?" Redderick answered.

"Demon, you's are the one the song is about. You's are the prophecy," Ter-Ra said. His tone snapped Julie back into paying attention.

"Don't make me laugh. I am no prophecy."

"I's assure you's it is nothing to take lightly."

"I have heard prophecies before. They are all just nonsense."

"This was passed down to me's from the Elder, Ostram. Can the other prophecies you's have heard say the same thing?" Ter-Ra gave him a confident look.

"Ter-Ra knew the Elder, Ostram?" Julie asked Redderick.

"Yes, he and I spent some time together," he answered. "And you just saw him."

"Huh?" Julie cocked her head to the side.

"The priest, he was no ordinary priest. That was Ostram in disguise."

"What, why would he do that?" Julie asked. "And why would he let Marcus kill him?"

"All exceptional questions, my dear. Now, listen."

The old Greagon began chanting, "Five are the Elder's with their gifts born in the black of night. Five are the Elder's gifts hidden to set Seras right. Five Elder's pitted beneath an angry sun. Blood will flow. Flesh and blade become one. The blood given to ease time; the breath known to free men's minds; the bones to merge distance and space; the body a destined warrior, the Solia Custor, out of place, forged in battle with one true oath – protect Tolth's final gift, the Heart of Seras, our final hope."

"I've heard that before," Julie said. "It's supposed to explain who we are, but it's never made any sense to me."

"You keep talking," Redderick said. He placed a finger over his lips.

"Okay, okay," she said, then mocked him by pinching her lips with her fingers to close them, twisting an imaginary key, and throwing it over her shoulder.

"Yes, yes, yes! I killed a priest. I have no idea who he worshipped. But I do not worship the Elder, Eryx. I worship no one," Marcus said. His voice raised in frustration.

"Let me's ask you's a final question. Did the priest say anything to you's?"

"He said, 'It is you,' and he called me the Solia Custor."

Ter-Ra grinned. He opened the box and took out a large bottle of liquid.

"You know what that means?" Marcus asked.

"Yes. This is the "Breath of Ostram. I's am to give it to the demon who comes to Sychar after killing the Elder's priest."

"Why would I be rewarded for killing Ostram's priest?"

"It is only a sign that he's knew you's were the Solia Custor."

"See, the Greagons understood," Redderick Bobo broke their silence. "And so did Callista."

"Callista hated the Skorei. She told me how they destroyed her land and her people," Julie said.

"True, she had every reason to hate the Skorei. She had every reason to hate Marcus, but she didn't," he said. "Have you ever asked yourself why she didn't tell you Marcus's secret?" They moved to the sight of Callista riding a black stallion being chased by a band of men out from a wooded area and over the dunes where they were standing.

One of the horsemen caught up with her, and dove, knocking them both to the ground.

Marcus ran toward them with an oar in hand. He hit the man as he stood up. The rest of the men closed in on Marcus and Callista. Callista unsheathed her sword, and Marcus used the boat oar to fight the attackers. He picked up the sword of one fallen man.

In the middle of fighting, Marcus changed from his human form to the demon. He and Callista finished off the men, then she turned her attack to Marcus. Before she could strike at him a third time the Greagons appeared on the beach. Two Greagon children ran up to Marcus.

They fade into the campsite where Marcus and Callista argued. "Listen carefully, Julie. You will learn a bit about life on Seras," Redderick told her.

"There was never a place so beautiful," Callista said before turning to anger. "And you destroyed it! You should pay for what you did!"

"You pretend that you were a peaceful village. I know better. I know what you did to your prisoners. I know what you did to men and male babies," Marcus yelled. "I know how your people enslaved men captured in battle."

"You know nothing," Callista argued. "They wanted to do the same to us every chance they could."

"Of course, they would. That is the nature of war!"

"Those men were weak and pathetic. They deserved what they got."

"What are they talking about?" Julie asked, as they watched the two argue back and forth.

"Callista's Hemoor tribe wasn't as innocent as you would think, or as she would like for people to think. Any child not born female was...sacrificed. I will leave it as that. They also conquered and captured men to become prisoners, and use them as slaves for physical labor and reproductive labor. Then when they were finished with their work, they would kill them."

"Oh my god!" Then she saw Marcus and Callista's argument turn.

"Enough!" Callista said, kissing him.

After watching Marcus's startled look, she threw her arms around him and smashed him against a tree trunk.

The impact caused Marcus to let out a grunt. He and Callista stared at each other, then they began to kiss.

"Okay," Julie said. "I don't need to see this." She saw Redderick was enjoying the display. "I said, we don't need to see this."

"Very well," he said. "One more." With a wave of the hand, they were gone. "This is the Forest of Tunlaw. The Tunlaw sisters were demons created by Eryx, and they guarded the entrance to the cave Eryx entrapped Vestus. No one had every passed their wooded domain."

The forest was dead with brown and blackened trees, dirt, cobwebbed and shrouded in hazy mist. Julie saw Callista, Jakob, Argos, Freya and a blonde she didn't recognize. "Who's that?

"She is Alanas. She was an Evandell warrior, and admirer of Marcus."

Julie stopped and took him by the arm. "Wait, you said was?"

"Indeed," Redderick said.

Julie heard the voices nearly the same time as Marcus and his companions. It interrupted her continued line of questions.

"He is here," came a whispered growl.

"Impossible," answered another.

"It is the witch playing with us." The voices grew louder.

She watched the warriors draw their swords and entered into forest.

"There are more," a voice said with glee.

"Wonderful," another said.

"Where do we start?" The trees carried the voices of the mysterious women.

"Let us start here." Behind Argos a dark figure appeared. Its skinny, gray fingers wrapped around him and pulled him closer. *"He has a secret,"* the creature said.

Julie looked at Redderick Bobo. "What is that thing? It's hideous."

"It's one of the sisters," he answered.

"What secret does Argos have?"

"I don't know," he answered, though Julie didn't believe him.

"Delicious," another said. Argos swung his sword at the shadow, hitting nothing but dark fog.

"We know all of your pasts and all of your futures," one of the sisters taunted.

Another voice appeared behind Callista. *"Very unhappy, this one."*

"Poor pretty girl," a sister uttered sardonically.

"Indeed."

"She is…"

Julie wanted to help Callista. She felt helpless.

"Remember, they have already been here. Marcus and Callista survived this encounter," Redderick reminded her.

"Show yourself!" Marcus shouted. Julie saw the anger in his eyes.

"There he is."

"That is not him."

Julie kept her eyes on Marcus. He was sweating, obviously nervous. "I've never seen him nervous," she said to Redderick.

"Maybe, because he is worried about the people under his charge," he answered.

"It is, sister."

"I thought he would be taller."

"I agree sister." The air around them was stifling.

"I command you to show yourself!" Marcus yelled.

"It is him." The sisters disappeared, then reappeared seemingly at will from the ground to the trees.

"What arrogance." Their voices filled in the dread soundlessness of the forest and carried on the wind.

"I sense evil."

"He is a demon."

"I say we kill him now."

Three dark figures appeared. They were cloaked in black; two arms protruded from each side of their bodies. A veil of cobweb hung over their bald heads and into their faces. They had wings like those of a bat sticking out from their backs. Their eyes were void and seeped a yellowish substance. They were crouched in a near sitting position on tree branches just out of range of the warriors' swords.

"What are those things?" Julie asked.

"Evil, pure evil. A little gift to Seras from Eryx," Redderick answered.

"Demon, we could kill you now if we wanted," one sister emerged behind Marcus, knocking the sword from his hand. She then materialized back on the branch, rejoining her sisters.

"We are not here to fight you," Freya tried to sound diplomatic in the face of danger.

Marcus summoned his sword back into his hand.

"We know what you want, witch."

"Sister, does she remind you of someone?"

"Yes, sister she does.

"That is rich."

"Tell us what we need to know and we will leave," Freya asked.

"We will not tell you."

"Then tell me," Marcus begged. He took a deep breath to conceal his anger.

The blonde named Alanas notched an arrow and shot it toward the sisters. One of them caught it with long boney fingers, the color of death.

"There will be a price for that," it said with a hiss.

"Hold your fire!" Marcus ordered.

The band of warriors readied their weapons, and made a circle.

"I thought she was going to attack you," Alanas said.

"Safe passage will not be granted demon."

"We are looking for--"

"We know what you are looking for."

"We will not tell you."

"Please," Marcus said.

The sisters made Julie angry. She wanted to kill them.

"The demon is weak."

"He will never succeed."

"She will kill him."

"Who will kill me?" he asked.

"Ask too many questions."

"We should kill you."

"You cannot win."

"We should let her."

"No! I want death," two sisters shouted in unison.

"No, she should get the honor of killing the son of the scorned."

"The 'Warrior of Eryx'."

"The 'Body of Eryx'," a sister corrected one of the others.

"The 'Solia Custor'," the third one laughed.

"Who?" Marcus asked loudly.

Julie felt sorry for him. She wanted to help.

"Enough questions."

"More, more, more, always wanting more."

"We will be leaving now," Marcus stepped back forming a circle with the others.

"Safe passage is still not granted." The sisters cackled.

"On my command," Marcus said, then yelled, "Run!"

The company of warriors ran through the woods. Jayna took flight as a hawk, narrowly escaping the grasp of the sisters.

The sisters appeared, disappeared and reappeared at will, grabbing soldiers then tossing their bodies to the ground. Alanas screamed as the sister she tried to shoot earlier with an arrow trapped her.

Marcus stopped running, and turned around to help her.

Julie watched in horror as Alanas took out her blade and swung helplessly at the dark figure. A slash marked Alanas's face from a mere gesture of the creature's hand. A cut gashed her arm, then her chest. The sister was toying with the helpless Evandell warrioress. A large pool of blood spouted from Alanas's neck. Marcus leapt up the branches of the tree to help his friend.

"Can't we help her?" Julie screamed.

"I'm afraid we can't. This is the past, and the past is over."

Alanas looked at him defenseless. "Marcus," she cried. The sister motioned her hands to plunge deep into Alanas's stomach.

Julie felt the fear of the blonde girl, and started to cry.

"No!" Marcus yelled. Alanas's body fell to the ground. Marcus jumped to the branch the sister was standing, celebrating her kill. He sliced off her head before she could react to his presence.

The other two sisters screeched at sensing the death of their sister. Marcus leapt from the trees. He was now in his monstrous demon form. The astonishment of losing their sister caused them to lose track of him.

Julie watched Marcus as he moved quickly, striking one across the back with the full width of the cutting edge of his blade as she knelt beside her headless sister. The sword cut her in half. The final sister stood and faced him in horror. Before she could react, he grabbed her by the throat. His demonic claws dug deep into her veins as yellow pus oozed from the wounds. He plunged his sword deep into her body; a loud gurgling hiss escaped her crusting mouth and filled the dead forest.

Marcus picked up Alanas's body and sprinted out of the woods. The others had gathered the dead, eight in total; five men and three women.

The image faded, Julie and Redderick were back in Marcus's apartment living room. "I'm confused," she said. "Why did you show me those things?" She collapsed on the couch.

"You left. You thought you knew everything there was to know about Marcus and the Skorei. You misjudged who he was, and who he is. The Elder Ostram knew he was the right one to be your protector, your Solia Custor. He has the military leadership, the compassion, the honor it takes to help you," he said.

"How does a Skorei demon have compassion and honor?"

"You don't have to approve of everything he did. Nobody does that. Marcus doesn't do that. But he is making up for his misdeeds." Redderick sat beside her.

"Misdeeds? He was evil, and the only reason he is making up for them is because Ostram gave him...what...a conscience...heart?"

"Possibly," Redderick said. "Or, perhaps he has had it all along, but nobody tells those stories about a warlord, let alone a demon Skorei warlord." He patted her on the head. "Maybe you should ask those closest to him before Ostram. Pertheus, Griffus, Freya were all there to witness who he was when he didn't have to do what he did. I'm not saying he was good and righteous. I'm saying he deserves a second chance." He stood as if he was going to leave. "I'm not saying all four deserve a second chance, obviously William doesn't." He looked around. "Interesting home you have here. I'm afraid I have to go."

"Wait, I'm still confused. I've been gone for months, why did you come for me now?"

"My dear, Julie, I did not come to you, you came to me." He faded away.

"I did what? How is that possible?" she tried in vain to stop him from fading away. "Wait!" She reached out her hand in protest. "Why did you say four Skorei?"

"It's not important, my dear," the immortal said as he began to slowly fade.

"He's in trouble. I need to go to him," Julie said.

"No, the time isn't right," Redderick told her. He was barely visible.

"When will the time be right?" she scrambled to ask her question before he was gone.

"You'll know." Then he vanished.

Chapter Fourteen
Earth - Julie

A harsh wind blew through the crowd as Julie, Claire, Jimmy and Alex stood in line along with another forty people of all ages waiting to enter the haunted house. The house was off of a side road. The four of them drove together in Jimmy's parents' minivan.

"Oh man, I think I'm going to pee my pants," Julie said.

She squatted down as Alex wrapped his arms around her. The house was three stories tall, rundown, spray painted, with boarded up windows, and blasted loud music of howling wind, howling dogs, and ghost sounds.

"How did we let you guys talk us into this?" Claire asked, looking at Jimmy who stood rigid, fighting the cold on his bare arms.

"Because you love us," Jimmy joked. "It's going to be fun. Besides, all the parties have been lame. All anybody wanted to do was drink and party. This is going to be so much better."

"I hate being scared," Julie whined.

Alex rubbed his arms up and down hers.

"Remember, they can't touch you. It's just for fun," Alex said over the sound of clanging metal against the side of the wooden house.

"This is why I preferred being a kid and just going house to house for candy. This is going to suck."

It had been over a month since her encounter with Redderick Bobo, and his tour of Marcus's life. She had also avoided Mr. Christian's home, since he seemed to have a connection with Marcus. *"Was it the fact Marcus had sucked out his brains with the one of the Gifts of the Elders?"*

"Don't worry, I'll protect you," Alex said.

Julie and Claire looked at each other, and laughed.

"What?" he asked.

"Um, if we get in trouble, we're going to leave you guys in the dust," Claire said.

"Yeah, we don't just run track for our health," Julie added.

Obviously, leaving out the fact she is a trained warrior with fighting skills beyond her boyfriend, or any other person on Earth.

"Plus, look at these guns." Claire struck a pose to flex her muscles. Jimmy took the opportunity to squeeze her biceps.

"I feel safer already," he said.

Claire rewarded his statement with a peck on the lips.

The line moved forward. The closer they got, the more Julie could hear creaking doors, women screaming and pounding against the walls.

"I didn't think it was supposed to be this cold," Claire said. Jimmy attempted to wrap his arms around her. "You have to be freezing," she said to him.

"Not really," he answered. "I'm used to be out on the field during this time of year."

"That's true," Claire responded.

Julie and Claire had just wrapped up their cheer season, as Jimmy played his last football game, though it wouldn't be his last.

"I can't wait to watch you play in college," Claire said. "Even though you're going clear across the state." She gave a smirk.

"I know, but we have a lot of time before that comes around," he said. It was apparent he was trying to avoid an uncomfortable conversation.

"Okay you two, you're both going to have a blast in college. Jimmy, you are going to do great playing football and running track in college; and, Claire, you've already signed to run track in school," Julie tried to smooth things over.

"Yeah, you're playing in college. That's impressive," Alex added.

"It's division two, so it'll be fun. I've heard division one schools basically own you, so I'm glad I'll be able to play and concentrate on school," Jimmy said.

"Where are you going?" Alex asked Julie.

"I don't know. I haven't thought about it much," she answered.

"You can always join me," Claire said.

"I'll probably go to McPherson like Patrick does," Julie said. She saw the disappointment in Claire's face. "We'll see." She smiled and shrugged. "We're a long way off."

"Not that long off. It goes by quick." Alex said.

Julie grimaced in his direction. The line surged forward, saving him from Julie's wrath.

"Here we go," Jimmy said clapping his hands together in excitement. "Are you ready?" He shook Claire by the shoulders. Cobwebs filled the doorway.

Claire promptly moved behind him. "Now I am." She squeezed her shoulders together to make herself smaller and buried her face in Jimmy's broad back.

Julie held onto Alex's hand as he took the lead. *"Come on, I've faced worse than fake vampires, loud music, and fog machines,"* she thought, taking a deep breath, and allowing Alex to pull her into the entryway. To the left, there was furniture covered in white sheets covered in blood. The lights flickered. A centerpiece coffee table overturned suddenly, then ghosts arose from the furniture. Without warning, one of the ghosts rushed at them with a blood curdling scream.

Claire and Julie screamed. Julie felt Alex pull her hand down as he ducked from the danger. Jimmy and Claire flew back against the furthest wall.

"Keep moving," a separated voice commanded, low and grumbling.

Julie reached out in the sheer darkness. She couldn't see her hand in front of her face. She touched a wall, it was slimy. "Gross."

"What?" Claire practically cried from somewhere behind her, Alex, and Jimmy.

"Don't touch the wall," Julie called out. "How did I get in front?" she whined.

She felt Alex's hand on her butt as they moved through a doorway with black strips of streamers hanging down. In the next room, strobe lights flashed, everything looked as if it were moving in slow motion. Werewolves, zombies and ghosts moved toward them in rapid succession, making all four scream. Then the sound of a chainsaw being revved up came from behind them, and the man wielding it chased them up a flight of stairs.

They walked into a room with a witch sitting at a table, a large crystal ball in the center of the table with electrical shock zapping the inside of the purple glowing orb. "I'm here to tell your fortune," the lady said in a bad Transylvanian accent. "Your future looks bleak!" she cackled, as three monsters storm from closets and chased them to another room, where the only way out was to jump down a large slide.

It led them to a room with a mad doctor and his grotesque patient slowly turning toward them, then chasing them out of the room.

"I hate being in the front," Jimmy yelled at that point.

The girls and Alex were torn between laughing and screaming. Julie had tears in her eyes from both.

"I'm pretty sure I peed my pants," Claire said over the noise.

They entered a room. It had cages filling every wall, some hanging from the ceiling. The creatures growled and screamed and rattled the bars. As the doors opened, Julie had a vision. She saw Marcus locked in a cage. She saw William smiling and laughing at him beating the cage with a large stick. She felt pain from beatings, bruises, broken bones, and being trapped in the cage. "No-o-o-o!" she screamed. It stopped the advancing actors in their tracks.

Jimmy, Claire, and Alex grabbed her, pulling Julie out the final door into the fresh midnight air.

"What was that?" Claire asked. "Are you okay?"

"Huh? Yeah, yeah, I'm fine," Julie answered. "That was fun."

The three looked at her.

"What?"

"You kinda freaked out there at the end," Claire said.

"I thought you got hurt," Jimmy added.

"No, oh gosh, no, that was so much fun," Julie said.

The group started walking back to the parking lot. She looked up to the sky, and wiped the tears forming from her eyes.

"You're okay, right?" Claire asked.

"Yeah, that was a blast," Julie said. They got in the minivan, and as Jimmy drove them back to his house, they relived the entire experience. "This was so much more fun than going out trick or treating, or those parties we went to last year." Alex had cozied up with her in the back of the van.

"Heck to the yes," Jimmy said.

"We need to do that more often," Claire said, turning to the backseat, interrupting Alex who had started to make a motion to kiss Julie.

Julie leaned forward. "Yes, we do. I'd go to another next weekend."

"I'm in," Jimmy said.

He pulled into his parents' driveway.

They got out, Julie hugged Claire and Jimmy. "Thank you for driving, and for the fun." She joined Alex in his car. They pulled out, and headed toward her house. "Did you have a good time?" she asked Alex.

He placed his hand on her knee. "I did. It was a blast."

They pulled into Julie's driveway. Her mom had her yard filled with tombstones, ghosts, and witches. Her life size cutouts of Bela Lugosi's Count Dracula and Nosferatu had been joined by Frankenstein's monster and a werewolf.

"Are your parents' home?" Alex asked.

"No, do you want to come in?" Julie opened the car door.

"Yes." He got out and joined her to walk up the steps.

Julie turned to him. "Listen, I like you a lot, but nothing is going to happen. Do you understand?"

"Yeah, yeah, I understand," he answered.

"I'm serious. You've been all over me tonight, so I'm not sure you understand."

"Okay, wait, I don't get it. You like me, I like you. We've been together for six months. I'm not sure what you're waiting on?"

"What does that have to do with anything?" Julie asked, crossing her arms.

"Don't you want what Jimmy and Claire have?"

"Jimmy and Claire have been together since freshman year, and you don't know what they do," Julie argued.

"Come on, what's wrong with you?" Alex asked, his voice hostile.

"Nothing's wrong with me. What's wrong with you?"

"Nothing, why, because I want to have sex with my girlfriend, how is that on me? I'm not the eighteen-year-old virgin."

"Well, then I'll make this easy on you. I'm not your girlfriend. So, you can take your little hurt ego and go home."

"You're breaking up with me? After six months, just because you don't wanna…"

"Goodbye," Julie said firmly. He looked at her. "Go!"

Alex shrunk away from the porch, then jogged to his car. As he pulled away, peeling out in the gravel, he raised his left hand out the window and flipped her off.

~ * ~

The next morning, Julie bypassed her dad making pancakes, and went for a bowl of cereal. She opened a package of Swiss cake rolls, put them in the bowl, and added five chocolate chip cookies before filling it with cereal.

"Rough night?" her dad asked as he watched her.

She doesn't answer.

"Is everything okay?"

"Alex and I broke up last night," she finally told him.

"I'm sorry, are you okay? What happened?"

"Nothing, I don't want to talk about it."

She sat down at the kitchen table and ate her breakfast.

Phillip sat down across from her. He started eating his pancakes. "I love you."

"Love you, too."

Chapter Fifteen
Seras - Marcus

Marcus watched the little child run into the arms of his mother. It was Raewin. She looked beautiful, just as he remembered her. The little boy was Marcus. He remembered he was allowed to live with his mother for his first two years, after that he moved into the imposing Cauleta with his father, Canis. Canis allowed him to visit his mother on occasion until he celebrated his ninth tempora. After that, his raining would begin, and he would not be permitted to spend time with his mother until he finished.

As a child, Marcus loved hearing his mother tell stories. She had a breezy easiness to her. Wild with passion, she tried to undo the harsh training she knew her son was going through inside the city gates. Marcus had heard the story of how they met, how Canis fell head over heels in love with the young, brunette Corven maiden, and how he changed his rules about women living in his fortified city of Cauleta because of her. He also knew Raewin rejected the offer, which made him furious. To make their relationship worse, Raewin and her Corven tribe worshipped the Elder, Tolth. Canis didn't worship any particular Elder, but his men and the tribe of his birth were followers of Eryx. So, Raewin stayed away.

He had always enjoyed the visits with Raewin. The journey to her home was merely a day's ride from Cauleta, but the experience was worlds apart. It was much more peaceful than the training he was required to do with Canis. She told stories, they sang and danced and young Marcus would sit at the table in her little cabin and watch as she cooked.

It was even better after Darius was born, who was two years younger, and Freya who was born five years after Marcus. They played in the woods, swam in the nearby creek, played hide and seek, fished, and climbed trees as high as they could.

Freya, being a girl, was never required nor allowed to live with Canis like Marcus and later, Darius. She was expected to live with Raewin and learn the ways of womanhood, and Raewin taught her the ways of the Corven. When Freya was born, she took Freya to a Corven temple and performed the ritual of Corven maids. Raewin allowed Marcus and Darius to watch. She laid her in a basket placed in the middle of the chiseled symbol of the Elders, then poured the milk and water which was said to have been from the bath of Tolth, to welcome her into their care.

The visits to Raewin were a far cry from the time spent with Canis. There, Marcus spent his days learning sword play, how to use a bow and hunted. Canis made sure he had the proper early training until he was of age, and gave him over to the master trainer, Kralen. At age nine, Marcus said goodbye to his mother and sister. He would not be permitted to visit them until he finished his training which took five temporas. He hugged them both. Raewin wept, Freya didn't understand but followed in her mother's tears. Marcus ruffled his brother's blond hair. "I will see you soon my brother."

Marcus woke up when the wagon came to a stop. His body still tingled, and he couldn't move beyond looking left or right. He could wiggle his fingers ever so slightly. Opening his eyes, he could make out the three collectors who found him at the base of the cliff. They herded the others out of the cart before dragging him by his arms and legs.

"What are we going to do with this one?" one of the men asked?

"Not up to us. Let them figure it out," another collector said.

"What happened to this one?" a new voice spoke.

"Fell off a cliff from what we can tell," one of the guards answered. "Got some nice meat from the horse he was riding."

"Was not sure if he was going to survive the trip," another one said.

"Put him in a cage over there. We will let Lord William decide if he can use him or not."

"*Lord William,*" Marcus thought with a chuckle that made his head hurt. It was not the way Marcus saw him riding into William's fortress. He envisioned riding his horse swinging and slashing every man in sight until he could face his old friend face-to-face, kill him, then track down Pallanex. He wanted to end it all; the hurt, the pain, the torture for Julie. "Julie," he sighed.

The pain from being pulled out of the cart made his body crack. He gasped and groaned as he was tossed into a small cage, then hoisted upon the shoulders of two men. He lost track of where they were going as they left the blinding light of the sun to a dark chamber hall. The smell of rotted flesh irritated his nostrils.

Marcus awoke in a different cage. He could wiggle his fingers. He opened and closed his hands, but his arms failed him. He was able to move his forearm slightly. The rest of his arm wouldn't cooperate. His feet moved…no pain. He raised his arms up and down, he moved his feet. No pain. "Progress," he thought. He turned his head to the right. There was a stone wall. The wet stone smelled of mildew. He turned to the left, nothing but bars. The floor was rock. He followed the floor to a stairwell, a guard, and more cages. All of them empty. He started to lift his head. "How long was I asleep?" he worried. His head swirled at the clanging of a stick banging across the cages.

"Wake up," a deep growl commanded. "Time to see if you can walk." The beast of a guard flung open the cage door and pulled Marcus by the arm dragging him across the hard rock surface.

The jailer stood behind Marcus and reached under his shoulders, lifting him to his feet. Marcus stood for a moment before his hip gave out and his knees buckled.

"Better than yesterday," a voice behind him said.

"Yesterday?" he thought. "I don't remember yesterday." Then it occurred to him the voice wasn't the jailer. "William!" Marcus's hoarse voice scratched.

His arm reached for his sword but it wasn't there.

William laughed. "Hello, old friend." William's raven black hair was pulled back into a pony tail. He had his sleeves rolled up. It was stifling hot, so much so that William was already drenched in sweat.

"You will excuse me if I don't stand," Marcus said.

William walked in front of Marcus revealing himself. "No, no, perfectly fine. Imagine my surprise when I was informed one of my prisoners was nearly dead and asked what they should do with him…you." William paused. "At first I was just going to have my pet--," William stopped with a wicked smile. "I will come back to that later. You will get a kick out of it," he continued. "Then they showed me the weapon they found with you. I could not believe my luck, my good friend Marcus right here as my guest. Needless to say, I had to see for myself. I have to tell you, you have looked better." William walked around him. His footsteps echoed on the stone as he moved closer. "I wanted to kill you right then and there, but I have to ask what are you doing here, Marcus?"

Marcus cleared his dry throat. It hurt to speak.

William snapped, and the guard brought him a ladle of water.

Marcus took the water slowly, but choked as it hit his throat. When he caught his breath he answered, "I came here to kill you."

William laughed. "Well, maybe later but now let us talk about you. You have really been a pain in Pallanex's butt. She would kill me if she knew you were here."

"So why don't you kill me?" Marcus asked.

"All in good time, but I think I will wait until you can actually stand up on your own then I will kill you." William snapped his fingers; the guard grabbed Marcus and put him back in the cage. "I will be back soon. We can talk more then, goodbye my friend."

Marcus laid in his cage. Maybe an hour went by, he wasn't sure. He twisted and turned his neck. He could hear every bone crack. He tried to sit up, still no luck.

As promised, William showed back up. "Right where I left you. I have to tell you, that's kind of pathetic." He pulled a stool next to Marcus's cage. "Do you remember when we first met Kralen?"

Kralen was their former teacher. When Marcus and William separated, William chose Kralen as part of his unit. Marcus thought about it for a second, it was shortly after they both celebrated their ninth tempura.

Canus escorted the young Marcus to the arena. At the time Marcus thought it was the biggest thing he had ever seen. Marcus recalled the walls were thirty feet high. The arena was the size of three football fields, as he could compare it to something modern. There was an obstacle course and other large structures for training.

Boys of all ages fought with shields, spears, and swords. Another area was sectioned off for attacking on horseback. Still another had boys taking turns running through an obstacle course with a bow and arrows.

The massive Kralen was the scariest man Marcus had ever seen. He had thick black hair, a coarse beard, scars and pockmarks decorated his face. Kralen was one of Canis's most trusted commanders. He was there for Canis when he overthrew his older brother, and helped negotiate peace between the Skorei tribe and the Tarracks before Canis betrayed his brother, Theon. He met the new recruits and walked them through his domain. "I am the king here," he announced. "Canis is king everywhere else." When they got to their sleeping area, they were met by another man. "This is Marddek. He will be in charge of your early training."

Marddek was a broad man with short cropped hair, and a mustache. He was shorter than Kralen, and much rounder. "Welcome to my team." He showed them the way to their beds. They walked past the first wood slats with stuffed cloth and a blanket. "This is Fish and Hurvay."

Marddek was Kralen's right hand man. Hurvay and the one nicknamed Fish were third and fourth. Hurvey had deep black skin, and the start of a thick goatee. Fish, was a tall stocky boy with coarse blonde hair that stood up like spikes.

"Why is he called Fish?" Marcus asked no one in particular.

"None of your business, boy," Fish growled.

"You will hear all about it later," Marddek said, continuing. They got to the back of the room where a rolled blanket and a small pillow waited. "This is where you will sleep." The group of boys looked at him. "Not much. It will toughen you up. I encourage you to not talk to the others. They are tired, and will not be in the mood. We will begin at dawn." With that, Marddek left them.

"So, what happens now?" one boy asked, Thomen.

"I am Arthur," Arthur said. The young black boy was muscular even at that age.

"I am Angus," the wild haired boy introduced himself.

The group sat on the floor in a circle. Marcus, William, Arthur, Thomen, Angus, were among the dozen new boys, along with a thin pale boy with the blondest hair Marcus had ever seen. He introduced himself as Linus.

At the time, Linus wasn't a strong fighter. He was partnered with Marcus, William, Arthur, Angus, Thomen, and two other boys. This was before Darius, Malcolm, Chadrick, and Chaldrean joined them in training a year later. Darius, Justus, Parikus, and Galius were two years away. Petar was three years away.

The boys spent their days learning war strategies, battle formations, and most importantly, how to fight. They drilled fight sequences, different weapons, and played combat games from morning until night. Kralen and Marddek kept them in shape with very few days off.

One of those days off was Canis's wedding to Pallanex.

When Canis had first built Cauleta, he made his men promise not to take wives. That changed after he met Raewin. He wanted to wed her and make her his queen. She refused him, and he lived in Cauleta alone until the young Pallanex entered his life.

Canis wasn't a young man any more. His thick dark locks had all turned white. He walked with a noticeable limp, and he bent slightly forward.

The city and castle of Cauleta were decorated with flowers and silver and blue drapings. The entire Skorei tribe and their allies, the Tarracks, gathered in the arena. The weather was perfect. Girls lined the sides of the walls holding giant silver candles. The guards stood at attention in polished uniforms, their metallic armor shone in the sunlight.

A dozen women on either side held six-foot candleholders with five stems set with blue colored candles to form an aisle. Canis and Pallanex walked behind a bevy of dancers and military personnel.

Being the king, Canis reigned over the procession. He stood with his two most trusted men, Kralen, Master of Soldiers, and Reinwald, Master of the Guard. Reinwald's fiery red hair had yet turned grayish. Canis addressed the arena crowded with spectators, and introduced Pallanex as "the queen of Cauleta, the Skorei tribe, and the lands possessed by King Canis."

The newly appointed Queen Pallanex bowed to Canis, then repeated the motion to the audience. She nodded her head to one of ladies in waiting who in turn signaled to men pulling a cart; inside the cart stood a white marble statue of Canis.

"It is my gift to you, my King. It will go alongside the statues of your younger self; your brother, Theon; the Elderesses Eryx and Vestus; and, the Elders Tolth, Ostram, and Azahleah. I have commissioned more to be added later if it pleases you," Pallanex cooed.

"It pleases me very much," Canis answered. He turned to Kralen. "Are they ready?"

"They are," the thick bearded Kralen answered.

Marcus and the rest of the boys under Kralen's training were divided into teams for a display of games. The boys were armed with wooden weapons dipped in animal blood. When a player was struck, it was determined by Kralen or Marddek if the contestant was eliminated. The day came down to Marcus's team against an older team.

The battle was ending, the two teams were regrouping when Marcus pulled the small Linus to the side. "Here, hide here," Marcus told him. "Only come out when we yell."

He did what they said, and waited. In the game, Thomen, Angus, and two others got eliminated, leaving only Marcus, William, and Arthur against five boys from the other side.

"Three against five, Marcus, do you want to surrender now?" the leader of the other team asked with a crooked smile.

The rest of the camp looked on. Marcus could hear laughter from the gallery. The older boys of their camp were disgusted. He heard the one named Fish comment on being lucky his father was Canis. "Not yet," Marcus said. He, William, and Arthur were guarding each other's backs. "We need to get them closer to the wall," he whispered to William and Arthur. So, they maneuvered their position. Marcus had a wooden sword, Arthur had a spear, and William armed himself with a shield and sword.

"Follow me," William said.

He threw his shield at one of the boys blocking their path to the wall of skeletons. When the boy ducked the three scrambled. In the process, Arthur jammed his capped spear into the ribs of another boy, Kralen gave a thumbs down signal, eliminating him from the competition. William took a sword across the back of his leg, it didn't remove him from the game, but it limited his effectiveness.

The four boys converged on them. "Still outnumbered Marcus, and William is hurt. Surrender!" They rotated again. They wanted the four with their backs toward the wall. "Give up. You cannot outrun us, there is nowhere to go."

"What if I ask you to surrender?" Marcus asked.

The four just laughed.

"Now," Marcus yelled.

Linus popped out from the skeletons shouting and screaming at the top of his lungs. The four boys froze stiff, just long enough for Marcus, Arthur, and William to hit them with their weapons, eliminating them from the competition.

"Wait," the leader of the other team said. "That is not fair!"

"Why?"

"He has to be in the arena to count."

"He was. He was there the whole time. Maybe you should have counted how many men we had," Marcus answered.

Kralen stepped in. "Looks fair to me."

He named Marcus's team the victor. The boys celebrated. They were joined by their team members. The other team sulked away in anger.

"Linus," Marddek yelled, stopping the cheers. "How will I know what type of fighter you will become if all you do is hide among the bones?"

"Commander," Marcus said. "We wanted him to do that. It was part of our plan. It worked perfectly."

"Be careful, Marcus. Your little games will get you in trouble," Marddek said. "I do not know what kind of leader you are going to be, but you have style." He then turned to Linus. "And, you might look like a bag of bones, but that does not mean you can hide in them." Marddek left them to talk to Kralen.

Canis and Pallanex approached the victorious team. "You did well, my son."

"Thank you, Father. These are my friends, William, Arthur, Thomen, Angus, and Linus."

"The one in the bones. It was a clever move," Canis said.

"Yes, Bones, did his job perfectly," Marcus said.

Canis nodded, Pallanex followed his lead, and Marcus and his friends bowed. The friendship between the boys was forged that day. After that, they were rarely seen away from each other, and as often as they could, they would side with each other through competitions.

Chapter Sixteen
Earth - Julie

Late November and December brought the holiday seasons. "Why does this time of year always seem like a blur?" Julie asked, as she and Claire met at a little café in town to exchange gifts on the second day of their two-week Christmas break. The streets were slushy, the ground covered with a fresh layer of snow. They drank hot chocolate and ate a couple pastries.

"I know, it seems like once we get to Thanksgiving everything fast forwards," Claire said. "Christmas, New Year, back to school to finish our last semester." Her eyes widened at the last four words, and she practically squealed.

"Don't forget Halloween. That's when I think it starts. We have a party, then 'Bam!'" Julie threw up her hands. "Halloween was such a waste of time. I really don't want to think about it."

"I'm sorry. You're right. Alex was such an ass. Plus, this year the parties were all lame. All anyone wanted to do was drink," Claire said, recalling the misery of bouncing from one party to the next, and leaving disappointed when their friends and classmates acted like fools.

"That's why I'm glad I have you and Jimmy. At least there are three of us who still have sense." A waitress came up to them.

"Can I get you anything else?" the waitress asked.

"I'll take another cup of hot chocolate," Julie said.

"Me too."

"Two more cups of hot chocolate coming up," the lady said, and walked away.

"I'm glad we did this now before things get crazy with the family. I think I have three Christmases." Julie gave Claire her gift. It was wrapped and placed in a decorative bag. "Here, open it."

"Thank you," she said with a high-pitched voice. "I know, I have more than that with my mom's new husband, I think I have five."

Claire handed Julie her gift. Claire opened up lotion and a candle of her favorite scent, lavender. Julie received a package of scrunchies, a gift card, and her favorite scented candle, vanilla.

They thanked each other, and gave each other a hug. The waitress brought their hot chocolate and the girls drank it up. "So, what are you going to do now?" Claire asked, as they left the café.

Julie pulled down her warm cap with the ear flap and strings.

"I have a couple of errands to run before I go home with the fam. How 'bout you?"

"I'm going to Jimmy's for a few hours before his grandparents fly to Florida, then home," Claire answered. The girls hugged again before separating. "Merry Christmas, Jules."

"Merry Christmas. Love you!"

"Love you!"

Julie drove to Mr. Christian's. "Merry Christmas, Mr. Christian!"

Julie came through the door. She hadn't been to visit the old man in a few months. The last time he scared her when he told Julie about Marcus being in trouble on a horse, and she let her busy schedule of school work, cheer practices, Friday night football games and holidays get in the way before guilt took over.

"Hello, child," he spoke clear. "I haven't seen you in a while." He patted her hand with his wrinkly, large knuckled hand.

"You're looking good today. How are you feeling?"

"I feel wonderful. I love this time of the year," he said.

He sat in his rocker facing the large front window.

"I do too. Looks like I need to shovel your driveway, and sidewalk, huh?"

"No. You need to seek Marcus. He is in danger." The old man's eyes turned white. He spoke clear. "He went to avenge you and kill William. Marcus is injured, on the verge of death. William is dangerous to him. He will either kill Marcus, or worse."

"Worse? I don't know what you're talking about?"

"In his weakened state they could resume their friendship. Seras cannot afford that to happen. He needs you."

Julie stood there staring at Mr. Christian.

He stopped talking, and returned to normal. "Yes, that would be nice. Maybe next time you stop by."

"I-I-I have to go." Julie zipped up her coat and headed out the door. She sat in her car and cried. "What am I going to do?" She let out a deep breath, and wiped her eyes. Her chest closed in on her. She scrunched her face to keep the tears away, but they kept coming. "I don't want to go back." She slammed on her steering wheel with both hands. Another heavy sigh. "He's so stupid!" Julie pulled the car out of the driveway and headed toward Marcus's apartment.

When she got there, she was surprised to see to police cars in front of his building. Three officers were standing outside his door. One officer was knocking. Julie's eyes widened. "Now what?" She shook her head in disgust, as always, she went through the backdoor instead of the front. She waited for the officers to leave, but they didn't. "Great!" She trudged through the snow, opened the fence, when an officer yelled at her.

"Hey, what are you doing?" the officer asked in a deep, intimidating voice.

Startled, Julie stuttered. "I-I-I'm sorry. What's wrong?"

"We're looking for Marcus Campbell," he said walking up to her. "Do you know where he is?"

"No, I told another officer a few months ago, I'm just here to take care of his cat, and keep his place clean for when he comes back."

The officer radioed the others in front. "Can you let us in?"

Julie didn't want to say yes, but she didn't want to say no either. "I, um, sure." She shrugged. "I let them in before. What happened?"

"Nothing I can talk to you about."

Julie pulled out the key to the backdoor. Shakespeare appeared out of nowhere, as if he sensed Julie's presence. The officer looked at her. "He's outdoor trained." She smiled.

The officer told the others they were opening the front door.

"I remember you," one of the officers said as they entered the apartment. He looked at his notes. "Julie, right?"

"Yep."

"Still no word from him?" the officer asked.

"No, he's still at his sisters," she answered. Julie watched the officers as they looked for anything suspicious in the living room and kitchen.

"Do you mind if we look around?"

"No, go ahead." She smiled. Julie knew they weren't going to find anything. Since Halloween Julie had packed up the items in the basement, placed them in the trunk of her car, and scrubbed the basement floor clean with bleach water.

Two officers went upstairs. The meaner officer went down to the basement.

"Right now, he is a missing person, and you're the only connection to him," one officer began to say.

Another officer interrupted with a questioning tone. "The board games are still where he left them?"

Julie shrugged. "Yeah, I figured he would want to pick up where he left off when he got back." She turned her attention to the other officer. "A missing person? He must have had a family emergency. He'll be back soon."

"He just left you in charge of his house and never told you when he was coming back, and didn't tell you how to get ahold of him?" the gruff officer from the backdoor asked as he came up from the basement. "It's all clear down there."

"It was a family emergency," she repeated. "He left so fast he forgot his cell phone," she repeated her statement from the last time they were there.

"You keep saying that. You're the only one who has supposedly had any contact with him before he left," an officer said.

"Do you know how he's making his rent payments?" another asked.

She had never thought of that. It's a wonder they hadn't evicted him by now. "No, but he's a pretty smart guy. Autopay?" She shrugged.

"We'll have to check that out with the manager," Officer grumpy said.

"All clear upstairs, too." The officers came down the stairs. They gathered in the kitchen.

Julie listened as best as she could.

"What do we tell her?" one asked.

"This makes no sense, but everything checks out," another said.

"What checks out? The guy has been missing for almost ten months. He leaves in a rush. Leaves a girl in charge of his apartment. Now the school is accusing him of fraud, identity theft, and forgery. How does any of that check out?" the grumpy officer asked.

"Do we treat her like a suspect?" she heard one of the officers ask, but she could not hear the reply.

They walked back to the living room. The nice officer took over, "Listen, Julie, we can't let you come back here anymore. Your Mr. Campbell is in a lot of trouble, and his apartment is going to be a crime scene."

"What?" She covered her mouth with her hand, and sat down. "Can I ask what you think he did?"

"We can't really talk about it, but if you know anything, even if you don't think it's important, please tell us, or call us if you think about it later."

Just breathe, breathe, she thought. "Okay, um, yeah, can I take Shakespeare with me?" The officers looked at her. "His cat," she clarified. "If I can't come here, I don't want to leave him alone."

"Yes, of course," the nice officer said. He looked at the others. "I don't think it would hurt anything."

Under their watchful eyes, Julie gathered up Shakespeare's food and bed. She picked up the cat and walked out the front door.

One of the officers followed her out the door. "I have a question for you. Isn't that Mr. Campbell's car." He pointed at the old, white car sitting in Mr. Campbell's reserved space.

"Um, yeah," she said. *Crap!*

"Why do you think he would leave it here?" the officer asked.

"Pick up service…He probably got a ride to the airport," the nice officer answered. "You did say his sister lived pretty far away, didn't you?"

"Um, yeah, she's really far away."

"Where's she from again?" the other officer asked.

"I don't know. He just said he was leaving and didn't know when he would be back. Family emergency."

"Does his sister have a name?" the nice one asked.

"Yeah, Freya," Julie answered.

"Unusual first name. Last name?" He waited to add to his notes.

Julie wrinkled her nose, juggling the cat, its food and bed. "Campbell, I guess."

"Make sure you stay in town," the grumpy officer started.

"Okay, thanks, we'll be in touch," the nice one continued.

"Thanks." She sat in her car and watched the officers put caution tape across his door, and take information on his car. "Now what am I going to do?" she asked Shakespeare. The cat placed its front paws on the dash, and meowed as if to answer her.

Fifteen minutes later Julie entered her house. "Mom, Dad," she hollered from the doorway.

"What's wrong?" her mother answered.

"Nothing...well, everything. Mr. Campbell is missing."

"Missing, I thought he went to his sister's to take care of something?" she asked. Julie's dad entered from the garage.

"What's going on, Jules?" He obviously noticed the cat and its belongings in her hands. "What'd we have here?"

"This is Shakespeare. He's Mr. Campbell's cat." She let the cat leap to the floor. "He's outdoor trained and really good," she started to plead her case.

"What happened to Mr. Campbell?" Michelle asked.

"I don't know, mom. It sounds like he's in big trouble. The police put yellow tape around his apartment, and were asking me all kinds of questions."

"That's weird. I knew he was gone, but now the police are involved?"

"I hope nothing happened to him," Phil said, pushing his glasses up his nose.

"It sounds like they are trying to find him, I heard them mention fraud?" Julie told them.

"Fraud? That's scary. He always seemed so nice, and he saved you from—"

"Okay, we know," Julie stopped her mom. "I'm sure it's just a misunderstanding. He's been gone for a while, and probably forgot to pay a bill or something."

"They don't call the police for not paying a bill," Michelle said.

"I'm going to put this in the kitchen." She held up the bag of cat food. "He can sleep with me."

"Okay, but he's your responsibility," Phil said. "You have to take care of him."

"Yep." She put the food in the kitchen pantry and rushed up the steps to her room. Shakespeare followed her up the stairs. "We have work to do," Julie said, holding the cat face to face and shaking her head.

Chapter Seventeen
Earth – Julie

Julie stood back to admire her handy work. It had taken three days for her to drag pieces of a broken-down barn a half mile away from her house to the woods behind her home. The old farmer would never miss the faded red barn siding. She fashioned it along with parts of her old tree house from her younger days into a makeshift cabin. She finished the project the day after Christmas. It stood just over seven feet inside, so Marcus wouldn't bump his head. It was smaller than Marcus's cabin, but it would do to travel back and forth. "Here goes nothing." She sliced her hand with one of her mother's kitchen knives. She let the blood follow the trace she had made of the Elders' symbol on the dirty wooden floor she made from pallets she took from behind a grocery store. After she filled in every bit of the symbol with her blood, she wrapped her hand in a cloth and placed the three rocks in their position around the markings.

It reminded her how crazy she thought Marcus was the first time he took her into his basement. When he flipped on the light and she saw the Elder's symbol on his floor. "What in the world is that?" she had said.

"Do you trust me?" Mr. Campbell asked. Looking back, she was foolish trusting him that far. She remembered arguing back and forth, praying he wasn't some kind of satanic murderer. Marcus had begged her, "Julie, please trust me."

"Having a little bit of trouble with the whole trust thing right now," she recalled saying.

When Mr. Campbell tried to reach out and grab her by the shoulders, she backed down the stairs. "I swear to God if you take another step, I am going to scream my head off."

"I am not going to hurt you," he said at the time.

"You lured me down into a dark basement with a freaking pentagram on the floor and you want me to trust that you aren't going to hurt me?"

"Julie, I would never hurt you; and, it's not a pentagram…at least I don't think it is." He turned on a second light.

"What are you doing, Mr. Campbell?"

"Listen, I can explain everything if you would just relax."

He had moved toward her as she backed away from him.

"You can explain from over there," she pointed to the basement steps.

"What is the problem?"

"The problem? The problem is you brought me down to this basement and you have some kind of Satan-worshipping drawing on your floor. Did you think you could just lure me down here and kill me without a fight? How many other girls have you done this to? Is that why you don't tell anyone about your family?"

"What? No. I have never…Julie, I am not going to kill you. I told you I am not going to hurt you. I can explain everything, please!" He sat down on the steps. "Okay, remember the naked guy you saw in the woods?"

"Yeah?"

"I was that guy."

"What! Oh, my God!"

And that was it, Mr. C. explained to her, or tried to explain to her everything he could about being the naked guy her dad almost ran over, about being from a different dimension, and how this marking on the ground became a portal which transported him back and forth from Seras and Earth. With that, she shook her head in the amount of trust she had in him. "It must be the connection people keep telling me about."

Here she was, getting ready to trust that the markings she designed herself would take her where she wanted to go. With one more week left during Christmas break it was the perfect time to see what was going on with Marcus.

She ignited a handheld candle lighter and watched the red and blue flame grow. Next, she lit the candle; the purple smoke filled the room and quickly spread to the outside world. Julie knew in a matter of minutes, time would slow down for Earth allowing her to spend as much time needed in Seras.

Julie felt the wind whip around her naked body, an exercise she had never gotten used to. Seconds later she was standing in Marcus's cabin. It was darker than normal, no candles lit, only the fading blue flame illuminated the small room. She could see cobwebs gathering in the corners. "He hasn't been here in a while," she said aloud.

Her clothes were hanging on the deer antler racks as they had since after her first day arriving when she first met Gwendolyn and Leyta who helped bring her clothes, and Marcus gave her the gross drink that allowed her to understand their language.

Julie quickly dressed and left the cabin. The Allon villagers in the streets and market place stopped what they were doing as she walked by. Julie greeted them awkwardly. She made her way to Freya's cabin in the quarters reserved for women of the town. Allon was divided into specific areas. Marcus's cabin was in the male area. Argos and Gwendolyn, and Griffus and his wife were in the cabins in the married personal quarters. All three areas surrounded the marketplace and had separating walls between them.

"Julie?" Freya met her at the door. "When did you get here?"

"Just now. Have you seen Mr....Marcus?" Julie asked, as Freya ushered her into her cabin.

Freya's room was simple, but colorful. Her different scarves adorned the wall closest to the door. It had a small wooden table and a single matching chair. A four-foot bench leaned against one wall. Her bed was in the furthest corner of the room, unlike Marcus's whose bed was situated near the door. Freya's room was filled with flowers, as was the garden outside her door

"Not since he went after you when you found out..." Freya sat in the chair by the table.

"Yeah, I know, but I wouldn't talk to him, so he left. I haven't seen him in months," Julie said. "In fact, he hasn't been anywhere I know of. He's missing."

"He can't be missing. It's his duty to look after you."

"Well, he's not...looking after me. I'm telling you I haven't seen him in forever." Julie put her hands on her hips and blew out a deep breath. "He never came back after I chased him away."

"I don't understand," Freya said.

"Okay, listen. I have a pretty reliable source who told me he was in trouble. First, there was a horse, then he was in a cage. I'm no genius, but my guess is he jumped on a horse, rode off, and got his stupid butt captured. Now, he's in big trouble on Earth, and serious trouble here. Where do you think he would have gone?"

"If what you are saying is true--"

"It is," Julie interrupted.

"Then there is only one place he would go."

Freya stood and left the cabin. Julie followed after. She got the attention of a passing by soldier. "Go sound the meeting signal." The soldier hurried away. Freya started walking.

"Wait! Where are you going, where would he go?" Julie scrambled behind her in a huff. Freya continued. "Freya, stop!" Freya obeyed. "Where-are-you-going? Where-is-Marcus?"

"If Marcus left, he left for one reason. He left to put an end to this," Freya said.

"What does that mean?"

"It means he could be in grave danger, or we are."

Freya and Julie made it to the council cabin. They were joined by Argos, Griffus, Redderick Bobo, Jayna, and Seren. They each greeted Julie. Griffus picked her up and spun her around.

"Hello, my dear," Redderick said with a smile that told Julie he remembered her dream.

"It's so good to see you again," Griffus said. "Pertheus and Otta are on patrol." He placed Julie safely on the ground. "I think we are all here."

"Marcus is gone," Freya said.

She looked at Julie.

Julie took this as her clue to begin. "Marcus never came back to Earth. He's been gone for six months or more."

"Impossible, my child, I saw him leave," Redderick said.

"He never came back," Argos said. "We would have seen him."

"He left on a horse. He had an accident, and is being held as a prisoner," Julie explained the visions Mr. Christian shared with her.

"I'm afraid this could go very bad," Freya said. "I'm afraid he left to find William."

"William? Why would he seek out William?" Jayna asked.

"To kill him, obviously," Griffus answered.

"It's never that easy with Marcus and William," Freya said. "If Marcus is really William's prisoner, he will try to convince him to rejoin him, and if that happens it would be worse than Marcus dying."

"What could be worse than Marcus dying?" Julie protested.

"Joining William," Freya said. "If William and Marcus got back together--"

"It would be the end of all of us," Griffus finished.

"He wouldn't do that?" Julie asked in a voice filled with confusion and near disgust. "Would he?"

Chapter Eighteen
Seras - Julie

Julie followed Redderick. "He wouldn't do that, would he?" she repeated her question to the immortal.

"It is hard to understand what is in his heart," Redderick said as he walked toward his tent. "The prophecy says he will protect you."

"I don't believe in prophesies," Julie argued.

"No, but the prophesies believe in you, and so does Marcus."

They arrived in his tent where the beautiful women were lounging, waiting for him to return as the slave, Charlena, was tending to the firewood.

"That sucks," Julie exclaimed.

"I am not sure what that means, but I am sure I agree," Redderick chuckled.

"What does that mean?" Julie asked as Redderick sat down between the women.

"He will do whatever he thinks he needs to do to protect you. In this case, he wanted to face William with the hope of killing him and eliminating that problem from your life. He just doesn't realize--"

"He doesn't realize?"

"Nothing, nothing," Redderick answered.

"Okay, whatever, so what was the deal with my dream?" Julie asked as she looked around, moved a few pillows and sat across from Redderick and his harem.

"As I said, you called for me." He signaled for Charlena to bring food.

Julie rejected the tray with a polite wave. "No thanks."

Redderick grabbed a handful of nuts and popped them into his mouth.

"How is that possible?"

"My dear, I wish you would understand your power. You are capable of so much. I understand, Marcus understands, Freya, Argos, Griffus, Pertheus all understand, Callista understood. You refuse to understand your power and what you mean to the people of Seras, not just Allon, but all of Seras."

"I'm just a girl," Julie argued. "I can't do anything for Allon or Seras. Heck, I can't do anything for Marcus."

"You can, you already have. You signaled for me. You have come here on your own. You have warned us of what Marcus had planned, and what has happened to him."

"But how is that going to help?" she asked.

"Now, it is possible to go after him and save him from William or himself," Redderick answered.

"Okay, is he my teacher, my mentor, or what?"

"I do not know what you are asking, child. He is your teacher, your mentor, and so much more," Redderick said.

"See, what does that mean?" Julie stood. "Nobody tells me anything!"

"Perhaps you are not asking the right questions to the right people," he said.

With that, Julie fumed out of the immortal's tent.

~ * ~

Freya stormed into her tent crying. She had held back a secret from her brother. A secret she was positive he would never forgive her for.

All those years ago, in the forest outside of Fort Madena, she made the decision to find Darius. It was after he and Arthur fought. The mighty Arthur laid dead. Darius was bleeding out from the wound across his chest.

She knelt beside her brother and ripped off the remains of his shirt. He looked at her with anger. Freya packed mud on his chest just above the open wound. She pressed the separated layers together, and began to hum. She massaged the mud around the cut and watched as it started to close. Freya lifted her brother's head, and gave him water from her side pouch. As he began to choke, she pulled it away, then whispered in his ear. "Marcus is the prophecy."

Freya left her brother where he laid. Her mission was to get what was left of Marcus's army, Griffus and Pertheus's men as far north as she could. The immortal Bhjuda Heilshorn had spoken to her in a dream several days earlier. The mysterious immortal was gathering tribes from territories attacked by Marcus's Skorei army, and William's army. Between the two of them, many villages and homes had been destroyed.

Heilshorn had recruited the well-known Letite warrior Argos to assist him in the task assigned to him by the Elders. Argos operated as Heilshorn's right, and rode to rescue survivors of battles, or, when lucky, get to the places before the Skorei. They would take whomever they could back to an undisclosed fortress deep in the northern mountains.

In her dream, Heilshorn revealed the location, and the fate of the Elders' plans were tied to Marcus's survival and the people of Allon.

Chapter Nineteen
Seras - Marcus

Marcus stood. He kept his eyes on William. He was not ready to fight, but knew William's patience would come to its end. "Okay, I'm ready."

"Ready? You are nowhere close to being ready," William growled. "Look at you!" He struck Marcus with a stick across the shoulder at the base of his neck. "Fine, fight me," William commanded.

Marcus wobbled toward him, and swung his fist at William.

William deflected the punch and hit Marcus in the gut, then across the back of the knees with his stick.

Marcus dropped to his hands and knees.

"Stand up, stand up," William ordered.

As Marcus did, William kicked him in the ribs. Marcus tumbled to his side. "Ready to fight? You are a joke." William struck him over and over with the stick. "Look what you made me do! You were my friend!" William continued the beating. "We are all dead because of you! It is all your fault!"

Marcus could taste the blood pooling in his mouth.

"Kralen and Reinwald did not deserve what happened to them!" He listed others who had died, "Hurvay, Chadrick, Chaldrean, Justus, Parikus…" With every word William lashed out at him with his stick. "Arthur, Bones…they were my friends, too! Freya told you about the priest, didn't she? You could have let me find him!"

Marcus lay crumpled in a ball.

"See, what did I tell? You are not ready." William turned to the guard. "Take him out with the other prisoners. Maybe some time outside will do him some good." He playfully slapped Marcus on the cheek.

Marcus was dragged to the courtyard with other starving prisoners. A guard was assigned to watch over him and the others who were nothing more than skin, bones, and sinew. Their job was to dig trenches. When they came across large rocks, they placed them in a cart to add to the fortress. It was hot, the prisoners received little water. They dared not faint. If they fell off the platforms they would die. If they fell in front of a cart or wagon, they would be crushed under the wheels. At night, they huddled together in shoddy wooden barracks, no pillows, no blankets, and only the ground to sleep. Men died daily in the trenches due to the lack of food, the sun and heat.

Once a week William would pull him to the side, and beat him severely. Marcus wanted to fight back, but while his body was getting stronger, it wasn't time. He took the beating and verbal abuses, went back to the trenches, and slept in the barracks with the others.

"Who are you? Why does William hate you so much?" one prisoner asked. "I have never seen him treat any of us the way he hates you."

"We go back a long way," Marcus replied. He took a small sip of the communal water jug.

"I am glad it is you, and not me," another said. "I do not think I would last a day with the beatings he gives you."

Instinctively, Marcus reached for the fresh wound across his shoulder. It would only be a matter of time before they realized he heals. It may not be as fast as normal with the effects of the huge fall, the beatings, and the lack of food and water slowing him down. But it will. "I have to admit, I wish I could make him stop."

A guard pounded on the wall of the barracks. "Stop talking in there."

"In due time, I will get my revenge," Marcus whispered. "But not now." He patted one of the nearby prisoners. "But not now." He found a corner to curl up and rest his eyes before morning came and he had to start all over.

Chapter Twenty
Seras - Julie

Julie sat atop a brown horse. Allon's full army gathered behind her. Freya, Griffus, Pertheus, Argos, his two sons, Julius and Jakob, the two Hemoor women Otta and Seren were shouting orders and telling loved one's goodbye.

Argos promised he would resume trying to find his youngest son, Edwin's killer when he returned. "I have to go, the fate of Seras is in trouble. Edwin's killer could be within these walls, or riding with us," he told his wife, Gwendolyn.

"Go, I will be here when you return," Gwendolyn told him.

She hugged her husband, then hugged Leyta, Edwin's betrothed before he died. She agreed Argos needed to ride with the battle party to escape Allon and the memories of Edwin for awhile. He eventually relented and conceded it would do them both some good.

Freya ordered Jayna to fly ahead. First, she had to find Tanda; and the Evandell spies charged with keeping an eye on Pallanex's home, Cauleta, and the Queen's coming and goings. Then the Tarrack was to fly to William's fortress to find Marcus and report back to Freya and the others.

Griffus hugged his wife, Laila, and his two children, the twins Tuco and Beahel. "I will be back soon," he said.

"You better," Laila told him. "I am not raising these two by myself." Tuco and Beahel found a mud hole, and pushed each other in. Laila scowled. "Hurry back."

"Yes, love."

Redderick approached Julie. He reached up to pat her hand. "My dear, I know you are mad at me and Marcus for keeping secrets, but it was for your own good."

Julie scoffed at him. "This doesn't change how I feel."

120

"I believe it will. Ask the others who have joined you on this journey. Why do they want to save a man so evil? A man who for many is responsible for them being here to begin with."

Julie glared at him. "I am doing this for Seras, and the people here. Not for me. I was way better off without him in my life."

She pulled the reins of her horse to move away from the immortal.

"I do not believe you mean that," he said, then she watched the immortal move to Freya.

"I think we both know it is time," he told her.

Freya nodded. With that, Redderick made his way through the crowd and disappeared toward his tent. Freya turned to Argo. "Are we ready, commander?"

Argos looked at Griffus and Pertheus. Both gestured their readiness. All three commanders raised their hands, and the men and women of the Allon army fell in tight formations. Many rode on horses, some in wagons. The rest would march or take turns on horseback. It would be a long journey, more than a month or more to get to William's fortress and save Marcus.

They headed out the gates. Julie could not help but wonder what she had gotten herself into. Eventually, the army made it to the fake walls they used to fool Pallanex's army when Callista died fighting in the Battle of Yellowfields to save Julie from the giant general. The same giant Marcus killed to protect Julie and avenge the death of Callista.

The party was solemn as the traveled past the walls which had been turned into a sentry post, ten guards continuously rotated their watch to protect Allon's southern most flank.

They marched up the hill, the yellow flowers were yet to bloom across the field, the fake shelters and cabins they built to were now used to house the guards who were off duty and their families. They made their way to the narrow passage that led to the woods. Four sentries stood guard over wooden barriers.

Julie heard Argos explain to Freya his men had set up the barriers as part of the construction to make sure another Battle of Yellowfields would never happen. The sentries removed the gates so the army could pass.

As night began to fall, Freya motioned for the company to halt. They dismounted, and started setting up camp. Firewood was gathered, tents put together, and soon campfires blazed.

Freya stood at a highpoint. The commanders gathered around her.

"What's wrong?" Argos asked. He looked around, knowing the mysteries of these woods and the rumors of unexplained deaths of Pallanex spies found butchered.

"What are you doing?" Griffus pulled out his sword. "Is there something out there?"

"There is," Freya said. "Unfortunately, I believe if we are to defeat William, we are going to need help."

"Help?" Argos asked.

The group looked at her incredulously.

"What are you talking about, Freya?" Pertheus asked.

"You will see, and I just have to ask for your forgiveness. There was no other way."

The party stopped their chatter when they heard noise coming from the cover of the trees. The warriors drew their swords, other notched their bows, ready for an attack. "Hold!" Freya ordered.

They waited. Each man and woman worked to control their breathing, and slowing their heart rates as the movement came closer. Griffus and Pertheus did double takes as a familiar image appeared.

Chapter Twenty-one
Seras - Pallanex

Pallanex watched as the crew of the *Sea Tiger* prepared to dock. She walked around the deck of the ship anxious to get back on land. The blood red sails were pulled down, along with the spider flag.

"My queen," Javan said as men fastened ropes to secure the ship before lowering the walking plank. "This is going to take a while, as we unload. Why not join me for a drink one last time?"

"I have so enjoyed my time with you, captain," Pallanex cooed. "But there are many other things that require my attention." She walked to the bow of the ship where the figure of the curvy woman with the head of a tiger, and a shark's tail overlooked the village of Tribulite.

Captain Javan ran his hand across the top of his head and down his tightly pulled pony-tail. "I understand, it has been so nice to have you on the *Tiger*. I wonder if there is a way to convince you to stay."

"No," she said. "I have plans, and they need my full attention."

"What can I do to make my queen's life easier?" He touched her shoulder. "I want to prove my love to you, and that I am worthy of your love. Even more than William."

"I am glad you asked. I do have something you can do, and prove your love to me. If you can do this, I promise I will give my love to you, and you alone."

"Anything my queen."

She watched as the slaves were moved from beneath the cargo deck. They looked sickly. "*I hope William's serum works on them,*" she thought before continuing her conversation with Lord Javan. "The fortress where my enemies, Marcus, and the whore of Tolth hide is deep in the mountains of the north. A place called Allon from what my spies have told me. My armies have failed many times to penetrate the forests and passages coming from the south, east, and west. I want you to take your ships up along the coast as far north as you can travel, then attack them from the rear. Perhaps their fortifications are weak, as they would not expect anyone to attack from there."

"Do you know what you are asking?" Javan looked at her, he cocked his head. "There are no maps to show me where we are going. There is no way of knowing how long it will take, or what the currents, the depths, the weather, or the terrain will be once we get there."

"You are right, my lord," Pallanex said. "If you are not able. I understand." She turned to walk away.

"My Queen, I did not say I was not able. I merely stated the dangers." He bowed his head. "I am your humble servant. I will sail my men north, and bring you the heads' of your enemies."

"I knew you would not disappoint me." She kissed him passionately. "When will you be leaving?"

"Give my men time to rest, and reload the ships."

"Of course." She leaned in to kiss him, as he prepared for her kiss, she grabbed him by the ponytail and bit his lip. "The sooner you accomplish your mission," she purred. "The sooner I am yours."

As Pallanex left the captain, she heard him yell out to his crew. "Rest up, we leave again in the morning." She couldn't help the wicked smile that crossed her face.

Chapter Twenty-two
Seras - Julie

The figure moving through the dense forest got closer until the army of Allon could see the image of a man walking toward them.

"What is he doing here?" Griffus yelled as he recognized the bearded man standing in front of them.

"He's dead," Pertheus added.

Both he and Griffus had their swords drawn and at the ready.

"Obviously not," Darius said with a grin. He held his Skorei sword across the back of his neck and shoulders.

"How about I come down from here, and wipe that smile from your face," Griffus growled.

"I would love for you to try," Darius taunted. "I haven't had a--"

"Enough," Freya said. "I asked him to come here."

"Why?" Griffus asked.

"How?" Argos spoke, moving in front of Julie, who had already dismounted.

"We need him," Freya answered.

"You've always needed me," Darius said. "Who do you think has been guarding your precious little fort all this time?"

"What?" Argos looked at Darius, then to Freya.

Freya nodded.

"That's right. All of those dead spies, me. The pack of warriors you came across bound to trees with knives in their mouths, me." Darius stroked his beard. "I'm not really sure what you and your men would have done without me?"

"You aren't helping," Freya said to Darius.

She rubbed her forehead. She turned her attention to Griffus, Pertheus, and Argos. "If we are going to be successful, we need him to help us. He knows William far better than any of us, and he's a better fighter than any of us."

"Who is he?" Julie chimed in as he moved from out of Argos's shadow.

"Darius," Argos said.

"Marcus's brother," Griffus added through gritted teeth.

"So," Julie stumbled to find the words. "You, you're…a…demon?"

"I've been called worse." Darius grinned. "You must be the Heart everyone's been talking about. Funny, I thought you'd be a lot more imposing."

The three men simultaneously positioned themselves to shield Julie from Darius.

"I had to save him. He's my brother," Freya explained. "When I found him dying in the woods after fighting Arthur, I had to."

"Why, I don't understand?" Pertheus argued.

"Because she knew all along this was going to happen. Haven't you idiots figured that out by now?" Darius scoffed at them. "She knew she was going to need a real warrior, so she kept me alive. And if anyone is going to kill Marcus, it's going to be me."

"I barely know who you are," Julie said, "and I definitely think you're a jerk, but, if you lay one hand on Marcus I will…" Julie couldn't finish the statement. She clinched her fists, seething.

"This is going well, Freya," Darius said.

"You are making it worse," she told him. She turned to her friends. "I'm sorry. We do need him, and I will take full responsibility. I promise."

Chapter Twenty-three
Seras - Marcus

A young Marcus and his little team of warriors earned the right to train with the older boys in the arena.

"Come on you maggots!" Kralen yelled. "Strike, strike, strike!" The boys looked at him with arrogant eyes. "Every time you miss a block, that is life slipping through your fingers, your blood spilled on the ground. Every time you swing your sword and miss, the warrior across from you will not. You are no good to me dead!" His eyes were black holes, darker than a starless night, as though he had no soul. "Get a drink. I am sick of seeing you!"

"Hard to say, but I miss Marddek," Thomen said, taking a long sip.

They peeked over the wall to watch the younger kids practicing. After two years they had become hardened warriors even at a young age. Marcus saw Darius, and smiled. The group Darius was with included Chaldrean, Chadrick, Justus, Angus, Parikus, Petar, and Galius.

"Stop dreaming about going back there," Hurvay said.

As an older warrior, they had privileges of getting better breaks and harassing those younger than themselves. He was joined by Fish and other older boys.

"This is your Scindo, right?" another boy asked. The Scindo is a time when the second-year boys are sent out to fend for themselves. They have to battle nature in its many forms, loneliness, and whatever else the nights bring.

"Try not to die," Fish joked.

Another boy shoved Marcus's head. "I hope your father does not try to save you."

Marcus stood up, ready to fight. Arthur, Thomen, and Hurvay back him away from the scuffle.

"Glad to see your friends have sense," the boy said. "I want you to live through the week so I can take care of you later."

"We should go," Fish said, "and stop harassing them."

"Hey maggots, why am I standing around waiting for you?" Kralen barked. "You have a lot of work to do before tonight."

~ * ~

The Scindo, a seven-day rite of passage after the Tempura, to go from childhood to manhood, even though they had only been in training for two years; and they were eleven years old. The boys gathered up all they were allowed to take: one blanket, one knife and the clothes they wore at the time.

All of the warriors from Cauleta gathered to send them off. Trusted guards would escort them on horseback, each knew how long they had to travel. The boys were given their final instructions.

"Welcome to the Scindo. In our tradition and culture, the Scindo is the first step to becoming a Skorei warrior," Kralen said from a script he had all but memorized. "You will be gone for seven days of Narkrios's passing. On the eight day, your escort will return. If you are not where he left you, you are either dead or will not be a Skorei warrior even if you make it back alive."

The boys present looked at each other. There were twenty of them in all including Marcus, Arthur, Bones, Thomen, Angus, and William. They stood at attention as they were inspected. Their weapons and uniforms were gathered and placed in a crate. They wore simple clothing, no armor and no weapons. They carried nothing as they marched to be greeted by Canis.

"You cannot receive any outside help. You cannot come back until your time is up," Kralen barked. "In the name of Cauleta, the Skorei warriors and the Elders, go out and conquer."

Canis, and Darius walked to Marcus, as other fathers and brothers approached their own. "You are my oldest," Canis said. "I am very proud of you. I know you will return a Skorei warrior."

Darius gave him a hug, practically latching himself to Marcus's side. "Come back."

"I will," Marcus said. "I will make you proud, father."

Canis rubbed his shaggy head. "You have keen eyes, boy. Use them, and be careful."

"Time to go," Kralen ordered. "Mount up."

Two warriors approached Marcus. Both bowed to Canis. "My lord."

"Azron, Cordar." Canis nodded.

The warrior named Azron, was a Tarrack, back when Skorei and Tarracks were allies. Cordar was a Skorei warrior who just completed the training. They were to be Marcus's escorts. They led him to his horse. They marched out of the arena, through the village of Cauleta to cheers and applause. They got to the gate named The Lion's Gate as the entrance to Cauleta in honor of Canis. "This is where we start," Azron said. He spurred his horse, and Marcus and Cordar followed.

The three had ridden for about a mile when they passed Raewin's home. From the corner of his eye, Marcus saw Raewin standing at the border of her cabin, still refusing to enter Cauleta. She waved and blew him a kiss.

Each of the twenty boys had different locations, none but their riders knew where. They did not talk the entire time. What felt like a full day's journey ended. Marcus saw a red archway.

Azron and Cordar brought their horses to stop. "Hear me now, we will return when the time is up. We will meet you here, and take you home. If you are not here when we return, we will go back without you. Understood?"

Marcus swallowed hard. "Yes." He dismounted.

Cordar took the reins of his horse.

"Do not disappoint me, son of Canis."

"No."

Azron threw him his blanket and knife. The two escorts turned the horses and rode away.

The shadows grew long as he felt he was being watched over by the tall conical pines. Marcus didn't have time to build shelter before the solitary moon made its appearance. He found the tree with the lowest hanging branches, and made it his temporary home for the night. Next, he collected wood, used his blanket to tie it into a small bundle, and took it to his camp. It took him more than a few minutes to start a fire, but eventually did.

In the morning, Marcus awoke with chirping and chattering of birds and squirrels. He broke off a sturdy stick, sharpened the end to a point with his knife, and went exploring. Marcus knew he needed three things: he needed to find food, a water source, and to build a true shelter. The woods were dead trees fallen from disease, limbs hanging on by nothing, roots barely making their way deep into the soil. Marcus kicked a few of the dying trees over for fun. His journey brought him to a nearly dried marsh. He had not found water. The salty sweat begun stinging his eyes. He came upon a broken stone wall, scars of old wars, the relics laid in ruin. Marcus saw a well, he rushed to it hoping for clean water. He pulled the weathered and fraying rope up, the only thing in the bucket were rats. He dropped the rope, and fell backward as the bucket plunged back down the well. He blew out a breath of air. "That was dumb." He picked up his self-made spear and pulled the bucket back up. He jammed the shaft into two rats, then cut the bucket rope with his knife. He carried the bucket back to the camp.

Overhead it began to drizzle as he made his way back to his camp. The blue and gray clouds swirled with impending rain. "This is going to work just fine," he said to himself as he swung the bucket. He cooked the two rats, and waited for the rain to fill up the bucket.

The sky turned yellowish green. A storm was brewing. Marcus put out his fire, and moved his camp to the stone ruins. He moved boards and bricks to make a roof and wall. Lightning flashed and thunder rumbled, they shook the forest. He heard tree branches cracked under the pressure of the wind. Marcus entertained himself by watching the sharp smooth rocks shimmer in the rain. He thought about the wars raged behind these walls. What stories they could tell?

For two days the darkened sky poured on top of him. He was in a continuous state of being soaked to the bone. He ventured out of his little camp to hustle under the canopied forest that gave him enough shelter from the rain to gather food. He tried to keep his fire going, though the wetness made it more difficult. Marcus did find a creek. It was a half mile from his camp. It measured twenty-five feet across. With the deluge, the creek rushed wild. "It will be good to have a source of clean water."

The rain eventually stopped. He was busy hunting in the woods when he heard a sound. From his left he saw a large brown object racing toward him. "What in the name of Canis?" he said aloud. "A bear!"

Marcus looked quickly at his options. He could not outrun a bear, and he couldn't fight a bear with a pointed stick and a small knife. He raced to the nearest tree with limbs low enough to reach. He pulled himself up, and climbed as high as he could. He heard the deep breathing, and the crackling of dead limbs under its weight. Luckily, the bear struggled navigating up the tree with the branches in its way. Marcus shouted, broke smaller branches to throw at the bear, and jabbed his spear toward the large beast. The bear must have decided Marcus wasn't worth the work, climbed down the tree, and slowly walked away from him. Marcus stayed in the tree until he was positive the bear wasn't returning.

He went back to his camp only to find the bear had beat him to it. It wrecked his makeshift home, ate the food he had stored, shredded his blanket, and smashed his bucket. Marcus looked to the sky, and sighed.

In the following days he slowly rebuilt his camp, gathered more firewood and scrounged for food. His rats in the well had given way to rabbits and squirrels. The dried marsh was still holding water and Marcus used it sparingly. On the fifth night, he saw smoke rising from the distance. The dead forest roared in flames. The smoke and heat began engulfing the ruined fortress. Marcus rushed out of the brick and rock before it collapsed around him.

"What did I do to deserve this?" he ran across a large open field away from one wooded area to another. Sweat stung his eyes. He hiked through the unknown; briar latched onto his skin, ripping and slashing him. Streaks of blood stripped his body. His legs getting the worst of it.

"The safest place to be is up there," he thought, looking at a large branch about fifteen feet off the ground. It appeared sturdy and thick enough to rest. He climbed the tree, settled onto the branch, and made himself a crude bed, wedging between two jutted limbs to keep him from falling out.

In the morning, Marcus climbed down from his perch. He cracked his neck, stretched and rubbed his muscles trying to work out the kinks. "I wonder how the others are surviving?" he said aloud. Starting from scratch, he broke a sturdy limb and chiseled it to a point. Blowing out a deep breath, "Time to start over."

Investigating the new surroundings he gathered firewood, before finding a small entrance embedded in a rocky hill. "Shelter." He yelled inside the cave. No sounds. Good news. Marcus had to crawl on his hands and knees to enter, the cave opened enough for him to stand about fifteen feet through. He stood up, dusted off his hands and knees, then busied himself starting a fire. "Okay, now I need to find water." As he headed out of the small cave entrance, he stopped as he saw the image of a man. "Azron, you are early?"

"I am sorry, son of Canis, but I wish you would not have seen me," Azron said. He unsheathed his sword.

Marcus scrambled backward into the cave. Azron surged at him. Being smaller in size, Marcus quickly maneuvered the distance from the opening to his little site. He grabbed his wood shaft and knife.

Azron pulled back.

"Why are you here?"

Marcus's question was met by a low growl. Azron had turned into a cougar.

Marcus jabbed his stick at the cat as it crawled through the entrance. Azron hissed and clawed at him. Azron backed out again.

Marcus grabbed a fire log. When Azron made a second attempt, Marcus pushed the fire into his face. The cat roared, and retreated.

"I cannot let you return," Azron said, turning back into a man.

"You were the bear, you wrecked my camp, and you caught the woods on fire," Marcus accused the warrior who was supposed to be his escort home.

"No, but the bear was a friend. He was supposed to do this for me. But I had to check, and here you are. Now you definitely cannot return," Azron said.

Marcus heard large crashing; the unmistakable growl of the bear, and pounding at the top of the cave entrance. Soon, the crashing of rock, and the light from the opening slowly went dark.

"Goodbye, son of Canis," Azron said muffled from the stone.

Marcus waited until he was certain Azron was not waiting outside and could not make his way in. "Now what?" He rubbed the tears and sweat out of his eyes. He crawled to the end of the entrance, there was no way to move the rocks from his crouched position. His heart pounded, and the pores on his body opened. He wiped his palms on his pants. "I need food and water." He fanned the flames of his fire to keep light around him. He took one of the longer sticks, cut his pants at the knees, tied the material around the stick, and lit it on fire. He went deeper into the cave using one hand to hold the torch, the other holding his spear and feeling the rough rock wall.

He stumbled under the loose footing, dropping to his knees. His stomach grumbled. "I have to hurry. There has to be something in here." He pushed on. He only stopped to rest when the level changed, or he had to add more clothing to his torch. It paid off. First, he felt the dampness on a rock. He followed the little trickle to a small pool. He blew out a breath of air. Relief.

He kneeled down and took handful of the cool drink. The question he had to ask, "How long can I last down here?"

Chapter Twenty-four
Seras - Marcus

"Do you remember what happened next?" William asked.

He hovered around Marcus who was on knees, his arms were laced through a board across the middle of his back, his hands tied in the front. Marcus's right eye was blackened, and blood oozed from his nose and mouth.

"Of course, I do," he answered through a hoarse voice.

"You have no idea how we felt," William yelled. He hit Marcus across the back. "Nineteen of us came back. Only you were missing. You father was crushed. You failed. You were dead to him." He hit him across the neck and shoulder. "We risked everything to bring you back. Thomen, Bones, and I knew something went wrong." He got in his face. "We begged Canis to go find you."

William, Thomen, and Bones huddled together with Arthur and Angus. They were in shock when Marcus's rider, Azron returned with an empty horse. Azron looked at Canis, and shook his head back and forth. Darius burst into tears.

Canis stood rigid. "Welcome back, brave warriors. You have now passed the Scindo. You are ready for the next phase of training so you can join the honored ranks of the Skorei." At that the men lined in black and red uniforms snapped to attention. There were ten thousand warriors watching the procession, and all villagers sat in bleachers around the arena as the boys were recognized. They stripped off their shirts, and took turns walking up to Kralen. As they did, he dipped an iron rod in hot coals. He pulled it out, and placed the hot iron on their back at their right shoulder blade. The heat sheered their skin, and they winced from the pain. When Kralen removed the branding, an emblem of a pattern of two Zs at one hundred and twenty degree angles crossing twice blazed on their backs.

The ceremony ended. Thomen, Bones, and William rushed to Canis. "King Canis," Thomen started. "Please, something happened to Marcus. You need to find him."

Canis was no longer the young dashing man who had made a truce with the Tarracks, betrayed his brother, and seduced the young Raewin. He was older. His dark locks now white, and he moved a little slower. "I do not have to do anything such thing," Canis roared. "He failed the test. He is dead to me. He is dead to us." Canis turned and walked away from the group of boys.

Thomen reached to grab the king's arm. Canis's guards began to react, William and Bones pulled him away before they hurt him. "We have to get him," Thomen said.

Canis turned. "You are forbidden to find him. He is dead to us."

The boys waited until the arena emptied. Since they had just completed the Scindo, Kralen gave them time to rest and recover. They ate silently in the afternoon as there were too many eyes and ears on them. When they returned to their barrack, the group huddled close.

"Something happened to Marcus. The Scindo was not that hard," Bones said in a whisper.

"You heard Canis," Angus said. "There is nothing we can do."

"Of course, there is," Thomen said. The boys looked at him. "We can go to the one person who is not afraid of Canis."

"Who is that?" Arthur asked. "I do not think that person exists."

"Raewin," Thomen said.

"Marcus's mother, yes!" Bones patted Thomen on the back.

"We need to sneak out, go to Raewin's cabin, and ask her to convince Canis to find Marcus," Thomen said.

"Count me in," Arthur said. He stood in the dark.

"Me too," William added, joining Arthur.

Angus paused.

"What?" Arthur asked.

"I am not sure about this," Angus said. "What if we get caught?"

"Never mind, you do not have to go," Thomen said. "In fact, you stay here and cover for us."

"I am coming, too," Bones said. He joined William and Arthur.

135

They stuffed their blankets with clothing. Angus stayed behind to make snoring sounds, and answer roll call. The four boys snuck through a wooden slat, then scrambled to the city gate. They ducked and hid from Cauleta guards and patrols, making their journey to Raewin's home.

The boys lurked in the shadows for two patrols on horseback to pass Raewin's front door before knocking.

Raewin stuck her head out the door. "Boys?" She opened the door wider. "Come in, come in before you get in trouble." Once inside, Raewin sat them down at her table. Her eyes were swollen and puffy. "I was hoping you were Marcus." She poured them water from a ceramic pitcher. "Why are you here? Do you know how much trouble you will be in, if you get caught?"

"We understand," William said. "We had to do something."

"We are hoping you can talk to Canis," Thomen started to explain.

"What makes you think Canis will listen to me?"

"Please, he has to listen," Arthur said. "There is no way Marcus did not pass the test. It was too easy."

"I appreciate your faith in my son, and in my ability to sway Canis, but--"

"Please, he has to listen, he has to believe you," Thomen said.

The four boys pleaded simultaneously.

"I will try," Raewin said.

"Thank you, thank you," they exclaimed.

"I said I would try. Canis will not listen to me any more than he would listen to four boys. He is with Pallanex now. She has a hold on him I do not understand." She got up from her seat. "Come with me." She threw a cloak around her back and raised the hood.

The boys followed. Raewin escorted the boys back to the city. They hid behind a merchant's stable.

"It will not be dark for a while, so stay here until I return," Raewin said.

The three shook their heads in agreement.

~ * ~

Canis and Pallanex were in the meeting quarters in Canis's chambers. Dark brown pillars were posted every eight feet. A fire burned from a stone fireplace. Large slabs of rock tiled the floor. Two guards were posted outside the door. He stood at a carved table. Three advisors waited for him to consider their recommendation.

"No, I do not want negotiations. I want their fidelity. Either they will submit to me, or I will destroy them."

"Lord Canis," one of the men began, "the lands south of Puri near the port village of Tribulite and beyond are vast. You will be spreading the army thin. It would be almost impossible to keep it under control."

"Besides, my Lord," a second added, "there is nothing to gain. We have fields for grain, cattle and iron for blades. Their resources are not important to us. We do not want their port. We do not need their ships." He glanced at Pallanex.

The other two shifted their eyes to him, then her.

Pallanex moved to her husband. "My Lord, listen to them. Ozmos, Harold and Bellar are your friends, and they want what is best."

He slammed his fist on the table littered with papers and maps. "You want me to look weak. We need more resources. We need to build a bigger army. We are growing fat and comfortable," Canis argued.

Pallanex took one of the men by the arm. "Give Canis some time to think about it. I am sure he will come around."

She escorted them to the door. They bowed to her, then to Canis, and took their leave.

Pallanex turned to him. "My husband, you are under stress," she cooed, "and it is understandable."

"Do not patronize me!"

"I do not, I just know the pain you are feeling," Pallanex said. She eased him into a chair and sat on his lap. "I want you to feel better." She stroked his white hair. "You do not want to spread the army thin. We need to keep the men close, and use them to clean out the enemies inside our territories."

"You mean the Corven," he said, putting his hand on her knee.

"*Indeed,*" *she answered. She moved his hand up her thigh.* "*It would benefit you,*" *Pallanex said in a suggestive tone. She stood, adjusted her dress.* "*Come with me.*"

"*I will be right there.*"

She left the room.

Canis got up, straightened up his old body as there was a knock on the door. "*Yes,*" *he said loud enough for the guards to hear.*

One man entered. "*Lord Canis, there is someone here to see you.*"

"*Who?*"

The guard gritted his teeth. "*It is your wi...Raewin.*"

Canis was puzzled. "*Send her away.*"

Raewin stormed in the room. "*You will not send me away.*"

"*Raewin, I do not want you here,*" *Canis ordered.*

He waved his hand to dismiss her. The guards moved to grab her.

"*Do not touch me,*" *she hissed. She turned to Canis.* "*We need to talk.*"

Canis dropped his shoulders. He held out his hand to stop the guards. "*You can go,*" *he told them. Once the door was closed, he walked to a food table and poured himself a drink.* "*What do you want?*" *He took a drink, then popped a grape into his mouth.*

"*You know why I am here. Marcus is our son,*" *she said.*

"*He is not my son,*" *Canis said.* "*He did not come back. He is no longer welcome in Cauleta.*"

"*He may not be your son, but he is mine.*" *Raewin moved closer to him.*

Canis sat in his chair.

Raewin walked to the window, lighting the dozen or more candles as she did. She pulled the dark green curtains together.

"*You know I cannot go back on the rules of the Skorei.*"

"*You made the rules of the Skorei, my Lord.*" *She took a pillow from the chair beside him, and placed it on the floor in front of him.* "*Canis, please, you must go find him. Even if it is just his body. You cannot leave him there, dead or alive.*" *She unclasped her gown.* "*Canis, please.*"

Chapter Twenty-five
Seras - Marcus

As Canis slept on the rug in front of the fireplace, Raewin fixed her gown, covered the old man with a fur blanket, and tiptoed to the table. There, she grabbed maps and rushed out the door.

Pallanex entered the dark chamber. She saw Canis lying on the floor. She rushed to him. "My Lord, Canis, are you hurt?"

"Raewin," the old man mumbled. "Come back."

"Raewin!" Pallanex seethed. She slapped Canis.

He shook his head in shock. "Pallanex?"

"Tell me that whore wife of yours was not in here!"

"Pallanex? I do not know what to say," he stumbled out the words.

"You will destroy the Corven, and all of their kind," she hissed out the command.

"My Queen, I am sorry," Canis rose to his feet.

"Promise me you will kill them all," Pallanex said. Her eyes flashed menacing as the candles flickered. "I want them all dead." She whipped around and left the room with a slam of the door.

~ * ~

The boys huddled in the dark as Raewin told them.

"How much longer should we wait?" Bones asked. "We can't stay out here forever."

"Raewin will return," Arthur said. "You can go back if you want, I am staying here."

"I do not want to go back," Bones said. "But I am getting hungry."

"We will get food soon enough," William told him. "Raewin will

139

return. We will go back to her cabin, then we will find Marcus."

They heard noises coming from outside the stable. "Hide," Thomen whispered. The boys moved behind the stalls.

Raewin opened the stable door quietly. "Boys," she whispered. "William, Arthur, Thomen, Bones."

They peeked their heads out to see Marcus's mother, then straightened up.

"How did it go?" Thomen was the first to ask.

"Did Canis agree?" Bones asked enthusiastically.

"No, I have bad news for you. Canis did not relent."

"No," Thomen began to protest.

"But I do have good news," She continued. "Here is the map of where he was taken."

"The map?" Arthur questioned. "How did you get that?"

"Never mind that, you just have to follow it, and please find my son."

"Wait," Willian said. "What happens when we get back and we have Marcus?"

"Find him. Find out what happened, do not worry, I will take care of Canis."

Raewin helped the boys gather four horses. They snuck out when the sun went down, and rode off in the direction Marcus was supposed to be.

They arrived at the red edifice where Azron had dropped off Marcus. "What happened here?" Arthur asked, looking over the collapsed structure. "Azron did not mention there was a fire."

"He did not say anything," Thomen reminded them.

"We are going to have to wait until morning," William said. "We will never find him in the dark."

"We are dead. Angus will not be able to keep Kralen and Marddek from finding out we have left," Thomen added.

"We have to do this for Marcus," Bones said.

"Prepare for the night," Arthur said. "We will take shifts." He threw Bones a rolled bedding. "I will go first."

In the morning, they started combing through the ashes of the burnt woods. "I have to say, I am not sure he could survive this," Arthur said.

"He had to," Bones said. "Do not lose faith in Marcus."

"Keep looking, there has to be something here," William said.

"Wait, come over here," Thomen yelled. The other three ran to the fallen wall where Marcus had built his camp. "He was here."

"So where did he go?" Bones picked up the shredded blanket, tossing it down in anger.

"What kind of an animal did this?" Arthur asked. "Bear, wolf, cougar?"

"What would you do if you were attacked by an animal then caught in a fire?" William asked.

"Run," Arthur answered.

"Run…" Bones looked around. "Run where?"

"Follow me," Thomen said. He started walking. "He would run away from the fire, so he would go this way."

They crossed over the narrow creek, and into a clearing. "Look," Arthur said, pointing to the entrance of the cave which had been demolished.

"Marcus," Thomen yelled.

The others began doing the same. They searched high and low for several hours.

"Listen," William said. He lowered himself to the pile of rocks at the cave entrance. "I think this is a cave. What if he is in here?"

"How would he…" Arthur stopped talking as Bones, Thomen, and William began frantically moving rock and dirt from the entrance.

"Marcus, Marcus," they shouted. The opening emerged. Bones crawled in first, followed by William, Thomen, and Arthur. They continued hollering until they heard a muffled sound.

"Here." Marcus's voice cracked. He was deep in the cave, sitting on the rough surface, back against the trickling water. He coughed. "Here."

The four friends rushed to him.

"What happened?" William asked.

They stood him up, one boy on each side, as the other two dusted him off. They moved him through the cave, and pushed and pulled him out of the opening.

Marcus was barely breathing. He could not speak. They put him on the horse with Arthur, who was the strongest of the group, and could hold him in place as they rode away.

They arrived at Raewin's first. She came out of the door and hugged her son as the boys brought him down from the horse.

"I was so worried," she said. "You boys are going to be in trouble. I have heard patrols riding through the country looking for the runaways. I do not know if I can help you."

They looked at each other. Their faces grim.

"I wonder how long Angus kept us out of trouble?" Arthur asked.

"Not long, I bet," William answered.

"We are dead," Thomen said.

"We got Marcus back, that will be worth it," William responded.

Marcus sat up. "He must listen to me." His voice hoarse and weak.

"What happened to you?" Raewin asked.

He told them about the bear, the fire, and Azron's deception. "Canis has to let me back, right?"

"Canis is a difficult man, but I would think even he would find it in his heart to allow you to return."

As the boys entered the gates of Cauleta, they were met by Kralen, Marddek, Reinwald, and four guards. Marddek was holding a bloodied Angus by his arm.

"I told you I saw boys entering the home," one of the guards said.

"Indeed," Kralen said. His voice a low grumble. "Take the four back, they will be dealt with soon," he told Reinwald. "You." Pointing at Marcus, "you are not welcome here. You are dead to us, boy."

"No," Marcus barked. "I demand to speak to Canis."

"You cannot demand me," Kralen yelled. "You are forbidden to enter the city. I do not care who you are!"

Raewin appeared behind the boys. "I do care who he is. I demand you listen to him, and take him and these boys to my husband."

"You have no authority here, woman," Kralen scowled.

"*No, but he is my son…and the son of Canis. You will do as I say.*"
Raewin held firm.

Kralen began to protest, but obeyed. He led the boys under guard to Canis. Raewin followed the procession.

Canis sat in the throne room. Pallanex was by his side. Guards were listening to his orders. "Why are you disturbing me, Kralen?"

"*Lord Canis, Marcus has returned." Kralen thrust the boy in front of his father.*

Canis looked at him with anger. "I no longer have a son named Marcus."

Raewin marched in, followed by the other boys and their captors. "He is your son! He is our son, and you will hear him out!"

"*Woman, you have no rights here," Canis roared.*

"*Arrest her! She stole from your king," Pallanex screamed.*

She looked at the guards in the room.

"*You should not be here," Canis ordered. "Kralen, remove her!"*

"*No, listen to him," Raewin begged.*

"*Why would I listen to you, or anything this child has to say?"*

"*Because he is your son, and I am your wife, and there was a reason he did not return. Please listen to him," Raewin demanded.*

The boys took the commotion as a chance to wiggle free from the guards. Reinwald, Marddek, and Kralen grabbed at them as they pleaded Canis.

"*You will not tell me what to do!" Canis roared.*

"*Father, please," Marcus begged. "Azron attacked me!"*

The chaos of the room fell silent.

"*What?" Canis ordered.*

"*Azron, the Tarrack, he attacked me three times. Once he had a bear attack me and it destroyed my camp after he chased me up a tree, then he caught the woods on fire trying to kill me, before he trapped me in a cave, and demolished the entrance so I could not escape."*

"*Kralen, is this true?" Canis asked.*

"*I have only just heard this, my Lord," Kralen said with a frown.*

"*Bring Azron to me," Canis ordered.*

Kralen motioned for Reinwald and the guards to let the boys loose, and retrieve the Tarrack warrior. When they returned, Azron took one look at Marcus. He stopped at the doorway, fought off the guards who reached out for him, and ran toward a window.

Marddek grabbed his leg just as he turned into an eagle. The bird flapped wildly, striking and pecking at him.

Reinwald jammed a spear into the large bird, killing him. Azron returned to human form.

"Why did you do it?" Canis asked, but it was too late.

William hit Marcus with a stick, snapping him back from the memory. "We fought for you. We risked our lives for you." He hit him again. "And how do you repay us?" he hissed in his ear. "Look at you." Another strike across the back. "You betrayed us all." William backhanded him in the mouth.

Marcus collapsed on the hard surface.

"Take him away."

A guard carried him to the barracks over his shoulder. He threw Marcus headlong into the room and closed the door.

Marcus stood up, wiped the blood from his face. His lip started to heal. He smiled. "Oh, William, it won't be long."

Chapter Twenty-six
Seras - Marcus

When Marcus saw William's personal guards coming for him again, he walked over to the biggest man in his company of workers. "You know what to do," Marcus said.

The man stood up, he was six inches taller than Marcus, and built like a bull.

"Where do you want it?" the man asked in a quiet voice.

Marcus pointed at his left jaw and left eye. "Here and here," he said. Then he pointed to his back. "Hit me here with a board until it swells."

The big man punched him hard in the face.

Marcus shook it off. "Again."

The man did what he was asked. He hit Marcus three times before he collapsed to his knees. He spit out blood. "Don't stop."

The man punched him over and over until the left side of his face turned crimson.

Marcus held up his hand. The man stopped, and blew out a breath of air. "Now the back, hurry."

Taking a board from the makeshift table, the man crushed it over his back.

Marcus tried to muffle his pain. "Again, hurry." Another strike, and Marcus went down.

The big man helped Marcus to a seat. He looked at Marcus with a combination of sorrow and confusion. "I do not understand?"

"Thank you," Marcus said as the guards entered the room.

"Back away," one guard ordered.

"William wants to see you again," the other one said, lifting Marcus out of his chair.

"It does not look like you recovered from his last beating," the first guard laughed.

"Not sure what he sees in you," the second said.

They dragged him out of the barracks across the long courtyard and down the rock steps to the cells.

Marcus felt his body slowly recovering, but he would look like he had the day before. "*William cannot know yet,*" he thought.

William stood in the doorway. His eyes were dark and soulless. His austere appearance let Marcus know he was in for a long night. "Where were we, my friend?" he asked with a sardonic smile. "Your wounds are still not healing." William shook his head. "Maybe I broke you." He laughed. William traced Marcus's shoulder blades. He stopped at the spot the branding mark should be. This made William reach back and touch his. "I forgot, you did not get the mark, did you?"

"You know I didn't," Marcus answered. "Canis wouldn't let me. It was my punishment for being trapped by Azron."

"That was when you became the friend I loved."

"That's when I became a monster," Marcus said.

"I know." William laughed. "Remember what happened after that?"

Young Marcus stood before Canis, Kralen, and the others. "So, it is true. You survived an attack from a Tarrack." Canis shook his head.

"My Lord, what do we do with him?" Kralen asked.

The King looked at the dead body of Azron, then to Raewin, before fixing his gaze on his son. "I will let you back in. You will be my son. You will be a Skorei. I will not let you bare the mark of the warriors. You did not complete the Scindo. Perhaps you will at a later time."

"But, Father!" Marcus dropped to his knees in front of his father. His eyes welled with tears.

"No, I have commanded it," Canis stayed rigid.

Raewin helped Marcus to his feet, and gave Canis a nod of approval.

He looked at his mother, then turned to C kjanis. "Thank you, my King. I will make you proud," Marcus said.

Canis waved the gathering out of the room with both hands. "Big words from a little boy."

When he returned to the barracks, a few older boys began harassing him. Marcus punched one in the face and a brawl broke out. Kralen, Marddek, and other guards separated the boys. Kralen ordered Marcus to barrack clean up as the rest were taken to the arena for training.

Marcus grew stronger and angrier. In two years, he was among the tallest of the boys. He watched in a mix of pride and jealousy as Darius and the younger boys returned from their Scindo, and received the mark of the Skorei.

It was then when his friend, Fish, made a mistake. "Marcus, why do you not ask Canis to let you try again?"

"Shut up," Marcus said. "It means nothing to me."

"You are not fooling us," Fish said. "You want that mark so bad you can taste it."

"I said, shut up!"

"I know who your father is, and you might be as tall as me, but that does not mean I cannot beat you to a pulp."

"Really?" Marcus asked.

"Yes, really. You walk around here like a prince, but Canis does not even recognize you. You mean nothing to him."

Marcus lunged at Fish. The other boys pulled him away.

Marddek intervened. "What is going on?"

"Nothing," Marcus growled.

"Why would you be interrupting the Scindo?"

"Fish will not shut up about my father," Marcus explained.

Fish mimicked Marcus.

"I challenge him to First Blood," Marcus demanded. First Blood being a sport competition where two or more boys meet in a circle carrying small blades. The contest ends when only one boy remains without a cut. The sign of blood eliminated the wounded.

Fish and his group laughed.

"Marcus, no," Arthur said. "Fish is one of the best fighters here."

It was true. Fish was thick muscled. Short for his age, but still as tall as Marcus, he was stocky, and knew his way around the different styles of fighting. He was also two years older than Marcus with only one more year remaining until he completed training to join the Skorei army.

After the ceremony, Marddek set the two boys up for the competition. He gave them both blades and gave the instructions. Fish's friends aligned on one side of the circle. Marcus's friends on the other side.

They took their positions. Fish smiled the whole time, while Marcus showed nothing but anger.

"Come on, prince, this is what you wanted," Fish teased.

They circled and slashed. Neither made contact.

Marcus grabbed for Fish's knife hand, when he pulled back Marcus jammed his knife in Fish's ribcage.

Fish looked at him. His eyes enlarged with shock and terror. Blood seeped from the corner of his mouth. He dropped to his knees, and choked out a breath. "Why?"

Marcus twisted the blade. "I win," he said, and walked away as Fish collapsed on the ground.

Both groups of boys stood silent as Marddek rushed to Fish's aid.

Chapter Twenty-seven
Seras - Julie

"Welcome back," Freya said as Julie walked through the flames of the Elders' symbol.

"vvbfg! What the heck?" Julie screamed. "You scared the crap out of me!" She put her hands over herself to hide her body. "What are you doing here?" She ran behind a blanket laid over a rack to get dressed.

"I'm sorry, Julie. I was just waiting here until you returned."

She sat on a bench wearing orange and red robes with a yellow sash tied around her waist. Her hair was pulled back with a red scarf.

"How long have you been waiting?" Julie asked, surprised by Freya's response.

"Does it matter?" the Oracle answered.

"Well, it's kinda creepy," Julie said.

She could tell by Freya's face that she didn't understand.

"We just made camp for the night. I figured you would be back soon."

"Good guess." Julie came out from behind the makeshift dressing room.

"How was your visit?" Freya asked.

"It was good. I went back to school, hung out with friends, did some running to get ready for track season. It's my senior year and I think we are going to have an even better season than last year." Julie stopped. "You probably don't care about any of that do you?"

Freya just looked at her quietly.

"And I was able to do some thinking," Julie said. "Can I ask you something?" She sat beside Freya on the bench.

"Of course," Freya answered.

"I was thinking about this while I was gone," Julie started. "Do you know why Marcus and Darius hate each other?"

"I do know," she answered. "But it is not my story to tell. If you want to know, you need to ask Darius."

"I was afraid you were going to say that. He just seems so…"

"He is, but he was not always that way, and these years being alone in the forests have mellowed him out. I assure you, he will tell you what you want to know. Give him a chance."

The next morning, the group packed up for another day's ride. As they traveled across a slightly worn dirt road, Julie trotted her horse next to Darius. She felt the eyes of the others staring at her. He turned his head her way with a sneer.

"Uh, hi, Darius," Julie started.

"Freya told me you wanted to ask me something," he said. He looked straight ahead. "Well, go on then."

"Okay, so, why do you hate Marcus?" she blurted out, not knowing how to start the conversation with the intimidating man.

"That's rich coming from you," he answered, still facing straight ahead.

"How so?"

"You hate him too," Darius said, he stroked his beard.

"I do not," she protested.

Darius finally looked at her with a smug expression. "Yes, you do. That's why we are here. You found out he was a monster, excuse me, a demon, and you left. He wanted to prove to you that he wasn't evil, so he left to do what he probably should have done a long time ago, kill William and Pallanex. The idiot got himself in trouble, and here we are getting ready to bail him out; or worse…he and William reconnect their friendship, and he turns evil again, and then we have to kill him too."

Julie stared at him. Her face flushed and her eyes watered. "Shut up! That is not what happened, and we are not going to kill him!"

"You don't know them like I know them," Darius reminded her. "I've watched them together since I was half your size." He continued, "They were like brothers, and William was like the brother I wish I had."

"See, that's what I mean. What are you talking about, what happened?"

"I don't know how much you know about Marcus, and our

family," Darius said.

"That's easy, Redderick told me about your dad, Canis; your mom, Raewin; Pallanex, and how she seduced your dad, then there was a battle, and…" Julie hesitated saying she knew they were unable to reproduce, then something occurred to her. "Wait a sec! Bobo told me the curse was something about never being able to have kids, so the army would die out…"

Darius smirked and shook his head.

"The curse turned you into demons."

"Now you're getting somewhere," Darius said. "Pallanex convinced Canis to attack, and kill all members of the Corven tribe. He gathered about one hundred of us. It was Marcus's fifth year, my third. Canis wanted us to be part of it, a proud moment for him. We requested to bring in our friends. It was going to be fun." He smiled at her.

"It was going to be fun slaughtering helpless women and children? You're sick."

"We didn't know it at the time. It was the first real action we were allowed to be part of. Canis told us the Corven represented a danger to us, Pallanex had said so." He chuckled. "As it turned out, he was right. Because of our attacks, especially on their main temple, we became cursed. We got hit so hard with whatever type of spell they did, it knocked us off our feet. We didn't know what happened obviously, until later. The first time I saw it was when Canis got angry. He stormed through the Corven temple looking for something, something…about the Heart of Tolth." He looked at Julie. "He was looking for you." Darius shook his head. "Now I am sure Pallanex put him up to it. When he couldn't find it, he went berserk. He broke anything he could get his hands on. Then, out of nowhere, he started screaming in pain, and we watched as his body started to change. I think he killed two of his men just because he couldn't control himself at first. As our blood started pumping, getting all nervous, scared even, we started changing. It hurt like you would not believe the first few times." He turned to Julie. "Eventually we learned to control it and it became part of us. The rest, well you know…"

"But I don't know. What were you, what are you?"

"We were the Skorei tribe, so we became Skorei demons. Same

thing, only we were monsters. It made us more powerful than normal humans. We could also heal quicker, I mean, like never before: broken bones, stab wounds, anything. If it didn't kill us immediately, we could heal from it."

"I get that. I think I have some of that too. It must be a Tolth thing," Julie added. "What I don't get is what happened? So, you became evil, or were you always evil?"

Darius looked around. "I don't know. I know we had an army. We were allies with the Tarracks. We destroyed the Corven. But during Canis's time, I don't know what happened before the curse. I was what, twelve? I know we had a lot of land, and no one ever tried to attack Cauleta that I can remember."

"Okay, so why do you hate your brother? Why do you hate Marcus?"

Chapter Twenty-eight
Seras - Julie

"You think you have it all figured out, don't you?" Darius laughed at Julie. The two had let their horses fall behind the marching army to cover the rear. It also allowed them to talk in private, though Julie noticed Freya hanging back to keep an eye on them.

"I don't have anything figured out," she protested. "I want to know why you hate him?" Julie wore a thick fur cloak. The late winter snow was gone, but the chill of the day remained.

"Why do you hate him?" he asked.

"I don't. You keep saying that, but I don't hate him."

He ignored her.

"Are you going to tell me why you do?" she asked.

"My reasons are simple."

"And?"

"He killed our father," Darius said with a grimace.

Julie was taken aback. "That can't be. From what I've heard, Marcus loved his father. He would have never killed him."

"There's where you are wrong. It was sometime after the attack on the Corven witches. The Skorei were divided between those who had been cursed and those who had not. At first, it was difficult to learn to control the power of the demon. Canis insisted we learn to transform back and forth and to only do so when we needed to fight. Others wanted to use our newfound ability to become something different, to establish a new Skorei. We went to battle with the others to keep Canis in control. It was a bloody time. We began killing our own people because they wanted to overthrow Canis. Those warriors who were not with us when we got cursed fought by Canis's side. The Tarracks refused to take sides. They wanted to see who would come out on top.

Eventually, our side won out, but it came at a great cost. Our numbers were cut in half. Canis had the leaders of the rebellion killed. That was when Marddek and the other non-demons plotted against us. They had the numbers in their favor and decided it was time to take advantage, and kill us presumably before we killed them. Which, if I had my way, we probably would have. I wasn't alone. Kralen and Reinwald both begged Canis to attack. He refused, wanting to keep the Skorei as it was, and learn how to make others like us. He had his new queen, Pallanex, but she was not able to duplicate what had happened. The next civil war began. We lost more men. Again, the Tarracks refused to help. But, again, we were victorious.

"It was different, though. During the worst of the battles. Raewin was killed. It wasn't by the non-cursed. It was by one of us. Canis had ordered her home to be moved within the gated walls, no human could have gotten through to get to her. The non-demons did break through Cauleta's gated walls, and nearly had Marcus, Freya, and myself. Luckily, William arrived in time to help us regain footing inside the halls and stairwell. We rejoined our friends, and killed the last of the traitors.

After our victory, we learned of Pallanex's betrayal. She was the one who convinced the non-cursed to attack us, and try to overthrow Canis. She was the one who deceived one of our own to kill Raewin, she tricked Marddek into betraying us and let the non-demons inside the gates. And, she was the one who poisoned Canis, leaving him blind, and nearly crippled. That was when Marcus chased her down, slit her throat, and flung her from the cliffs to her death.

"Okay, I didn't need the gory stuff. But I don't understand why you hate Marcus. He didn't do anything to you, and he revenged your father."

"Canis was blind and crippled. Marcus decided for himself, and all of us what was best. He gave Canis a sword, marched him into the woods, tied one end of a rope to his ankle, and the other end to a tree. Canis would fend for himself against nature, wolves, and anything else that came his way to die a warrior.

I watched as Marcus walked the old man toward his death. I knew Canis could recover. We can recover from anything, but he kept saying Canis must have a warrior's death. He just would not listen."

Chapter Twenty-nine
Seras - Canis

The great Skorei King Canis laid in bed. Pillars of gray stone blocks supported the high beam ceiling. His bed was eight feet long and six feet wide. Marcus, Darius, and Freya by his side. Flames flickered from large candelabras throughout the room.

His surviving commanders, Kralen, Reinwald, and Hurvay stood near with the friends of Marcus and Darius: William, Thomen, Arthur, Bones, Chadrick, Chaldrean, Justus, Petar, Galius, and Parikus.

"I am as useless as a woman," the old man coughed out. "I was a fool, Marcus. Look at what I have become. Crippled, blind, and helpless. Tell me what I used to be. Tell me I was brave and strong. Tell the world I was the king of all warriors."

Marcus had never seen his father like this. He was so fragile. So pale and weak. "Canis, you are our king. There was no one braver. The Skorei are the revered throughout the lands of Seras, and that is because of your leadership and vision. Look what you have built."

Canis winced with pain. "Raewin, come here my love." His right hand reached out for someone not there.

"Father, Raewin is dead," Marcus said. "She was killed by a coward during the attack on Cauleta."

"No," Canis cried. "Not my sweet Raewin." He put his hands over his face. "Get out, get out." He waved his hand at the audience around him.

Marcus nodded, and everyone began to file from the room.

"Not yet, Marcus." He grabbed his son by the hand.

Darius and Freya looked back at him.

When the room was empty Canis took a deep breath. "I am dying, son. Let me die with purpose. Let me die an honorable death. A death worthy of the Skorei."

"Father, I cannot agree to that. What if you heal?"

"I am too old to heal from this. I need you to promise me you will let me die a worthy death," he whispered.

"Father…"

"I am your king, I am your father, I have spoken," Canis said.

He pressed on his chest to suppress a cough.

Marcus relented. He left his father's bed chamber. As he closed the door he was met by Darius and Freya.

"What did he say?" Freya asked.

She was pacing back and forth. Tears stains streaked her face.

"He needs to rest," Marcus answered.

"He wants to die a warrior?" Darius asked. His face was flush, and his eyes were puffy. He was sitting on the floor of the hallway, his arms resting on his knees.

"He does," Marcus answered.

"What did you tell him?' Freya asked. She wiped her eyes on the sleeve of her frock.

"I agreed with him. He is our king, and he should dictate how he dies," Marcus explained to his younger siblings.

"He can heal," Darius yelled.

He stood up to his brother.

"I will make arrangements. He has until then to heal. After that, I will give him his desire."

"You are killing our father!" Darius stormed away.

Marcus walked to the window and stared out at the arena, his home the past nine years.

"What if he can heal, Marcus?" Freya asked. She placed her hand on his shoulder.

"I will be glad." He turned to her. "Make him understand this is not what I want to do."

"He will," she said.

~ * ~

Marcus took his father by the arm. "It is time," he told the old man. Marcus took two days to prepare the spot he would take his father. When he returned, he checked on his father. Canis continued to lie in bed

He wrapped a cloak around his father's shoulders and lifted him to his horse. Fog clouded the streets as they exited Cauleta, his father's home for the last thirty years, the one he had built to honor his mother. It matched the fog in his eyes, while not completely blind, nothing could come into focus. His sharp blue eyes were grey and dull. His once dark brown hair, white and thinning.

They passed by their friends, Kralen the thick bearded commander in charge of training the younger warriors. Reinwald, captain of his personal guards with his reddish hair. Both men had served him well. He touched them on the arm as he went.

They walked by Marcus's friends: William, Bones, Thomen, and the others. His son's friends who had argued so valiantly when Marcus did not return from his Scindo. The same boys defied orders not to retrieve him, and they did. He then learned about the plot of the Tarrack warrior who tried to kill Marcus. That had made Canis rid Cauleta of all Tarracks in his service, and sent them back to his old friend, Urvasus. The Tarrack who helped him defeat his brother, Theon, in battle to take control of the Skorei. Urvasus had turned his back on Canis when Marddek led his revolt against Canis, and when the non-demon Skorei tried to overthrow him at the bidding of Pallanex. As it was, Canis would never see his friend again.

Canis then passed by Darius and his friends. He could sense the anger raging from Darius. His young son seethed as each warrior saluted their king by pounding their right hand across their chest. Daruis would not understand this was the way it had to be. It had taken a lot to convince Marcus it was the way he wanted it. Marcus argued, begged, and cried not to do it, but in the end he resigned himself to follow his father's final orders. Darius was inconsolable. Canis hoped he would forgive him and his brother someday.

They slowly rode past the cottage where Raewin, had lived. It was a mile from the castle. Canis ordered her to move to a small cabin inside the gates of Cauleta during the attacks. Was it his fault she was killed? That was where Freya, his youngest stood. She hugged him, clutching at his cloak, sobbing, not wanting to let go. A pearl of a tear made a wet path down his cheek. He loved her, and he loved her mother. If things would have been different, or if he could rewind time, he would have moved mountains to have them live with him in Cauleta. Maybe things would have ended another way.

Marcus led him through the path away from the villages, now all but deserted. The men and women who made Cauleta live and breathe abandoned them out of fear. Once Canis and the Skorei returned from their raid on the Corven, at the wish of Pallanex, the people they protected turned on them. Led by one of his highest-ranking commanders, Marddek, the non-demon warriors and village men attacked the castle, not once but twice. Bloodshed on both sides took their toll.

In his heart Canis knew Pallanex was behind everything. The witch gained his trust, seduced the old man, and became his biggest traitor. She caused the rift between two factions of the demons, she caused the civil war between Canis and his followers, and Marddek and his followers. She led the civil unrest between Skorei demons and Skorei humans. She poisoned Canis, a poison his newfound healing powers could not recover from. His bones hurt, his body ached, and his sight was gone.

By his request, they rode up the eastern cliffs where Pallanex's body was thrown over after Marcus chased her from the gated walls, caught her and executed her from her treasonous plots. Canis spit on the ground where the blood stains of her neck still covered the ground. Did he even really love her or did she cast a spell on him? He will never know.

They marched in silence. Canis could hear his son ahead of him, leading him by rope, his nose sniffled to suppress the sounds of crying. He let the boy lead him. In time, Marcus would become the man he wanted him to be. He would lead the Skorei warriors to victory against their enemies, bring honor to his name, and he would rebuild Cauleta.

In the quietness of the ride, Canis could reflect on his mistakes. He felt guilty about what he did to his brother. Theon was satisfied with building a strong army from the Bukaras tribe, then staying put in the land of their mother and father. Canis had wanted more, he wanted to conquer lands, and have as much control over the land as possible. As it turned out, after he killed Theon, and with the help of the Tarracks defeated Theon's army, he did just what his brother had wanted. He built Cauleta and made it his home. Yes, he had conquered several kingdoms in the south, but he always returned home.

Home...Raewin was his home. He loved her. She gave him two strong sons, and a beautiful daughter. He remembered the first time he laid eyes on her. Her golden-brown hair, her hazel eyes, the way her hips moved beneath the red frock with a strap hanging off her shoulder. He fell in love with her in the moment he saw her.

Before he met her Canis had forbidden his men to marry. Raewin changed everything. They snuck out and had a private ceremony committing their love for one another, becoming husband and wife. If only she would have accepted his ways, and not the Corven ways, she would have been the perfect wife. It was his love for her that convinced him to allow his men to marry and settle down. But she refused to move into Cauleta.

That brought him to the bed of Pallanex. The beginning of all his troubles.

"We are here," Marcus said, stopping. Marcus helped his father dismount.

Canis felt around. His son had stopped by a pine tree. He sat down while Marcus gathered firewood, soon he was feeling the warmth of the flames and the smell of meat cooking.

"Here is your sword." Marcus took him by the hand and placed the hilt in his hand. The swords forged by Evandells. When Canis had heard about the magical blacksmiths he made sure they were captured and enslaved with the sole purpose of crafting weapons for the Skorei.

"It will be getting dark. Stay by the fire until you are ready."

"It is cold out here. I would say a three or four whore night," Canis said.

It took Marcus by surprise. "But I thought your speciality was virgins?" Marcus joked back to his father.

Canis laughed. "Thank you, Marcus. This is more than an old fool deserves," he answered, his voice catching in his throat.

"You are not a fool. She was clever..."

"But Cauleta paid for my mistake in trusting her; now the Skorei are shattered. All I have worked for wasted."

"I will bring the Skorei and Cauleta back to glory. I promise," Marcus responded.

"May I ask one more favor?" Canis asked.

"Yes, of course."

He took his son by his arm. He pulled him close, and hugged him. "I am proud of you, Marcus. Follow your own path. I made too many mistakes, and there are things I would take back if I could do it again." A tear formed, and ran down his cheek. "Now go. Let me die a warrior's death."

They pulled away from the embrace. "You have your fire, you have your sword, and I left water. I will be back in the morning."

"Thank you."

Canis heard Marcus mount up and ride off with the two horses without another word. That was it. He was on his own. He sat near the fire. Feeling around, he located the water pouch and a bundle of sticks to stoke the flames. The burning wood reminded him of nights with his own father and brother. Times spent hunting and traveling before his father died in battle. A battle axe to the chest, then to see his father's head on a pike. Canis shook his head to erase the memory. Death, death, and more death. His father, his mother, his brother, Raewin, now it was his turn. Hopefully Azaleah's Speculus would be more kind to the warrior.

Canis ate the meat Marcus had prepared, deer. He placed his sword across his waist as he waited. He used his cloak as a blanket. Somewhere in the dark he heard a howl. It would not be long.

As he thought, he heard the low growl of a lone predator. Canis forced water into his mouth and used his sword to get to his feet. His clouded eyes were even more useless in the dark. Maybe if he survived the night, survived long enough for Marcus to come back to him he could convince his son he still had purpose.

He heard the wolf move slowly behind him. In the darkness, the old man grew began to feel a chill. The heat of the fire subsided. The awful cold of the night crept on him just as the hungry animal did. He scrambled to add dry grass and twigs, hoping there was still enough ember to build up the flame.

The sound of the lone wolf multiplied. Its friends had arrived. How many Canis could not tell. He held his sword with trembling fingers. Listening to the snarling predators he wondered which would attack first. The animals had him surrounded. Canis slowly turned to face which ever growl was the loudest and closest.

One wolf lunged at him. Canis felt the pain as it struck his leg just above the knee. Flesh tore. He was frightened, and in that moment, he turned into the monster. He laughed at his foolishness in forgetting he had this power. Now it was the wolves that were in trouble. Their barks faded briefly as they retreated from the sight of the demon. He was still weak from the poison Pallanex gave him. He cursed her.

Why had he trusted that woman? She never loved him. She only loved his power. From the instant she entered his life, wearing a white frock that taunted his senses. Her slow, teasing manner, and her raven black hair with blue streaks was enough to make him forget himself. She stroked his ego, building him a large courtyard with marble statues to honor him, his men, and his family.

She had stood by his side when he became a demon. In fact, it did not bother her at all. Something he wondered about, but never confronted her as to why she was…happy, yes, happy with the idea that he and his men came back from the attacks on the Corven tribes, no longer men, but demon-cursed. She was the only wife of the men who returned to greet him in such a way. The others were abandoned by their wives out of fear. She asked for the names of the men who had gone with him. Another odd occurrence he never questioned. The Skorei warriors who did not go with them were also scared of their comrades. That was what led to the revolt from the non-demons. Or, so he thought, until Pallanex gave him a drink to calm his nerves during a night of intense fighting. After he had drank it, he began to feel numb. His body convulsed as he collapsed to the floor. She confessed everything. How she sent Azron to kill Marcus. She orchestrated the attacks on the Corven, knowing their ability to make such a curse happen. Her ordering Raewin killed. Leading both the revolt of the curse demons, then the revolt of the non-demons to weaken their numbers and destroy him. How Pallanex seduced his old friend Urvasus, to make sure he and the Tarracks did not get involved. Her final betrayal, poisoning him and ordering the deaths of his children. Luckily, she failed. She underestimated his children's resolve; Marcus, Darius, and Freya were able to stop the assassination attempt as they were able to defeat the fifty mercenary warriors sent to kill them.

Canis's anger spilled. Soon, the wolves gathered their collective courage to make another attack. They swept in from the left, then the right. Teeth and claws met. The old man fought off the horde with bravery. One wolf knocked him off his feet. A second ripped at his arm, while a third pulled at his leg. In the scramble, he lost the grip of his sword. He would never find it again. Canis slashed with his free arm, but another wolf tore into his bicep. Canis reached for the wolf's underbelly, causing the animal to shriek away. That would be one more predator denied the taste of this victory. He kicked and clawed long enough to get to his hands and knees.

He felt around for his sword. He opened his hand to have it return to him, but the Evandell magic failed him. Canis thought of the Evandells. A proud people he conquered and imprisoned before the curse, before Pallanex. Their genius being magic and forging. The swords they were forced to make for the Skorei warriors were brilliant. Connecting the hilt of the sword to the hand of its master made each warrior even more fierce in battle as they could quickly retrieve a fallen sword, never or hardly ever leaving them unarmed. It made his men nearly unbeatable.

He wiped his face, replacing the sting of sweat in his eyes with mud and blood. The wolves were ready to strike again. His eyes began to clear...could he be healing? Canis could not rise to his feet. He straightened up his body with both knees on the ground. His muscles and sinew were barred from his flesh. The wolves advanced with relentless tenacity. There were too many of them, and he was too weak to continue. Canis, King of the Skorei, Lord of Cauleta, Father of Marcus, Darius, and Freya, and Master of the Eastern Lands battled to his final breath. He would die a warrior's death. Canis closed his eyes and gasped, "Raewin, I am sorry."

Chapter Thirty
Seras - Marcus

Marcus is dragged to the cell away from the slaves and other prisoners. He pretended to be hurt, and still recovering from his fall off the cliffs.

"I have to say Marcus, I am rather surprised and disappointed in you," William remarked as the guards tossed his body on the ground.

Marcus rubbed his chin, feeling the tenderness from the beating he had the biggest slave inflict on him before the guards arrived at the barracks to pick him up.

"I expected more from you," William continued. "You are dismissed," he said to the guards after they finished tying his arms up on an overhead beam. Then he turned his attention back to Marcus. "Do you want to know what I am most curious about?

"Not really," Marcus said. He pretended to be weaker than he was.

"Tell me more about the other world?" William circled him. "What's it like?"

"You wouldn't like it. They frown on killing. You can't carry swords wherever you go. They throw you in prison for being as ugly as you are."

William chuckled. "I know you are playing with me."

"I would never be able to explain how different it is there," Marcus said.

"Fair enough. Tell me more about the Heart?"

"Nothing," Marcus growled. "Don't ever say her name!"

"My, my, my I ruffled a feather," William said. He grinned. "What is it about her?"

"Shut up, shut up!" Marcus started to rise to his feet.

William smacked him across the back with his stick. "I think you told me everything I need to know."

"You know nothing," Marcus spit out the words.

"I disagree. Do you remember how good we were together? Do you remember the fun we had and the terror we spread across Seras?" He placed the baton across his shoulders.

"That was a lifetime ago," Marcus said. "We were both different people back then."

"Speak for yourself," William yelled. "I am the same! I have not changed!"

"What do you want from me?" Marcus asked.

William slammed his baton across Marcus's back. "I told you what I want. I want to go back to way things were. Remember when we defeated the Tarracks? Remember the fun we had afterward?" William finished each question with another lash from his stick.

Marcus struggled to keep his feet under him. The memory of the Tarrack war flooded his mind. Can a heart turned cold by anger and grief be blamed when it leads to destruction?

After Canis died, the surviving Skorei gave their king a warrior's funeral. They built a large pyre inside the walls of Cauleta. Young Marcus was surrounded by his friends as the tall wooden structure went up in flames.

"He died a good death, one to be proud of," William said. "Three wolves died at his hands."

"What are we going to do now?" Bones asked.

He looked at Marcus, as did the rest of the warriors present. Marcus caught Darius's glare.

"I will tell you what we will do. We will avenge Canis's death. The Tarracks said they were our allies. Where were they when we were under attack? Where were they when our men turned on us? They sat, waiting to see who would become victorious. Their allegiances floated with the wind. They are not our allies! They must pay for their betrayal!"

The men roared with approval. Marcus would get his revenge for his father's death, and for the torment of the Tarrack guard who tried to kill him.

The warriors gathered their weapons, and began their march east to the Puri River where the Tarracks made their home. It took two weeks of traveling to arrive. The men met in camp. They divided into three units. Marcus would lead the spearhead into the center of camp. William would take those under his command further south, and moved up river to block a retreat, trapping them between the two forces and the river. The third unit would be led by Kralen. He took the best archers and set across the river from the north. They would make sure any attempt to cross into safety by water or air would be blocked.

The Tarrack lands were set on the plains by the Puri River. A mountain formation rose where the village was hidden by trees. The mountains protected those unable to or not ready to fight. The rest of the ground were rolling hills of green grass. A land vital for survival and cared for by the Tarracks.

Uravus and his generals met Marcus and the leaders he chose for the assignment; Bones, Thomen, and Arthur. The others were already in place, or near to it. The grass was wet from the morning dew, fog was beginning to lift.

"I was sorry to hear about your father," Uravus said. "He was a good friend." The King of the Tarracks was a bear of a man, even when not in that form.

"If he was such a good friend, why did you abandon him in his time of need? He called out for you, and you ignored him," Marcus said.

If he could, he would have cut off the man's head right there.

"I am sorry you feel that way. You do not know what you are saying. You are in grief," Uravus said.

He looked at his generals and laughed.

"You betrayed him. You let the witch convince you to betray your friend and let the Skorei die," Marcus continued.

Uravus's face turned from mild amusement to grave. "Why are you here, boy?" he taunted.

"You left us to die," Marcus yelled his response. "Canis is dead because of you!"

"Go home, Marcus! You do not belong here. You are children playing adult. Canis was my friend, and I am sorry he is dead, but if you insist on continuing to insult me, I will kill you!"

"You betrayed us, you abandoned us, and we will not forget what your actions have done. Revenge will be ours!"

"You will regret this. We will not show you mercy, and your first act as the Skorei's new king will be the last of the Skorei," Uranus said. "Go home, boy."

"You will regret those words," Marcus said.

He dismounted and rushed toward Uravus.

Uravus got off his horse to meet him face to face. "I will regret nothing, unlike you, you miserable brat," he said.

Marcus moved to strike the much bigger man, but Thomen and Bones took him by the shoulders. Arthur stood rigid facing the Tarrack leader.

"Hold your temper," Thomen said.

"He is goading you to make a silly move. Do not fall into his trap," Bones said.

Marcus shoved his way past is two friends, and joined Arthur. "Make your peace with the Elders, and prepare to die."

Uravus laughed. "You would have made a good king someday, if you did not die today."

He turned with his generals to join his men.

Marcus, Thomen, Arthur, and Bones returned to their army. Being split into three factions, Marcus realized it appeared small, which probably gave Uravus even more confidence. The two armies faced each other. "When I say the word, give the signal."

Bones nodded. He overlooked the men and boys preparing for battle. Marcus joined him. Some of the warriors trained with them. That seemed a lifetime ago. Others fought alongside his father. Marcus worried what kind of leader he would be.

"How do you think they will attack?" Thomen asked, keeping his eyes on the front line of the Tarracks.

Marcus looked across the field. "They will storm us as hawks. That will make them small and hard to hit, then change to bears and cougars to break through our line."

"We have to take them out before they get too close, and force them to shift early," Arthur said. "Should we initiate?"

"That would surprise them," Bones said. "I can lead a charge.

They can take the brunt of the attacks, then we can ride down to face them after they change."

"Make it so," Marcus said. "Check the range of the archers we have. Give Bones cover until they get close."

Arthur rode away as asked. Marcus watched as his friend talked to the head of the archers, then Arthur gave him the approval.

"It is time." Marcus raised his right hand.

The archers took aim toward the sky. He clinched his fist. The archers let off a volley of arrows. He pointed forward. Bones led the charge toward the Tarracks. Marcus nodded to Thomen. Thomen sent a fire arrow to the sky. That was the signal for William to begin moving up from the river to flank the Tarracks.

The Tarracks split into two waves. The first wave changed into bears and cougars to take on the charging men under Bones command. The second wave became hawks to attack the archers. Arrows rained down on them. Bears and cougars dropped, as did many of the hawks. The hawks that made it through quickly changed and wiped out the front row of archers. Marcus, Thomen, Arthur, and the Skorei present turned into demons as fast as they could to counter the viciousness of the Tarracks.

Marcus felt the power of his demon form. His Evandell sword in his right hand, and a spear in his left. He jabbed his spear into a charging cougar, then sliced it down the shoulder to finish it off. Men and beast alike screamed. Blood was everywhere.

The Tarracks were fierce. They could change from one animal to the next in a blink of an eye. The hawk was used to shorten the distance between foes and make themselves small targets. The cougar would spring and explode with reckless abandon, moving, twisting, attacking with bared claws. Bears were thick skinned; they could take the results of an arrow without much damage. Their power and strength shredded many men.

Most of the non-demon Skorei, and humans who gave their support to Marcus, fell with little resistance to the onslaught. Marcus and his Skorei demons fared better. Their monstrous forms were equal to the viciousness of the bears and cougars. Marcus continued to hack his way through the horde. He lost his spear in the hide of a bear but cut the beast in half with his sword.

Marcus heard the war cries from William and his army storming from behind the Tarracks. They were caught by surprise, just as he had hoped. The tide momentarily turned back into their favor with William's arrival.

The bloodshed, mud, and increasing dead bodies made moving harder.

The Tarracks responded by taking flight, soaring above their opponents, then swooping down with the sun at their backs. The blinding attack gave them the advantage over the Skorei, again.

Marcus's men didn't have time to string their bows before the Tarracks crashed down on them, then took flight again. Some of the Tarracks stayed in hawk form just to tear at the face and eyes of the men.

Luckily, Kralen and his archers made their way across the Puri River in time to fill the air with arrows. His archers were the better skilled of the army, and were able to down many of the Tarrack hawks before they could swoop down on them.

The three-pronged attack Marcus devised worked as hoped. They had the Tarracks trapped on three sides with the Puri River being the fourth barrier. There was nothing they could do to stop the Tarracks from flying but he hoped his archers could take them out before they escaped. He also hoped the proud Tarracks would not retreat but see the battle through.

A new wave of Tarracks charged into the battle. They had come from the village, when Marcus killed one of the attacking hawks it turned back to its human form. "A woman." He saw another fall; it was just a child. Marcus then realized the incoming reinforcements were the women and children from the Tarrack village. The proud people were going to fight to the death.

It was up to the men to finish the Tarracks. He wanted to find Uravus. In their animal forms it was impossible to tell them apart. When he saw a giant brown bear with graying fur Marcus knew it had to be him.

Marcus began to close the gap between him and the bear. Navigating through the fighting and ground soaked in mud and blood was difficult. The bear charged. Marcus rolled his neck and braced for impact. Uravus plowed into him. The two tumbled to the ground. Uravus stood on hind legs, at least four feet taller than Marcus.

Uravus shifted into a man for a brief second. "I told you, boy, now I am going to kill you." He changed back into a bear and swung a powerful paw at Marcus.

Marcus blocked it with his left arm, fortunate to avoid the claws, unfortunate as he heard -his arm snap at the impact. Even in his demon form, the pain seared through his body. He whirled his sword wildly, more to keep out of Uravus's reach than an attack. His left arm dangled as he brought it close to his side.

The bear gave a mighty roar, teeth bared, and saliva spilling from its mouth. He stood again. In the distance thunder clouds rolled across the sky. Lightning flashed across the black, gray, and blue backdrop.

Marcus rushed the bear. It caught Uravus off guard. He lunged at the bear, knocking Uravus off his feet.

Uravus changed to a cougar to scramble up to his feet. He faced Marcus and growled. His teeth bared, blood and saliva dripped from his mouth. He leapt toward Marcus in two easy bounds. He clasped Marcus's right arm in his mighty jaws forcing him to drop his sword.

Marcus screamed. He punched the great cat with his free hand. He could hear bone break and flesh being ripped from his arm. Each punch with his already broken arm shot waves of pain through his entire being. One punch landed in the cat's eye, and Uravus released his bite.

Marcus opened his left hand. His sword returned to its master. He gripped it with both broken arms and swung at the cat blinded in one eye with all his might.

Uravus tried to change into a bear to protect himself. He wasn't in time. The blade caught him at the shoulder.

Uravus roared.

Marcus rammed the sword deep into the belly of the animal. Both man and bear laid stunned.

Uravus grabbed at the sword, unable to free himself with his paws. He turned into a man once more. As he started to pull the blade out of his stomach Marcus grabbed him by the throat before he could finish.

Marcus clasped the Tarrack king with his right hand and swung his broken arm across Uravus's face. His monstrous hand ripped Uravus's face nearly in half. Marcus dropped the man as the pain paralyzed him.

Uravus kicked at Marcus, knocking him off his feet. He pulled the sword out of his gut, and swung it toward Marcus catching him on the thigh.

Marcus grabbed a broken spear within reach hitting Uravus across the hand and arm until he let go of the sword. Marcus dropped the stick and opened his and to retrieve his sword. The mystical weapon returned to its owner.

Uravus changed into his cougar form and lunged at Marcus. His claws dug deep into Marcus's chest, but pain coursed through Uravus's body. Before he could clamp his teeth around Marcus's neck, he yelped in sudden realization of the sword now protruding from his chest.

Marcus had been able to maneuver his sword between himself and the leaping cat just in time.

Uravus shuddered and fell. His breathing quick and shallow. He changed to his human form.

Marcus removed his sword from the Tarrack King.

"Spare my people, son of Canis," Uravus pleaded.

"You had your chance. You wanted to destroy me," Marcus said. He held Uravus by his hair as the man was on his knees. "Show no mercy, leave no survivors!" Marcus yelled, taunting Uravus before swinging his sword, taking the head of the Tarrack King.

Marcus yelled and raised the head of their leader. He tossed it on the ground for all to see. It splashed in the mud and turned face up.

The Tarrack people were stunned to see Uravus fall. The Skorei did not relent. They took advantage of the Tarracks despair and slaughtered every Tarrack man, woman, child, and human slave who fought alongside the Tarracks.

"Revenge has been made, Father," Marcus said as he overlooked the destruction in front of him.

The Tarrack village was burned. Any Tarrack who surrendered was butchered. Blood and fire mixed as one in the wake of the Battle of Puri.

Chapter Thirty-one
Seras - Marcus

After the defeat of the Tarracks, young Marcus became obsessed with doing what his father had not, conquering the surrounding areas, and destroying any people who defied him.

"So, what is the plan now?" William asked as the group of leaders sat around a fire drinking ale from a leather pouch.

"What is wrong with what we are doing?" Marcus answered with a smile.

"We have conquered the Tarracks, the Corsains, and the Estars," Thomen said. "The other tribes will fall in line."

The surviving Skorei numbered forty-seven. The battles against the non-demonic Skorei led by Marddek, Cauleta's Civil War, and the Battle of Puri as it was called, took its toll on the warriors.

Marcus led the men north. "There are territories there my father wanted to conquer but never took the time," he had said.

As they marched, they would come across poor travelers. Those they found worthy they recruited into their company. The man would have to be a warrior, good with a sword or bow, and be able to provide food for the small army. Those they found unworthy were bound to a tree and forced to swallow a knife, pinning the man's head to the trunk.

"Do you remember the tribe we conquered?" William asked.

"There were a lot," Marcus answered. His face was bloodied from William's stick and fists.

"The one where the only way a man could mate with a daughter was to kill the father in battle," William said. He was sitting on a bench, one leg propped on the bench. His baton rested at the side. "We had some fun there, didn't we?"

"You could say that," Marcus said. He saw an opportunity. "How about the time we went to that small village…oh, what was its name?

Never mind, you know, the one with the bar maidens with loose morals?"

"Yes, yes." William howled with laughter. "What did Bones say the next day?"

"He said, 'It is a good thing we heal fast'," Marcus said imitating his old friend's voice. "Because that girl ripped my back to shreds."

William roared with more laughter. "Yes, because of them we did not destroy the town."

As William was distracted, Marcus made a move for the stick. Unfortunately, William was quicker. He snatched it up and struck Marcus unconscious.

The Skorei army was camped, poised above a valley of two shared kingdoms. The two kings of the land had built an alliance with one another for protection and shared the wealth of the territory.

"We have nothing to prove," Arthur said during the talks about attacking the two small kingdoms.

"There is always something to prove," William argued.

"I am listening," Marcus said.

He poked a stick into the fire. Sparks rose into the starry sky.

William shrugged. "I just do not want to sit here getting fat and bored."

"Fat, maybe; but never bored," Bones joked.

He looked at Marcus, who was staring at another fire pit forty feet away with Darius, Chaldren, Chadrick, Petar, Galius, Angus, and Malcolm. Marcus noticed his stare.

"He still refuses to speak to me or acknowledge me," Marcus said.

"He is young," Thomen said. "He does not understand you did what had to be done. Canis wanted you to fulfill your duty."

"It will take time," Arthur added.

He took a drink from a jug and passed it to Thomen.

"Then we should have some fun," Marcus said, biting a piece of meat then taking a drink.

"What kind of fun?" Arthur asked.

"I could go for a fighting game," Thomen said.

"Perfect. It will keep us sharp," Bones added.

"I think he has something different in mind," William said. "I have seen that look before."

"Yes!" Marcus said. "I want to do something different." He looked at his young friends.

"I am not sure what you are asking?" Bones asked.

"Simple," Marcus explained. "I take a group of you into a town and torture each king until I get everything I want."

Thomen put his hand on Marcus's shoulder. "I think you are drunk."

"Possibly." Marcus laughed.

"You should sleep this off," Bones said.

"I think it's a great idea," William said.

The men around the fire stared at him.

"Yes!" Marcus yelled. "Finally."

The troop traveled to the first village, Brekenpot.

They rode into the village, killing the guards and any man who opposed their entry. Once inside the main hall, Marcus ordered his men to bring the chieftain's seven sons to the hall. Their hands were bound behind their backs. Marcus nodded to his men. They executed them in front of their father; simultaneously having spears jammed from behind through their chest. Next, Marcus took out his sword and playfully hacked of their heads one-by-one while mocking the grief-stricken chief. He then had the chieftain taken out and dragged behind a team of horses through the village.

Next, Marcus and his men went to the neighboring village, Ralhaven. There, Marcus discovered the chief took pride in the purity of his daughters. After taking control of the village, he gathered the daughters into a room. There he has the four women dressed in white frocks, tied with rope under a wooden post. He had the chief brought into the chamber bound in chains. Once there, Thomen held the chief's head up by his hair to force him to watch as Marcus walked up to each one. He started with the eldest daughter, and kissed her. "Tell me, which daughter is your favorite?" Marcus chided the old man. He moved onto the second eldest, and kissed her. "Which one should I make my wife?"

"None," the chieftain yelled. "I command you to stop."

Tears ran down her face as Marcus continued to kiss her.

William cackled with laughter.

Marcus moved to the third daughter. "I am a fair man. I will let you pick." He kissed her and licked her face slowly from jaw line to temple.

"Save one for me," William said.

The Chief moved. William pulled on his chain to stop him.

"Which will it be, old man?"

Marcus stopped at the fourth daughter. A girl slightly younger than himself.

"No, stop. I beg you to stop!" The chieftain blubbered wildly.

He dropped his head down, but William yanked it back up and placed a knife just below his eye to keep him from closing them.

Marcus sensed the additional importance of the youngest daughter. "I am insulted," Marcus growled. "I would think you would want me as a son."

He smiled as the old man trembled. He took the girl by her arm, removed her ropes, then with one eye on the chief, bent over to kiss the girl as he did the other three.

The young girl closed her eyes. Her face flush with horror.

Marcus reached up and pried her eyes open with his rugged hands and as she looked into his blues eyes, he smiled a demonic smile and changed into the beastly cursed form. The girl screamed in terror. Her sisters cried louder. Her father quivered in dread and regret. She squirmed to free herself. Marcus held her in his clawed grip. He laughed at her struggle.

The young girl screamed again then fainted. The sight of the monstrous form was too much to bear.

Marcus let her body fall to the ground. He walked to the chief. "I am not finished, yet."

At that his men pulled on the ropes binding his daughters. They hung helpless with their arms tied over their heads. Then his men gathered the body of the youngest and strung her back up to join her sisters. Marcus nodded to Bones who then lit the posts that held them on fire. The chief was forced to watch his daughters, the loves of his life,

174

burn in the flames. Marcus finished his act of cruelty as he gouged the man's eyes, then plunged his claws just deep enough into the man's ears to cause permanent damage. "This will be the last thing you will ever see or hear," Marcus said with a laugh.

That first taste of having so much power over humans began Marcus's reign of death and destruction. To no one's surprise, Marcus promoted William to be second in command. They rode across the countryside burning, looting, torturing, and killing any village they came across. The Skorei only stopped long enough to eat, sleep, and sometimes pursue women of the different villages. The young warriors made a game of their conquests.

In the heat of battle, Marcus would spit out the blood of worthless men as sweat busted out of his body in his lust for war. The Skorei scorched the lands of Seras. Blood rained down and covered the ground wherever they decided to venture.

As the company celebrated one such victory, William suggested to split into two groups. "Traveling back to the southern lands makes sense to me. It is close to Cauleta, and there are a lot of tribes to conquer."

"I have already been to the south, and I have no desire to return to Cauleta. I never want to see that place again." Marcus rose from his seat and went to the fire to warm his hands.

"But there are warriors amongst us who wish to return to their homeland," William said. He joined Marcus by the pit.

"Who?" He looked at his friend.

"I, for one. Reinwald, Kralen, Darius..."

"Darius just does not want to be with me." He motioned at his younger brother who was busy setting up a tent for the night.

"Possibly, but would it not be wise to let him return to his homelands? He is young. Kralen and Reinwald are the two most experienced warriors, they would give him the training his needs."

Marcus walked over to his brother. "You are determined to leave."

"I am," Darius answered, the most he had spoken to Marcus since their father died.

"I will not stop you."

He marched away in anger. That was the end of the true Skorei army. William took Darius, Kralen, Reinwald, Angus, Malcolm, and Parikus. Arthur, Bones, Thomen, Chadrick, Chaldrean, Petar, Hurvay, and Galius stayed with Marcus. They split up the rest of the army to balance both sides. "We will meet up before the next snow fall," Marcus told William. "We can celebrate our victories." The two friends clasped arms.

William smacked Marcus with his staff. "Wake up, wake up," he said. "Where were you?" he asked with a grin.

"Nowhere."

"You lie. I heard you. Cauleta, Canis, Darius. Why don't you admit you miss the life you used to lead?"

He offered Marcus a small portion of a loaf of bread he had in his hand. Marcus refused. William shrugged.

"Do you remember when we split up? You went south, I continued north?"

"Of course." He took a bite of the bread to taunt Marcus.

"You did it just to poison Darius against me, didn't you?"

"That was a big part of it. You see, I couldn't kill you. I tried. Trust me, I tried. She was disappointed in me, but I had a plan. If I could make Darius angry enough, maybe he could do it for me."

"Why did you want to kill me? Who is she? Who was disappointed you couldn't kill me?"

William paused as if he was thinking about lying, then grinned. "Yes, I returned to Pallanex."

"How, I killed her. I watched her die. I threw her body off a cliff."

"You did. Unfortunately for you, she is much more powerful than that. She was…is a follower of Eryx, and the Elderess found her worthy of life."

"So, is she Pallanex or Eryx?"

"Yes…I suppose she is both. She is still the same Pallanex I fell in love with; the same Pallanex who convinced me to turn on my king and my best friend. She had me kill your mother. She had me create a rebellion. She had me lead the attack to overthrow Canis to keep you occupied while she killed Canis. I convinced Marddek to take the fall.

The oaf was too foolish to know what happened. I did all of that for love."

Marcus lunged at him to no avail.

"I know, I know, you are angry with me, disappointed. Sometimes I was too. That is why you are still alive. I could not let you die at the hands of those lesser soldiers. After Canis died and we left Cauleta she spoke to me through the wind. Imagine my surprise to hear she was still alive. I had to return to her and nurse her back to health. I thought I could convince you to join me, to join her. But you just would not. When you decided to keep traveling north, I took my men to Cauleta. They never knew it was she who gave us our orders. I kept her a secret until she was strong enough to rise up from the dead. She began making plans to create her army. I conquered tribes, taking prisoners, turning them into slaves. Then she sent me to Madera, and she told me I had to call for you. I was supposed to find the priest and kill you and your men. I let her down twice that day."

"You bastard! You did all of that and still think we could ever be friends?"

"No, I suppose we will never be friends. I...I just wanted you to know the truth before I killed you."

"You better do it quick, because you will not get another chance."

William nodded in agreement. He walked to a shelf and picked up his sword. A knock on the cell door stopped his progress. "What?" he yelled.

A guard entered, then said something to William that Marcus could not hear.

"I almost forgot." He waved the guard to enter. The guard motioned four more men to the chamber. They were carrying a large wooden crate on poles. They sat the box on the floor and left in a haste. "I couldn't let you die without showing you this." He struck the corners of the crate with the hilt of his sword. The walls collapsed revealing a cage. In the cage a hideously disfigured half-man, half-dog, shriveled and naked, stared up at Marcus with pained eyes. It looked like a skinned wolf without a tail and the face of man. A man Marcus knew.

"Thomen?"

Chapter Thirty-two
Seras - Julie

The army stopped to camp. Their march toward finding Marcus brought them out of the worst of the mountain passages.

"We are stuck here," Argos said. "The ground is too wet, and water has flooded a lot of the area."

"My wagons will never get through there like that," Griffus said.

"We need to hurry," Freya said with a tinge of panic. "There is no telling what is happening with Marcus and William."

"Freya, if we try to navigate through that we will be stuck even longer, and we will lose a lot of time and equipment," Griffus explained.

"Fine." Freya slid off her horse. "Let your men know we are camping here indefinitely," she told Argos, Griffus, and Pertheus.

"Will do." Argos rode off.

"My men already know," Griffus said.

"As do mine," Pertheus said.

Darius smiled. "Better for me." He looked at Julie. "The longer Marcus is with William, the better chance I have at--"

"Do not finish that sentence," Julie ordered. She had her sword pointed at Darius's throat.

Darius moved it away from him. "My, my, my, the Heart has some bite."

"Darius," Freya yelled. "Come with me."

"Mother's calling," he said with a wink. "Lucky you."

He dismounted and followed his sister away from Julie.

As the men and women began unpacking the supplies and building tents for the night, Julie made her way through the darkness to interrupt Griffus and Pertheus.

"Julie." Pertheus nodded at her to recognize her presence.

"Is everything okay?" Griffus asked.

He was holding up a large pole as Pertheus hammered the structure tight.

"Yes…you guys have been with him all this time?" She blurted out not knowing how to begin.

Both men stopped their work.

"Yes," Griffus answered.

"Why?"

"We've been waiting for this conversation," Pertheus said.

"He warned us you ask a lot of questions." Griffus added. Pertheus grabbed a log and took a seat. Griffus grabbed two, he sat on one, and offered Julie one for a chair.

Julie sat down. "Okay. But why?"

"At first it was for survival. We saw an opportunity to live and took it like many others did," Pertheus said.

"I don't understand. He was evil. He was a demon. He killed lots of people," she said. "It didn't bother you that he was all, you know, grrry?" She opened her mouth to show her teeth, and held her hands in front of her face to mimic his protruding jaw.

"You're not wrong," Griffus answered with a bit of chuckle at her comical display of Marcus in demon form. "I don't know what life is like where you come from, but here, we have to decide when to fight and when not to." He looked at Pertheus, who agreed with him. "If you decide to fight, is it worth dying for?"

"You see, when we met Marcus, we were already in the service of another warlord, Bellor. Laila lived alone while I took the ballaters to battle. I would be gone for months if not years. Same with Pertheus," Griffus explained.

"Except, I didn't have a wife at home. It was the only way we could protect ourselves and our loved ones," Pertheus said.

"Bellor was panicked, as he should have been. Marcus and his men were killing everything in sight. He destroyed every place and every person that opposed them," Griffus said.

"After we joined his ranks we stayed because of respect," Pertheus said. "He has a brilliant military mind. He was also convinced that what he was doing was for the best. It was all he knew. How he was raised and trained."

"We didn't respect what he was doing…what we were doing. But because of his leadership, well, we would fight for him, and we would die for him."

"And we almost have," Pertheus added. They both held up a mug and toasted their good fortune. "Many times."

"It didn't bother you that he was evil?" Julie asked, not convinced.

"It bothers you, doesn't it?" Pertheus asked.

"Well…"

"We are men of war, and being so we have long known that as warriors we must abandon some of the things, we hold dear. Such as peace, kindness, happiness, and love... for they hold no meaning to those who we consider enemies. We become what we despise, and that is how we survive," Griffus said. "Hoping that we live long enough to forget what we did, what we became, and what we did."

"The one thing we always had was our faith. We followed the teaching of Tolth," Pertheus added. "We know the stories. We know the prophecies and that is what led us to Marcus."

Julie smirked. "I don't understand?"

"That's your story," Pertheus said to Griffus. "I'm going to get some food." He got up and left the two alone.

"Bring me something," Griffus yelled to his friend. He turned his attention to Julie.

"When Belltor called on us, we were forced to gather in the Daya Valley. Belltor gathered more than a thousand men. We were dressed in full battle armor. I had my ballaters at the ready when we saw the enemy we were summoned to battle. The Skorei."

We had heard what they did throughout the Dar-Zak territories, defeated the Hemoor, the Pron, the men of Gizele. Not to mention the rumors of killing the Tarracks and the Evandells. Needless to say, we were not excited about meeting them in battle. Belltor was convinced their reputation was exaggerated. When we faced them, we were surprised when their leader, Marcus, rode out alone to confront our generals and Belltor. We were even more shocked when they returned, leaving Marcus on the field.

180

Joe Evener

"I need a champion," Belltor commanded. He was a wide man who took pleasure in the excesses of his position. His thick long hair and beard were graying, and his skills as a warrior greatly diminished, if he ever had true skills, and not just the product of a powerful family name. "I need a champion," he roared again. "The demon has challenged the integrity of you men. Their leader will face one challenger. If he wins, he wants us to surrender all we have in horses and weapons. If our challenger wins, they will lay down their weapons and never return." He turned to his generals. "Either way, our army will kill him and his men."

"Why did you except his terms," one general asked.

"Easy, it is worth one man to either kill him or wear him down before we attack," Belltor answered. "It should be fun sport for the men before the slaughter."

As it turned out, Belltor picked me as no one stepped forward. "You, the one they call Griffus. You are a giant of a man. Their champion is half your size. You push the wagons and ballaters around daily. You will have no trouble beating him."

So, I tightened my armor, drew my sword and was given a shield. I walked out to face Marcus. Belltor was wrong. Marcus was not half my size, well, you know. We are the same height, and I might have a little more meat on my bones. Griffus laughed.

He had a sword and long spear. "What is your name big man?"

"I am Griffus. And you?"

"I am Marcus, Son of Canis. King of the Skorei."

"That is quite the title," I said with a smile. I think it took him by surprise.

We tapped blades and began. We fought for most of the day. He never once turned into a demon. He wanted to beat me fair and square, as if he had something to prove to himself. At one point he removed his chest plate and shirt. I felt compelled to do the same. It was freeing, and I could move quicker.

We fought hard. Sweat was pouring from both of us, and the sun beat down on our tired bodies.

He stuck his spear in the ground on purpose. "You impress me," he said.

"Thank you?" I kept my shield. We commenced to fight more.

Then he started carrying on a conversation with me. "Tell me Griffus, do you like fighting for Belltor?"

I paused. "No, he is incompetent."

"How would you like to join me?"

He swung his sword. I blocked it. It wasn't an aggressive attack, just enough to keep me on my toes. "It depends?"

"On?"

"On if you kill me or not," I said.

"I do not plan on killing you." He stopped. "Unless you are planning on killing me?"

"I would prefer not to." Marcus continued to strike at me, but it was more like he was playing with me instead of trying to kill me.

"Good." He moved into position to retrieve his spear, which made me nervous, but he just held it in his left hand as he went through the motions of fighting. "Do you think most of his army would join with you or would they stay with him?"

"I cannot speak for them," I told him.

"Fair enough. Would they follow me if he was dead or would they want to avenge his death?"

"I doubt they would avenge him. He is an idiot full of himself."

"That is what I thought."

That is when I noticed how close we were to my army. My men cheered me on as we continued to talk more than fight. In one quick movement he dropped his sword, switched the spear to his right hand, threw it at Belltor, then opened his hand and his sword returned to him. The spear sailed into Belltor's chest before he knew what happened.

The men looked surprised. That's when I noticed his bare back. He did not have the mark of the Skorei demons. I remembered the Tolth prophecy about the unmarked demon, and I knew who he was.

"Who?" Julie asked.

"The Solia Custor, of course. All the people in my village worshipped the teachings of Tolth. In one of the scrolls written by Redderick Bobo tells of the unmarked demon who looks like a man. He will be the Solia Custor and bring the Heart of Tolth to Seras to save us from the Wrath of Eryx."

"So, because you saw that he didn't have a mark you thought he was good?"

"Not good, yet, but he would become good, and bring the Heart…you to us," Griffus said.

Pertheus returned with three plates of food. Argos joined them with a plate of his own and a jug of water. "What did I miss?"

"I just told her about the missing mark," Griffus explained.

"Ah, you should have seen our faces when the spear went through Belltor." He handed Griffus and Julie a plate. "We looked at him, then to Griff, then back to Belltor. Griffus ran over to us and yelled, 'he does not carry the mark of a demon, he does not carry the mark of a demon.' We just stood stunned," Pertheus said. He took a bite of food, deer. "It took a little convincing, but when we finally understood what he was trying to tell us we were even more shocked."

"Marcus told his men why he did what he did, which we learned was to strengthen his army. They had been depleted by continuous battles. He fooled us by making his army look bigger than it was, so he could trick Belltor into a man-to-man fight. It played out just as he wanted," Griffus said with a laugh.

"Alainas was still with us then, remember?" Pertheus said.

"I do, poor girl." Griffus shook his head remembering the blonde Evandell warrior who died at the hands of the Sisters of Tunlaw.

"But it doesn't explain why you killed people for him?" Julie interrupted.

She took a drink to wash down the deer meat, not her favorite.

"It's hard to understand. Sometimes we attacked very wicked people. That was not a problem. Sometimes we had to attack places that we should not have. But we were still under the orders of extremely dangerous people. So, we did what we had to do to survive," Pertheus told her.

"They also contacted Bhjuda Heilshorn whenever possible," Argos added. "I rode with him across the north. We tried to get as many people out of harms way as possible. Sometimes we got there in time, sometimes we were too late, and had to rescue survivors. Bhjuda did not want to interfere with what Marcus was doing because it would eventually lead him to Ostram. Bhjuda knew he had to meet the priest, and Ostram would determine if Marcus was indeed the Solia Custor," Argos said.

"When we heard the news about the priest and Marcus said 'Solia Custor,' we knew we made the right choice," Griffus said.

"We saved him that day, too," Pertheus said. "We got to him just in time, put him on Wolfsblood, and sent that horse running."

"When Griffus and Pertheus finally made it to Allon with the rest of the men, Bhjuda knew he had to send Callista to get him from the Greagons," Argos explained.

"I don't know about the rest of you, but I want to see how this ends," Pertheus said.

They all nodded in agreement.

Julie sat watching these three men. "And you're all okay dying for him…for me?"

"We are," they said in near unison.

"I don't get it."

"You see, Julie, when Marcus killed Pallanex, Eryx consumed her body. We had been waiting for you. Marcus was the only one who could have w0ent through the portal. He was the unmarked demon. He was the one who allowed Eryx to return. Ostram did not see him when they met. He saw you, and he knew it was the only way to win the war against evil. We all did, and we all do. It was the beginning of hope for Seras. Without Marcus, Seras would have continued to plummet into darkness. Had it been someone like William, life for us would have ended violently long ago," Argos explained.

"Isn't it already? Callista, Alainas, Edwin, all the people he told me about…wait! Bones, Arthur, Thomen, all of his friends were demons, weren't they? They caused countless deaths. They destroyed all of those villages, killed all of Callista's people!"

"You are right," Pertheus said. "But we had the ability to make a choice. We decided to choose courage over being a coward, duty and love over fear. We chose to make the world we live in instead of being ruled. We made sacrifices, and decisions we regretted and still regret for the greater good of Seras. Us," he said, waving his hand to Griffus and Argos, them waving it bigger to encompass the entire camp, "we knew the risks involved, and we put our faith in Tolth, in Ostram, in Marcus, and in you. If you were us, what would you have done?"

Chapter Thirty-three
Earth - Julie

Julie sat on a bench in her makeshift cabin in the woods behind her parents' house. She had just returned to Earth. With the army bogged down until the weather cooperated, she could return home with a clear conscience. As she sat there tying her shoes, she couldn't help stopping, leaning back against the wall that used to be part of a neighbor's barn, and breathe. It felt as if she hadn't breathed in over a month. In her time of reflection, tears began to pool in her brown eyes.

Freya and the others had set up camp to wait for her return. "What if I don't go back? I'm a senior. I should be enjoying this time of my life," Julie said aloud. Then she felt guilty. "I promised them I would come back. I will keep checking on them until they are ready to start traveling again." She banged the back of her head on the wall and blew out a deep breath. "I'm going to kill Marcus when I find him."

She got up to leave the cabin. She was proud of its structure. It was about a half mile deep in the woods behind her parents' house. She had to cross over a little creek that was currently frozen over in the cold weather. While she trudged home, she thought about the stories she learned from Griffus, Argos, and Pertheus. These three men practically abandoned their lives to save Seras and the people of Allon. Griffus and Pertheus fought in battles waiting for the right time to make sure he became the Solia Custor so he could find her. Argos rode from one end of the north to the other with the immortal she never met, Bhjuda Heilshorn, to gather refugees of war. "How do people do it?" she asked herself.

She walked through the little path. It was cold. The trees were barren and brown with traces of melted snow. The ground outside her home was just like the ground on Seras. When I first got there the temperatures were completely different, she thought remembering how during the summer months on Earth, at least in her hemisphere, it would be blazing hot, and then on Seras it was completely opposite. Now, they were the same. "Weird."

She got to the door and took off her boots that she had just put on ten minutes ago. "Hi honey!" her dad called out from the kitchen.

"Hey!" She walked in and gave him a big hug.

"Wow, what's that for?" Phillip was flipping over some pork chops on the stove.

"Nothing, can't a girl hug her dad?"

"Any time she wants," he answered. "Where've you been?"

"Out taking a walk." She doubled checked the desktop computer in the living room for right day and time: four-thirty, February 27th, Sunday. "I have some homework to finish up before school tomorrow, and I wanted to clear my head."

"Okay, dinner will be ready in a few, so don't get too comfortable."

"I won't. Where's Mom?"

"She had a meeting downtown. She's supposed to be back by now. She was talking to someone about taking a writing course for her book," he said.

"Oh great!"

"I know, but let her have her fun. It keeps her happy."

Julie rushed upstairs. She checked her phone. Six messages from Claire. Seven from other friends. She texted Claire, "What's up?"

"Where have you been hiding?" her friend quickly responded.

"Working out. Gotta get ready for track practice."

"I know. It starts tomorrow. I wanted to work out with you today."

"Sorry!" Julie typed back. Shakespeare jumped on her bed. "Hi, Shakespeare. How's my pretty boy today?"

Marcus's pure white cat curled up on her lap, then rolled over on its back. "You're such a baby."

Chapter Thirty-four
Seras - Marcus

Inside the courtyard, Marcus stood with the other prisoners. The sun beat down on their backs. They were covered in dirt from head to toe, scarcely recognizable. The guards, each armed with a spear in one hand, a whip in the other, and a sword at their side watched as the prisoners carried planks of wood from carts brought in through the gates by other prisoners charged with the duty of cutting them down and stripping them of limbs.

Sweat streamed down Marcus's face leaving patterns of small crevices through his muddy face, arms, and bare torso. The wide-open courtyard was the perfect place for his plan. While the guards were well-armed, they weren't disciplined and hardly paid attention to the prisoners.

Marcus dropped his long piece of wood and pretended to topple over. When the guards moved to him, the prisoners who had been secretly positioning themselves behind the guards attacked. The skirmish was brutal, months and years of pent up abuse poured out from the prisoners. Marcus grabbed the spear of the nearest guard and rammed it into the man's chest. He took the dead man's sword and killed two more guards.

Within minutes the courtyard was covered in the blood of guards and prisoners alike, but victory for the prisoners. As the men cheered, their celebratory words were drowned out by the sound of dogs coming from the arena. The men braced themselves for the next attack.

Dogs rushed through the courtyard. The prisoners fought them off, but were soon overwhelmed by the bloodthirsty animals and another wave of armed soldiers.

Marcus tried his best to keep the men in a tight formation. The untrained prisoners allowed the soldiers to breach their flanks.

William rode through the frontline on his horse. As most of the prisoners fell or surrendered. William, dressed in his black Skorei attire with the purple head of a bull emblazoned on his chest, and purple undercloak, dismounted.

Marcus fought toward him, but he underestimated his strength. There were too many men to fight, and his plan failed miserably as the prisoners succumbed to their captors. Just as Marcus launched his final attack, three men grabbed him and readied to strike him down.

"No," William ordered as he pulled his sword out of one of the prisoners. "No!" The men stopped, but held onto him firmly. "I should have known you would try something stupid like this." He punched Marcus. "Now look what you did." He punched him again. Blood spurted out of his mouth and nose. "How many men did I just lose because you won't listen?" He punched him over and over until Marcus crumpled to the ground, then William continued by grabbing a spear and broke it across Marcus's back, then beat him until he blacked out.

~ * ~

Marcus thought of Julie for the briefest of time. He saw her jogging with her friends on the track team. He watched as she cheered on the sidelines with her best friend, Clare, as her friend Jimmy scored a touchdown. He remembered their sword fights in the forest behind Allon. And as she laughed at him for loving her mother's cooking. "Julie." He could hear his mind say in a fogged, far away voice. Then the images in his mind changed.

Marcus could see his old Skorei army camped inside a wooded area. He remembered this time; they had just finished winning a battle in the hills of Redleaf. A part of the north known for thick trees with large red leaves the size of a man's hand. Marcus looked over his handiwork. The bodies of the slain were littered throughout the land. The battle was a good one. He held a gash on his arm close together until the healing began to take hold. That was when he saw a woman walking through the trees. She was staring at the dead men. From where he was standing, all he could tell was she had light brown hair, and wearing a sheer white gown. "Who is that?"

Thomen was the closest to him. "Who?" Thomen sheathed his

sword after wiping the blood off on his arm sleeve.

"You don't see her?" He pointed in the woman's direction.

"I think the heat of battle has finally gotten to you. There is no one there."

Marcus looked at him in puzzlement and frustration. "Wait here." He walked in the direction of the woman in white. She moved deeper into the woods. Marcus followed. He quickened his pace to a jog to close the gap between them.

The woman looked at him, then disappeared in the darkness. Marcus stopped and waited. There was no sound, no movement, no smell other than the trees. A small wave of air rushed by him. A corporal spirit solidified into human form in front of him. "Hello Marcus."

The woman was beautiful. She had a thin band of gold across her breasts attached to her white gown which practically matched her skin tone. She was tall, nearly the same height as Marcus, and muscular.

"Do I know you?" Marcus asked, taken by surprise. His first reaction was to reach for his sword. His hand stopped just short of drawing his weapon.

"I am Rinna of the Deathwalkers," the woman said.

Marcus knew of the Deathwalkers. They were the female spirits of Azahleah who guided the dead to Speculus. Azahleah, the Elder of Seras's underworld created them as his servants.

"I have been watching you. I am impressed. You have kept my sisters and I busy."

She walked closer to him and enveloped him in a fog. The air around him was a sweet-smelling perfume of lavender. The Death Walker unclasped the gold of her gown and it fell to the ground. She moved even closer and kissed him. Marcus's breath caught. His body burned with desire.

Rinna was the perfect mate for Marcus. She enjoyed death as much as he did.

Marcus and his men spent their days conquering tribes and territories of the north while he and Rinna spent their nights together in the privacy of his tent. She was pleased at how efficient he was in killing. Marcus wanted to impress her more and more.

Until one night as they were celebrating another bloody battle wrapped in each other's arms when Marcus asked, "Why don't you stay with me?"

She sat up to face him. "I am here every night, my love."

"I mean for always…" He got out of bed and poured a drink.

"You are young, my love. We cannot be together forever." She joined him for a drink. "I belong to Azahleah." She took him by his hand. "Come back to bed."

"Be free from him. Join me. We are so good together," he begged.

"I cannot leave Azahleah." Her face contorted. She let go of his hand.

"We are so good together," he repeated. "We would be invincible. He is a hideous beast hidden from the world. We could rule this world."

"He is my lord. The Elder of Death. Do you know what you are asking?"

"That is blasphemy!"

She started dressing. It was not the white gown from their meeting in the woods. It was her black leather outfit. The same thing she wore when he fought her in the alley while saving Julie. She pulled on her long tight pants and fastened her crop top.

"You do not have to leave," Marcus said.

"If that is how you feel about Azahleah, I must. Otherwise, I would be guilty of blasphemy, too."

"Rinna, don't you see what he is doing to us?"

"No," she screamed. "You are doing this to us. We were doing great. I cannot leave Azahleah. Who do you think you are, what do you think I am?"

"That is why I want you to leave him. Be free from him. Join me. I will kill him if it means I can be with you," Marcus said.

Rinna's face turned crimson. "Do not ever say that again. I will forgive you this once, but we are finished. The next time I see you, you will be dead." Without another word the Death Walker vanished from his sight.

~ * ~

Marcus woke up in a cage. He tried shaking off the memory of Julie then Rinna. *"Why Rinna?"* He smelled foul breath on his face and neck. He sat up. "Thomen?"

The deformed man looked at him from another cage. "M-M-Ma-a-ar-cus?" he choked out.

"I thought you were dead?"

"N-n-n-o, n-n-n-o-ot de-e-ad. W-w-i-i-sh I-I w-w-as." His former friend's voice cracked and gurgled under the stress of trying to speak.

The heavy doors of the prison the two cages were in rattled open. William marched in. "Ah, I see my two favorite prisoners are awake and reintroducing each other. Surprise!" William clapped his hand once. "Marcus, Thomen, Thomen, Marcus." He gestured with his hands to each of them. "I bet you are wondering how he got here and why?"

"It crossed my mind," Marcus answered.

"First, let me say, I am impressed by how much you have healed since last night. I think the cage is much better for you than the barracks, wouldn't you say?" William gave him an evil knowing grin. "No hard feelings about yesterday. I understand it was something you thought you had to try. I should have expected it." He shrugged. "Now, on to other matters…if you remember, the last time you saw Thomen, he was racing off to tell me about your plans to have your men escape through the woods as you and your little gang kept us occupied. So brave," William said. "So silly. I appreciated his warning, but I couldn't keep a traitor in good faith. So, I stabbed him. But then, I got an idea. You see, Pallanex wants an unbeatable army. One that will defeat any army on Seras, any army on the world the Heart comes from, and any army from a world someone she worships is currently stuck in." He pulled up a stool. He threw a piece of uncooked meat at Thomen who gobbled it up without hesitation. "I thought, an army of Skorei soldiers would be perfect for Pallanex. After you escaped, and unfortunately all of your men died, I had Rinna." He paused. "You remember her, don't you?" He smiled. "She had a lot to say about you." He laughed. "I had Rinna keep him alive so I could use him for my experiment. I did not want to remake the normal Skorei. I wanted to create a new species of Skorei. I tortured him until what you see before you happened. The demon curse began to change to a lower being. One that is nearly indestructible, and ruthless. A perfect killing machine."

Marcus listened to William while looking at Thomen. "William what is this about?"

"Pallanex, it has always been about Pallanex. She was with Eryx from the beginning. Now she is Eryx. Join us, Marcus. We could do great things like the good days. We can make the Skorei army even better than it was. Look at him." He pointed at Thomen. "Imagine an army of him. That is why I have these slaves, and Pallanex brings me more. Together she and I will transform those useless humans into an army of demons. We will conquer all of Seras. Next, we will conquer the world the Heart comes from, along with the Heart. Then, we will conquer the worlds where Eryx and the Elders came from and where her lover is condemned. Once we do that, I will kill her lover, and she will see me as worthy to be her king." He moved to strike Marcus but refrained. "Join me. I will make you my right-hand man. We can finish what Canis started, then stopped."

Marcus looked at William, then to Thomen before looking back at William. "Okay."

"Okay, what?"

"I will join you," Marcus said.

Chapter Thirty-five
Earth - Julie

By the time school ended for spring break, Julie had four weeks of track practices under her belt. The team was looking great once again as her two State placing relays: the four by eight-hundred-meter relay and the four by four hundred relay were intact from last year. Expectations were high, and the workouts proved it. Mr. Langston harped on them about finishing every run hard, running through the line, stretching, icing anything that hurts, and drinking lots of water.

"Any of you going away next week," Mr. Langston said on the Friday before spring break, "You know how I feel about it, but I can't do anything about it. You better be in shape when you return because no position on the team is guaranteed. We have too much talent and too much potential to let a silly thing like lying on a beach for five or six days to ruin it."

"Are you going anywhere?" Coach Langston asked Julie at the end of the practice.

"Heck no. We took a big trip last summer, so we are staying home," Julie answered. "I'll be at every practice during the break."

"That's what I like to hear." Coach Langston smiled, then jogged to catch the next group of athletes before they got away.

Julie was semi-lying to her coach, but he wasn't asking about traveling to another dimension on her days off. When she got home that night after going to the Sullivan's to eat pizza with the team Julie was surprised to see her dad loading a suitcase in the back of the minivan.

"Hey," she said after getting out of her car, Jelly Bean. "Whatchya doin?"

"Did you get my text?" Phillip asked. "Or, my voicemail?"

Julie looked at her phone. Both were showing up. "I must have missed them."

"I decided since we couldn't go anywhere for spring break, I was going to surprise your mother by taking her to a little bed and breakfast for a few days. We'll be back on Monday."

"Wow, that's short notice. Good for you," Julie said. She gave him a hug.

"We aren't leaving just yet. She's upstairs grabbing a few more things, and we wanted to wait until you got home."

Just as he finished his sentence, Michelle came out the front door. "Jules, did your dad tell you?"

"He did."

Michelle hugged her daughter. "I left a few things in the refrigerator for you while we're gone."

"Thanks, I can take care of myself," Julie said.

"I know, I know, heck, in a few months we're going to be dropping you off to college...speaking of which, there's some mail on the counter for you. You need to decide where you want to go. Now would be a good time to do that."

"I will. I promise." Her parents gave her one last hug before getting in the car and pulling down the driveway. Julie waited until they were out of sight before going inside. "Well, that was easy," she said to Shakespeare as the cat greeted her at the door. Julie picked up the white cat. "I guess it's just me and you kid." She went upstairs. "I need a nap."

~ * ~

A few hours later Julie stood in the middle of her little cabin. She lit the portal then the candle that causes time to slow. "*My friends on spring break will appreciate the extra time,*" she thought. She walked through the flame. The wind whipped around her. She arrived in the tent the army of Allon had set up for her. Julie no sooner had her clothes on when Freya barged in the tent. "Uh, hello," Julie said, perturbed.

"I am sorry, Julie. I had guards watch for you to tell me when you returned," Freya said.

"Did they see me--" Julie felt her face flush.

"No, they were to wait for the flame. They had strict orders not to step inside your tent."

Julie blew out a breath of relief. "Good!"

"We are ready to travel again. The weather has broken, and the roads have dried," Freya said. She turned to leave. "I am glad you returned." Freya walked out before Julie could respond.

Julie stepped out of the tent. Two members of the party began cleaning out the inside of the tent as two others started tearing it down.

"Welcome back," Darius said as he rode past her on his horse. "I had started to lose hope in you."

"Well don't," Julie sneered.

"Pay him no attention," Pertheus said. "He just likes to get under people's skin."

"It's so easy to do," Darius said.

"Welcome back," Seren said approaching her.

She gave the honorary Hemoor warrior a hug. Otta followed, hugging her too. Julius and Jakob trailed behind with Leyta. The three nodded respectfully.

"I am so glad to see you. I would rather hang out with you than the older ones," Julie said.

"I don't blame you. They can be a bit serious at times," Julius said.

"All the time," Jakob corrected his older brother.

"Good, we shall ride together," Julie said. "So, what did I miss?"

"Not much. We still have not heard from Jayna or the other spies," Otta told her. "The scouts report we should be there within the week if the weather continues and the wagons don't bog down."

"Good, the sooner we get to Marcus, the better."

With that, a horse was brought to Julie. She mounted it, and the army began marching toward William's fortress and Marcus.

Chapter Thirty-six
Seras - Marcus

Marcus, William, and Thomen walked down a dirt road. Thomen was leashed. Marcus had chains on his wrists and ankles. Four heavily armed guards walked with them as they dodged a couple of dogs stretched out in the sun.

"I am so glad you have come to your senses and joined my cause," William said.

"If you're so happy about it, why do you have me chained and guarded?" Marcus asked as he shuffled along.

"I'm not a fool. I want to make sure you are being truthful, and not playing me to escape," William answered. "Of course, even if you did, you wouldn't get far." He pulled on Thomen's chain. "Thomen would be able to track you in no time."

"So where are we going now?" Marcus asked. "It's been weeks since I agreed, maybe months, yet you still don't trust me. I haven't tried to escape. I haven't tried to fight you. I've done everything you've asked."

"Well, I may not know what weeks and months are, but you have not done everything I have asked. First, I want to know the secrets of Allon. I want to know the secrets of the Heart. And, yet you refuse. Not to mention your little plan to escape, of course."

"I don't refuse. I told you, if anyone is going to kill the Heart it will be me."

"And this is why I must test you further," William responded. They arrived to the entrance of an arena. "Look familiar? It was designed to replicate our old one from Cauleta. In fact, many of the stones and logs are from the very same place."

"We spent a great deal of time behind those walls," Marcus said.

"Indeed. I thought it would be fitting to be the site of your final test." The large doors opened. Five men dressed in battle armor held on to two chain leashes a piece. At the other end of the leashes were large wolf dogs. They were practically pulling their handlers forward with their power. The animals' fangs in full view, barking wildly.

Marcus turned to William, "Only ten? You must think I'm getting rusty."

"Good. Then this should be fun." William moved up a set of stairs against the wall and took his place in the front row of the arena.

The men released the chains as soon as the gate was closed and secure. The ten dogs rushed toward Marcus. He looked around for a weapon. There wasn't anything to grab. "Not even a sword?" he shouted to William.

William shrugged.

Marcus leapt out of the way of the first dog. But it changed course quickly. Marcus ran from his position against the entrance wall toward the middle of the arena. The dog handlers had already cleared out of the way behind a gate to cheer on the action...cheering for the dogs.

One lunged at his arm. Marcus jerked away, then grabbed a handful of dirt and threw it in the dog's face. The animal stopped and shook its head wildly. The other dogs closed in. They surrounded him, braced for an attack. The hair on the back of their necks stood straight. Marcus saw nothing but open jaws full of teeth and saliva.

"Fine," he said. It took just a few seconds and Marcus transformed into the demon. "I gave you a chance."

He rolled his neck and arched his back to crack the joints. He lowered himself and spread out his arms to make himself look wider and more menacing. He roared as loud as he could. Three dogs turned tail to retreat. The other seven started barking uncontrollably. One took the lead and attacked. Marcus swung his right claw across the beast's neck. It dropped dead with a whimper.

The others circled, growled, and barked at him.

Marcus roared again.

The dogs ran to the gate holding back their masters.

He blew out a hard breath, and changed back to human. William smiled and waved his hand. Ten men dressed in metal battle armor came out of another gate. They had swords, spears, shields, nets, and maces.

One man had a bow and arrow.

"What is this?" Marcus yelled at his former friend. "I passed your test!"

William stood. "Technically you killed one dog, and scared the others. These men have been promised their freedom if they kill you."

"Why? What is the point of this?"

"I need to know I can trust you, and I know you have been out of the game for a while, but we still kill people. Do you have it in you, my friend?"

"I killed Angus. I killed Rinna. I killed General Juta. I don't need to prove my ability to kill!"

"Don't tell me. Tell them." William clapped his hand, and the men began to advance. "You might recognize a few of them." He smiled.

"You guys really don't want to do this," he said to the nearest man. The warrior did not respond. He caught the end of a spear as it was jammed toward his chest. He pulled the man closer and punched him in the face. Blood splattered from the man's nose as he let go of the weapon. He grabbed the man by the shoulders and turned him as a shield to catch an arrow in the chest.

The archer took aim again, but the spear ripped through his neck, pinning him against a wood post.

Marcus rushed at a man wielding a sword. The man swung, but he was clumsy and Marcus dodged the attack, kicking the man in the groin before he could regain balance. When the man bent over Marcus snapped his neck.

Marcus picked up the sword. He blocked an attack by another who had a long spear and shield. The warrior with a net swung it over his head, waiting for Marcus to turn his back. He blocked another jab, then grabbed the net as it closed in on him. He pushed the net holder into the shield, and drove them back until they lost their balance. Marcus stabbed both with the full length of the sword as they lied on the ground.

Marcus picked up the spear and shield. Sweat drenched his body. He wiped his forehead and wiped his hand on his pant leg. "Five more to go."

He picked out the man holding the mace. He was swinging it

around his head with both hands. As a warrior closed in holding a sword and shield, Marcus launched the spear into the mace swinger's chest. He then leapt up to kick the shield, knocking the man over before he could use his sword. Marcus drove his shield across the man's throat, decapitating him.

He had a sword. The next warrior fell quickly with two swings of the sword. The last spilling guts onto the blood and sweat soaked ground. Marcus picked up the second sword.

Marcus blocked an oncoming spear. He shook his head. The man had left himself unarmed. Marcus tossed him his sword, then proceeded to kill him. "Just you and me, pal."

The man took off his visor.

Marcus stopped. It was the prisoner Marcus had begged to punch him in the face to keep his healing a secret. Marcus looked at William in disgust.

William smiled and held out his hands.

"You don't want to do this," Marcus begged as the prisoner moved closer.

"I do not have a choice. I want my freedom."

"He will never give you your freedom. Either he will force me to kill you or you will kill me and still become one of his slaves," Marcus tried to explain.

Marcus dropped his swords.

"Pick them up," the prisoner ordered.

"No."

He swung at Marcus. Marcus backed out of the way.

He swung again. Marcus chopped down at his hand's holding the sword. He dropped the weapon. Marcus tackled him to the ground and held him in a rear bear hug. "You have to believe me."

Just then the nine living wolf dogs were released once more.

"Dammit!" Marcus let go of the man and scrambled to his feet.

A dog grabbed the prisoner by the leg before he could reach a sword, a second slashed at his arm, as a third leapt on the man's chest. He screamed in agony as the dogs ripped him to shreds.

Marcus got to his swords. He wielded both and hacked the dogs in half.

He stood in the middle of the arena, covered in blood. Ten dead men and ten dead wolf dogs laid around him.

"Finally, there is my friend." William grinned.

Chapter Thirty-seven
Seras - Marcus

"Ah, you were magnificent," William chimed as he led Marcus, Thomen, and two guards into the cells. "I knew my friend was in there somewhere. You just had to be convinced." He attached Thomen's chain to a ring on the wall. "Sit-down, sit-down Marcus." He pointed at a table with two chairs that had never been there before.

Marcus sat. The blood and sweat on his body dried with caked mud from the arena dirt. "If you're so pleased, why do I still wear chains?"

"All in good time, my friend." William motioned to his men. "Bring food, bring wine, bring some water. Marcus needs a bath." William sat across from him. "I can't tell you how happy you made me. It will be like the old days. Our names will bring terror to whoever hears it."

"Whom," Marcus corrected.

"Huh?" William started to ask, but was interrupted by his men bringing large portions of meat, cheeses, and wine. "There we are. Isn't this better?"

"I still need a bath," Marcus said. He scraped clumps off of his hands on the chair.

"Yes, yes, I will get that for you." William got up. The two guards followed.

Thomen looked at him. His eyes looked heavy. "Don't," he forced out.

"I have not done what you think I have done," Marcus said.

He threw some meat in Thomen's direction. The half-man, half-demon grabbed it choking on his excitement.

"I needed to convince him I was on his side. How else was I supposed to learn what his and Pallanex's plans are?"

"What is this other world she wants to conquer?"

Thomen just shook his head as he scarfed the meat Marcus gave him.

"You can tell me. You must know. It's the only way I can stop them."

"N-no. W-w-will-liam w-will k-k-kill you."

"I have to stop him. You can help me," Marcus pleaded. He gave his old friend more meat.

"No, you can help me," Thomen said clearer than he spoken before.

"How can I help you?"

"Kill me," he said. "I do not want to live like this."

"Thomen, I can't kill you," Marcus said.

"Yes, you can. You must. It will slow his plans with Pallanex and it will free me from this pain," he told his old friend.

"Are you sure?"

"I am, Marcus. Please."

Marcus stood and got behind Thomen. He wrapped the chains on his wrist around Thomen's throat. He took a deep breath. "Count to three," he told him.

"One," Thomen started.

Marcus pulled tight and twisted the chain as hard as he could. Thomen kicked and bucked, but Marcus would not let go. Thomen clawed at his arms. Then with a final pull, Thomen's neck broke. His rapid breathing came to an end as his body went limp.

"What have you done, Marcus," William said from behind him.

Marcus turned in time to see the hilt of William's sword crack him in the temple.

Chapter Thirty-eight
Seras - Julie

Argos raised his hand and the Allon army halted.

Pertheus and Jakob met the commander. "Just above the ridge," Pertheus said. "We took out the perimeter guard tower. As far as we can tell, they have no idea we are here."

"Good," Argos said as he dismounted. He turned to Julius. "Report to Griffus. He needs to get his machines in position before we begin."

Julius spurred his horse to the back line to find the ballater leader.

Freya caught up with Argos, Pertheus, Jakob, and Julie.

"It's time," Argos said.

"What do we know?" Freya asked.

Pertheus scratched the back of his head. "It's massive. Well fortified, Thirty-foot walls with four-foot-thick stones. I would guess three or four hundred men including prisoners and laborers."

"And Marcus?" Julie interrupted. "Have you seen him?"

"No," Pertheus said. "There was some commotion earlier, but we are too far away to see what it was."

Griffus and Julius rode up on the small group. "Where do you want me?" Griffus asked.

"We need you on the edge of the tree line to stay hidden until we are all in position to catch them by surprise," Argos said. "Julius, you ride with me."

His oldest son nodded.

"They aren't ready for an attack. While it should be hard to breech, the security is pretty relaxed," Pertheus explained.

"A trap?" Freya asked.

"No, I would say arrogant. Would you agree, Jakob?" Pertheus looked at Argos's son.

"I agree. They are acting normal. Prisoners are working. Men on the ramparts, but not at the ready. I don't think they thought we were going to come for Marcus," Jakob said.

"William is the most arrogant man I have ever met," Freya said. "It doesn't surprise me he wouldn't be expecting us."

"Then, I say we ruin his day," Argos said. "Let's get prepared."

Chapter Thirty-nine
Seras - Marcus

William throws a bucket of water on Marcus to wake him. He was chained from the ceiling, his toes barely reaching the floor.

William stuck him with a hot poker in his side. Marcus flinched at the searing pain.

"You know, I thought we could be friends again. I thought maybe you would see things my way," William said. He poked him again.

Marcus groaned in pain.

"What kind of hold does the Heart have on you? You left me. You left your father's dreams. So, I have to wonder...why?"

"I don't think--" Marcus started to say.

"No, you don't want to hear lies." William struck him with a whip. "I will get to the truth, the only truth we know, pain. Do you remember all the things we did when we were younger? Do you remember the fun we had?"

The sting of the whip cracked across his back.

"Do you regret it? Are you ashamed of what you are?" William struck him again. "Are you trying so hard to make up for what you did and what you are?" He hit him with the whip.

Marcus felt the skin of his back open. He tried to speak through the throbbing.

"Go ahead, I'm listening." William moved closer. He held the metal poker up to Marcus's face. "I want to hear what you are thinking."

"I am going to kill you, then I'm going to kill Pallanex," Marcus spat out.

"Oh Marcus. You had no chance. What did you think you were going to do, sneak in here and take us both on? You are a fool, Marcus."

"No, just an optimist," Marcus said.

"I knew the second I saw you, you were gone. Do you know how?

It was the brown clothes you wore. It was so fitting of what you have become, a dead leaf of your former greatness." He rammed the poker into Marcus's shoulder. "Do you remember William the Terror and Marcus the Bloody?"

"We were children playing childish games," Marcus said through the pain.

"You are going to die here," William said, his breath hot on Marcus's.

He pulled the poker out of Marcus's shoulder. "It's a shame I have to kill you," William said. "We could start over. Imagine the two of us together?"

"That's not going to happen," Marcus coughed out.

William hit him with his whip.

"Besides, I did my job. I found the Heart, and even if you kill me, she is going to kill both of you."

William's whip cracked against his back.

A guard rushed in. "My Lord. We are under attack."

Chapter Forty
Seras - Julie

The fortress was enormous, bigger than Julie would have thought if she would have spent any time thinking about it. The great fortification dominated the countryside, the scorched lands of Seras, with two large compounds, an arena, and a spiraling tower. A dried moat surrounded the fortress with one footbridge made of shell and stone at the front gate, and another smaller bridge in the back left unprotected.

"How are we going to get Marcus?" Julie asked.

"It won't be easy," Julius told her. "But trust us, we will." They shuffled back down the side of the rock and dirt canyon. Argos joined Griffus, Pertheus, and Freya. Darius walked over to Julie who was sitting with the younger warriors, Julius, Jakob, Seren, Otta, and Leyta.

"Why do you look at me like that?" Darius asked. "I am here to help. We should be friends."

"No, and I'll tell you why...one, because you're evil."

Darius opened his mouth, then shut it again.

Julie laughed at the comical display.

"I can't argue with your logic," he said.

"We are ready," Argos interrupted. His eyes drifted to the top of the ridge where Freya and her guards waited for the signal.

Julie cocked her head in curiosity.

The army of Allon was separated into three units. Griffus in full battle armor ready the catapults. Three wagons of ammunition rattled into place. Pertheus dressed in lighter more flexible clothing, as were Jakob and Leyta, moved his foot soldiers to the rear of the fortress and waited for the signal to move; and Argos, the leader of the mounted army, joined by Julius, wore uniforms for riding.

At Argos's signal, Freya raised her hands. She had taken her place on a cliff. She was surrounded by five armed warriors to keep her safe. A clouded fog encircled the tower. Under cover, Pertheus led his men across the rear bridge.

A fiery arrow informed Argos they were in position. He nodded to Griffus. Griffus raised his fist. The catapults were unleashed. They fired two at a time to give the others time to reload and continue the punishment against the high wall.

Pertheus and his men rushed through the unprotected gate and secured it from being dropped.

Julie watched the men. One warrior prayed with eyes closed, mumbling words to the Elders for protection.

Argos motioned for his men to charge. He looked at Julie. "Find Marcus." He spurred his horse.

Griffus's catapults blasted the high wall to distract the men inside the fortress. Freya's fog kept Pertheus's men hidden from archers.

Julie heard the primordial screams of dying men.

Darius smiled. "You know what's so dreadful about dying?" he asked her. "It's that you never know when it's going to happen, and you are completely on your own."

"You're a monster," Julie said. She gripped her sword, Pale Fire. The handle fit snug in her hand.

"Don't flatter me," Darius said. "He does not deserve your affection."

"What are you talking about?

"Marcus was one of the worst demons ever. You don't know him," Darius said.

"I'm afraid I know him better than you," Julie argued.

"You have never seen the real him."

Julie sneered at him. Argos and his men charge inside the gate.

Griffus ordered his men to stop. They mounted up, and Julie joined them, as did Darius, much to her chagrin.

They rode to the front gate where Pertheus, Argos, Julius, Jakob, Seren, Otta, and Leyta were already in the fray. Arrow after arrow soared by them. Julie crossed the front bridge.

Inside the fortress was a nightmare for Julie. Dead or dying men from both sides, fires roared throughout any wooden structure, the noise was deafening. If she had to draw a picture of Hell, this would have been it.

She dismounted, losing her footing on the blood-soaked ground.

Argos pointed in a direction. It was a spiraling tower. "That's the way to Marcus!"

The group surrounded her and moved toward their destination. Pertheus, Jakob, Seren, and Otta fired arrows to clear a path.

Griffus wielded his battle axe at the point of attack, while Argos and Julius flanked Julie's side. Darius held back for a moment to protect the rear of the group. Before they could make it to the tower, a large force bared down on them.

Julie watched as each one broke off to protect her, and fight off the charging warriors.

Pertheus waved Julie to follow him. Darius trailed behind them. Pertheus led her into the chamber. Five guards advanced on them. For the first time during the fighting, Julie raised her sword and killed one of the men. Julie, Pertheus, and Darius continued to move through the halls.

"Where is he?" Pertheus shouted. "We need to split up."

Julie's eyes grew large. "Okay," she agreed with hesitation. She went down a corridor to the right. Darius went left. Pertheus went straight. She turned a corner where two guards were coming out of a room. They drew their swords against her. "Please don't. I don't want to hurt you."

The two smiled at each other.

"Oh, we are going to do more than that to you," one of them said.

They started toward her.

Julie recognized the attack formation from her training, plus they were in a confined space. "Use your advantages," she repeated Marcus's teachings.

She moved past one as he tried to jab at her.

He was stretched out, and she was able to hug the wall. His partner was not.

Julie cut him across the arm. He dropped his sword. Julie picked it up. "Last warning, run!"

"Now you're dead," the armed one said.

He lunged at Julie. She twisted away.

The unarmed guard caught her by the throat. Julie rammed Pale Fire deep into his abdomen.

His partner scrambled forward. She threw the second sword at him, when he ducked to avoid it. She stabbed him in the chest.

She closed her eyes. "Oh God, what did I do?" She wiped the sweat from her face. Then opened the door they came out of, hoping Marcus was in there. He wasn't. She headed back the way she came, gingerly crossing over the two dead men. Julie ran down the hallway Pertheus went. She arrived at the bottom of a double staircase. She gasped when she saw Pertheus in the grasp of a darkly cloaked man she did not know at the top, looking over a banister.

"Julie, run!"

"Yes, Julie, run," the man said.

"Let him go," Julie yelled. She took her sword by two hands.

The man began to laugh.

"You don't know who I am," Julie said through gritted teeth.

"I think I do," he said. "You have the ego of a god, but do you have the power of one?"

"Let him go, and I'll show you," Julie said not moving, trying to control her breath.

The man moved Pertheus's head to face him. "Is this who I think it is?"

"Julie, run," Pertheus shouted one last time.

The man broke Pertheus's neck. "Now we are even." He let Pertheus's body crumble down the stairs.

"No!" Julie bellowed, sounding more resolute.

She started up the stairwell. The man pulled out his sword. It was exactly like Marcus's and her own sword. She stopped.

The cloaked figure scoffed with obvious irritation. He grinned widely; a sliver of candlelight caught a glimpse of his menacing eyes. His eyes were black holes where everything got sucked in and nothing came out alive.

Julie stared up at him from in between loose strands of her brown hair. "William?"

"Julie, the Heart, I presume," William said.

211

"Where is he?"

"I'm confused, am I just supposed to help you out of the evilness of my heart?"

"Tell me where he is, and I won't kill you," Julie said, snarling to hide her fear.

William just laughed. "Well, if you must know, he is just beyond these stairs. All you have to do is get through me."

"Fine." Julie started up the stairs. *He has the high ground, and he is a demon,* she thought as she tried to figure out how she was going to get by him.

Darius arrived. "Julie, stop!"

William leaned up from the balcony, "Darius, is that my old friend, Darius?"

Darius stepped between Julie and the staircase.

"What are you doing?" Julie asked him, her face contorted with a snarl.

"I'm keeping you alive," Darius answered.

"Now isn't that cute? First Marcus, and now you? Tell me…Julie, what type of power do you have over men?"

"William, this is between us. Leave the girl out of it," Darius yelled.

"I'm afraid you have that wrong. This is between me and the Heart. You are just in the way, like always," William said.

"I will show you who is in the way." Darius started up the steps.

"So easily fooled, Darius. I killed your mother. I turned you against Marcus, and you continued to follow me."

Darius stopped. "It was you who killed my mother?"

"Of course. Pallanex needed her dead, and I was more than happy to do it."

That made Darius sprint up the staircase.

Before Darius could reach him, William pulled hard on a cord attached to a door. The door opened and ten half men, half dogs rushed out. Their teeth razor sharp and white bore down toward Darius. He toppled over at the weight of their bodies crashing against his.

Julie went to the left set of stairs, and bounded up them as fast as she could.

William waited for her to get to the top. "I decided to wait, since you will never see another day after today."

Julie held onto Pale Fire with both hands.

"So, tell me, Heart, what powers do you have?" William asked. He tapped her sword with his. "Can you fly, can you turn invisible, can you turn into a demon like me?" William changed before her eyes, then changed back. "I think it is only fair since you know my abilities. I'm sure Marcus has told you all about me."

"Actually, he has never mentioned you," Julie said.

She swung at him. He blocked it.

"I find that hard to believe. Tell me, what would you have thought if it had been me instead of Marcus who showed up in your world?" William moved to her right and their swords clanged. "Would you have come with me?" Clang. "Would we be friends?" Clang. "Would you come to my rescue?" Clang. "Would we be lovers?"

"What!" Julie attacked him with a flurry of strikes.

"You know the old prophet, I'm sure. How does it go? Something about an ancient evil rising from the ashes of death, a ripple of time announces the Heart's birth, the Elder's gifts binding two lost worlds blah, blah, blah, get to the good stuff... The Solia Custor, chosen by the Elders is to seek out, train, and protect until the final rage. The two will fight side by side forever more – she is his betrothed."

Julie lunged at him, striking him across the arm.

William's anger spilled, healing the wound faster than she had ever seen.

"Everyone assumes I don't know who Marcus is or what he was. I'm tired of being treated like an imbecile. Now, where is he?" Julie continued her barrage. It caught William off guard. He stumbled back and leapt down the back staircase. Julie saw the door where no doubt Marcus was. She followed him and used everything Marcus had taught her. William was able to block most, but not all her attacks.

She caught him with a slice on his thigh, his shoulder, and his free forearm. She could tell he was getting frustrated since he stopped talking. Julie got careless and he hit her with a backhand that sent her sprawling to backward.

"I don't know who you are, Julie, but you are in over your head, and I am about to remove that pretty little head of yours."

"No!" Julie stuck out her hand. A force of air blew William off his feet and into a wall.

He laid stunned, then struggled to his feet, his eyes widened at her power, and he rushed away. Disappearing through the darkness.

"*There must be hidden tunnels*," Julie thought. She kept her guard up as she pushed open the door where she hoped Marcus would be. "Marcus?"

Chapter Forty-one
Seras - Julie

The room was darkened with black drapes over the windows blocking the sunlight. Julie heard a small groan. Her young eyes followed the sound to the center of the room where the large frame of Marcus was tethered to chains from the ceiling. Dark blotches of blue and purple camouflaged his back. She blinked in surprise. "Marcus...Marcus...please tell me you're alive."

He didn't say a word.

She moved to face him, horrified to see the bruising on his face and chest. Blood caked above his eyes, under his nose, and out of the corners of his mouth. He had a metal spike in each of his shoulders, another in his side, and a fourth in his thigh.

"Don't be dead, don't be dead, don't be dead," Julie repeated though she was certain Marcus was dead as she pulled each of the spikes out of his body.

"Stop," he whispered.

Julie jerked back.

"Leave me alone."

"No, if I leave you here, you'll die. I don't know if William is coming back or not."

"You have to go before he comes back. You can't face him. I'm a lost cause," he said. His words were blurred and shaky.

"Marcus, you have to be in pain," she said.

She found a chair and moved it beside him. She climbed up on it to undo his chains. Her body grazing his as she reached as high as she could to detach the looped ring.

"You should go. I can't be trusted," Marcus said.

"No, too many good men and women died to rescue you," Julie said. "Pertheus is dead."

215

Marcus let out a gasp. "I can't...be trusted. When I get mad people die."

"You're right. And it was dumb for you to come here. What were you thinking?"

She undid the rest of the chains holding him up. Marcus collapsed to the floor with a groan; arms and legs sprawled out like death.

"I'm sorry, Julie. I didn't mean to lie to you. I didn't mean to bring you here. The world is not a dark and scary place, I am."

Marcus forced himself to get to a seated position on the floor. He put his head in his hands.

"You're talking nonsense, Julie said. "I don't think you are dark and scary."

"You've never seen the real me."

"People keep telling me that. But, here's the thing. I saw you as a monster. I saw you kill people. I was scared at first...angry even. But here I am."

She could see the healing process slowly taking hold of Marcus. The bleeding had stopped, and the wounds were closing.

"You look like crap," Marcus said. His voice began to come back to normal, strong and rich.

"Well, I just helped take down a fortress and kicked William's ass in a fight. What's your excuse?" She fired back at his little joke.

"You beat William?" He looked up at her. She could tell he was impressed. "You are an amazing young woman," he said.

"I'm just a girl," she said. "Nothing special."

"No, you are much more than that."

Julie felt the blood rush to her face, but turned away as they were joined by Argos, Griffus, Julius, Jakob, Otta, Seren, and Darius.

Chapter Forty-two
Seras - Marcus

Marcus stared at his brother through the dimly lit room. "What is he doing here?" Marcus asked as he slowly started to recover. He stood looking for a weapon. "He can't be trusted. He is loyal to William."

Darius didn't speak at first, then he forced out, "Marcus, I'm--"

"Shut up!" Marcus moved to face his brother.

Julie stepped between them. "He helped us," Julie said. She put her hand on his chest. "I wouldn't have made it to you if it wasn't for him."

"I thought he was dead," Marcus growled, turning his attention to Freya.

"He was, or at least he almost was," she answered.

"We have to go," Argos said. "We have a lot to talk about, but you can explain it on the way back to Allon."

"Where is William?" Marcus asked.

His legs began to give out. Darius caught him. Julius and Jakob positioned themselves on either side of him and helped him out of the chamber.

They moved through the halls and down the stairs. Pertheus's body laid just a few steps down. Otta and Seren busied themselves wrapping him in a cloth, then Griffus flung his dead friend's body over his shoulder. At the bottom of the steps, the bodies of the half-men, half-dogs that attacked Darius lay.

"Those are what William has been working on. He used Thomen's blood and torture to turn men into these monsters," he said. He stopped. "Thomen is in one of these rooms. I killed him."

"We have to go," Argos repeated. "I will help get the dead. We need to take their bodies home. Griffus, after you take Pertheus out, destroy this place."

"There won't be a stone left standing," the burly commander said.

The group moved into the courtyard. A soldier approached Griffus and whispered in his ear. He turned to them. "Thirty men lost…thirty-one including Pertheus."

Marcus stood without help from Argos's two sons. "Thirty-one unnecessary dead. You should have left me here to die."

"We weren't going to do that, Marcus," Griffus said. "We all knew the danger. We all knew the risk. Protecting you and the Heart is our duty. We are honored to serve Tolth in this way."

"I don't understand. I guess I'll never understand," Marcus responded.

He saw Darius saying something to Julie. Marcus caught up with them. He grabbed his brother by the arm and punched him in the face. Darius fell to his back. "Stay away from her!"

"Easy there brother, I just saved your life and her's, if we're keeping count," Darius said, rubbing his chin and getting to his feet.

"Marcus, stop!" Julie reached out a hand to Darius. He waved her off. She turned to Marcus. "You should be thanking him."

"Thanking him?"

Julie turned to Darius. "Yes, thank you."

"I don't understand?" Marcus questioned her, then looked at Freya.

"I'm not surprised, brother. You were always the slow one," Darius said.

Marcus lurched forward to punch him again.

Darius held out his hands. "That's why she brought me," he answered. "I know its bit of a shock, but shouldn't you be happy I'm alive?"

Marcus stood and stared at his brother and sister.

Darius kept talking. "I admit, William tricked me. He was the one who killed Raewin."

"I know." Marcus shrugged. "William bragged about it."

"He manipulated me and made me hate you for what you did to Canis," Darius continued. "I wanted to kill you."

"I only did what the old man wanted me to do. I didn't want to do it," Marcus said.

"I now know that, too." Darius looked at Freya. "We have a lot to catch up on."

Marcus looked at her as well. "I have made a lot of mistakes, and as you can see, my friends have forgiven me even if I haven't forgiven myself. So, maybe we can forgive each other." Julie walked in front of them out of the fortress across the bridge. "It's going to take time but thank you for watching over her."

"So, she is really the Heart?"

"I hoped she wasn't for the longest time, but I'm afraid she is," Marcus answered.

"No, she is special. You should have seen her against William. She wasn't going to back down, and all she wanted to do was save you."

~ * ~

The somber army of Allon returned home after months of being gone. Marcus had tried to convince Julie to go back to Earth. "You don't need to be there. We are not coming home with good news. Good warriors died because of me, and just because Griffus said the sacrifices were worth it to protect me does not make it any easier. I cost them their lives."

Of course, Julie didn't listen. She rode back with the company. Wagons carried the dead home. Marcus and Darius spoke little. It would take time to heal their relationship.

When they entered the fortress of Allon, Julie could not help comparing it to the last time she returned from a battle. "It reminds me of when we came back after the Battle of Yellow Fields," she told Marcus as they rode together through the gates. Men and women waited to see their loved ones, hoping they weren't injured or dead. There were plenty of tearful reunions; unfortunately, there were equally many unhappy tears.

"You never get used to this," he said.

The death of Pertheus hit the leaders hard. "He was a loyal friend," Griffus said.

"He helped you save my life," Marcus said, patting the large man on the shoulder.

"He will be missed," Freya said with tears in her eyes.

Each warrior was given a proper burial in the pyre pits of Allon. They watched as the flames roared and smoke filled the air from each hole in the ground.

"I don't think I will ever be able to smile again," she whispered to Marcus.

"You have been through a lot, but you will find your smile again, you just won't be a child again," he said to her.

She walked to the spot where Callista was buried. "First soldier down," Julie said.

Marcus swallowed his thoughts. "Maybe for you, but not for me." He reflected upon the deaths. *Who was first? It had been so long it was hard for him to remember. Was it his mother, was it his father? Was it Arthur, Bones? Who, since this terrible journey began was the first soldier down? How many more would fall before it was all over?*

"I've killed people and I don't know how to feel?"

"You did what you had to do. In the heat of battle, you have to know what you are fighting for."

"Or who." He thought he heard her say.

"Huh?"

She held her tongue, but her brown eyes betrayed her.

"Here's the thing, Julie. You have to know or at least think you are doing what you are doing for the right reasons. As violent as I was, as bad or evil as I was, I never hated myself for what I did until now."

"What changed?"

"Being with William. Listening to him, remembering the old me. I hate what I was, I hate what I did. But I have to listen to what Redderick, Griffus and Pertheus kept telling me."

"What?"

"Those things that happened to me, the things I did, all led me here." He smiled. "And now I know why."

She smiled back.

"Come on, let's get out of here." The day's events left him feeling exhausted and empty. They walked back to his cabin. He started to light the Elder's symbol in the middle of his cabin to take her back to Earth.

Julie stifled a yawn. "Can we wait?"

He stopped.

"How is this going to work? I mean, you are a wanted man on Earth now. You can't really go back."

"I'll figure something out."

She sat on his bed and curled into a tight ball. "I really wanted you to give me my diploma."

"I know. I'm sorry."

Chapter Forty-three
Earth - Julie

Julie put on the required yellow gown and mortarboard.

"Just look at you," her mother said, helping Julie pin the awkward hat to her head. "Make sure you keep the tassel to the left until they tell you."

"I will, I will."

Michelle took another picture of her daughter. "Okay, we are going to go now to save seats."

Her father gently rapped on the door. "Is it okay to come in?"

"Yep, all clear."

"You look beautiful, honey," Philip said.

Julie turned and hugged him. "Thanks, Daddy."

"We have to go. We have to pick up Mom, and save seats," Michelle said.

"I'm ready to go. Just wanted to give my favorite daughter a final hug before she graduates." He gave her another hug, then they were gone.

"Meet us downstairs so we can take a few more before we leave."

"Okay, I'll be right there."

Julie finished in her bedroom and walked downstairs to meet her parents. They took more pictures on the porch, posing on the porch swing, and in the yard. Then they left to get Grandma Franklin and save seats in the Cedar Creek stadium.

After they left Julie took off the mortarboard and sat inside the Purple Jellybean. It had been a long two months since the attack on William's fortress. She returned to Earth without Marcus, but not before she fell asleep on his bed. She was confident she slept for two days before he woke her up and sent her home.

Julie's last season running track ended spectacularly. Both of her relays finished first. She won the four-hundred-meter dash, and Claire won the eight-hundred-meter run. Their forty points was enough to win the team State Title; the first time in school history. Jimmy added a first in the high jump and a second in the long jump. While atop the podium, Julie waved to her mom, dad, grandma, coaches, and friends. Through the sunny glare high up in Jesse Owens' Stadium she knew she saw Marcus. He was wearing a ball cap with the thick beard he had grown to hide his face.

The three friends celebrated with pizza and wings from Sullivan's, and they washed them down with pop. For Julie it was her first drink in two years, for Claire and Jimmy it had been four years. Both hated the taste and ordered water.

Prom was fun. She went as Jimmy and Claire's third wheel and spent the evening dancing with her teammates. Jimmy and Claire won King and Queen honors. Julie cried with Claire as she joined them after the customary dance. She was happy for her friend who had succeeded in the face of a difficult year. The trio headed to an after-prom, which Julie enjoyed more than ever. She even won a prize in the drawing for ten dollars at the Sunset Grill.

In a matter of hours, she would be saying goodbye to Cedar Creek. She drove to the high school, met Claire and Jimmy, and they lined up. *Pomp and Circumstance* played over the loudspeakers. The stadium where she and Claire spent four years cheering on the sidelines as Jimmy rushed for touchdowns was packed with family and friends. She waved at her parents and Grandma Franklin as the twelve valedictorians gave little speeches or motivational quotes. Her smile turned to tears as her mind drifted to her saying goodbye to Principal Frye; her favorite gym teacher, the grumpy Shultz with his ball cap on and a wad of something gross in his cheek and gums; her math teacher, Mrs. Larson; and her favorite history teacher and track coach, Mr. Langston. The only person missing was Mr. Campbell…he wouldn't dare try to sneak in here, would he?

The choir sang the school's alma mater. They sang the fight song. They sang a song dedicated to all the seniors. By then, Julie couldn't see through her bloodshot eyes. When it was time to stand and get her diploma from Mr. Frye, she was sure snot bubbles would make the graduation picture. Mrs. Larson gave her a tissue to clean herself up before the guidance counselor read off her name. "Julie Renee Ayers." She heard her family clap. Everything else was a blur until they moved the tassel from the left to the right, then threw them high in the air.

Afterward, her mom took pictures of Julie with all of her teachers, her grandmother, her best friends, her cheer teammates, her track teammates, and of course Claire and Jimmy.

Out of the corner of her eye she saw a familiar figure under the stadium lights, lurking in the shadows. She smiled knowing Mr. Campbell was nearby, doing what he always does supporting her and keeping her protected.

Also by the Author
at Rogue Phoenix Press

Journey to Seras
The Heart of Seras: Book One

Julie Ayers is a normal fifteen-year-old living in the quiet town of Sunset, Ohio. Her world is turned upside down by the arrival of the school's new teacher, Marcus Campbell.

Marcus Campbell has a secret. He is a warrior from a medieval dimension searching for the mythical "Heart"—a hero given to the people of Seras to rid their world of impending evil. Marcus's quest is challenged when he realizes that the "Heart" is the vibrant teenage girl. Now, against his better judgment, he must try convincing Julie to go to his world and begin preparation to face whatever evil lies ahead.

Journey to Seras is the first book in the five part The Heart of Seras fantasy series. It begins the adventures of the two unlikely heroes as they battle the dark forces of Seras.

Five are the Elders with their gifts born in the black of night.
Five are the Elder's gifts hidden to set Seras right.
Five Elders pitted beneath an angry sun.
Blood will flow. Flesh and blade become one.
The blood is given to ease time;
The breath known to free men's minds;
The bones to merge distance and space;
The body a destined warrior, the Solia Custor, out of place,
forged in battle with one true oath–
protect Tolth's final gift, the Heart of Seras, our final hope."

~Ancient Seras Prophecy

Prologue

"Why did that naked man look at me like that?" Julie Ayers thought to herself. At the time Julie was a thirteen-year old girl with vivid, curious, brown eyes the color of honey with flecks of gold, wavy brown hair, and a round face. Her friends would pick on her about how easy her creamy mocha skin easily tanned when kissed by the summer sun.

"I'm so glad we could have one day without cheerleading practice or basketball camps," Julie's mother, Michelle, had said from the front seat of her husband's newest purchase, a royal blue 1976 Chevy Nova.

"Me too," Julie answered. She nudged her older brother, Patrick, with her elbow. He was sitting quietly, listening to music through his earplugs, which annoyed Julie.

She began singing a song from the musical Oklahoma as she watched wave after wave of cornfields that stood up on both sides of the road like a wall of skinny green soldiers. Her mother joined in the show tune serenade.

"Dad!" Julie reprimanded her father when he came to a stop sign and played with the gas pedal just to hear the engine growl, distracting the mother-daughter duet.

"Phil," Julie's mother said, giving a disapproving stare.

"Sorry, I couldn't help myself," he weakly defended himself with a hint of humor.

Steam rose from the faded asphalt as the family outing continued toward the stone pebbled bridge that crossed over Cedar Creek. Cedar Creek served as the unofficial border to the western side of the town of Sunset, Ohio and wound its way behind the school that also acquired its name.

"Oh my god!" Julie screamed when a bright flash of light sent a crackle into the air directly in front of them, and the image of a naked man appeared out of nowhere on the edge of the bridge less than ten feet from the car.

Her shaken father blasted his horn as he swerved dangerously to avoid hitting the tall unkempt brown-haired man standing exposed on the side of the road. The disoriented stranger paused briefly. Julie's first thought, "Gross!" Then the unwelcomed visitor locked eyes with her, sending a wave of panic through her young body.

"What in the hell was that?" Julie's father shouted and jumped out of the driver seat.

Julie looked out of the passenger window to the tree line adjacent to the creek. The man was gone.

"He must've scrambled into woods," Phillip Ayers said, climbing back into his seat. "Is everyone all right? Julie?"

Julie refocused her attention to her father and nodded in silence. *Why did that naked man look at me like that?*

"It's okay, honey." Her mother tried to comfort her, reaching back and patting her leg. "He's gone." She turned to her husband. "Phil, we have to call the police."

"Already on it," he said, dialing his cell phone with one hand.

Julie heard her mother say, "Let's go home," through the mental fog enveloping her head. She pulled her knees to her chest and wiped the moisture from her eyes.

~ * ~

"Mom!" Julie yelled later that night after having a hideous dream.

Her mother and father burst into the room. "What's the matter, honey?" Michelle asked.

"I just had a horrible nightmare."

"It's okay, Jules," her father said in a calming manner. "You can tell me all about it."

"I was a monster!"

"A monster?"

"Yes! I was all by myself in this long hallway with torches on the walls. I heard people yelling and screaming outside. I was sweating like crazy, like I had been playing basketball all day. Then I saw a set of stairs, so I walked up to the top. There was a heavyset guy with gold-ish blonde hair. He was wearing a blue robe with green tassels and an embroidered red snake with the head of a lion across the front of his...shirt. Then he lifted up his arms to try to stop me or something."

Julie paused to make sure her dad was still paying attention. He nodded. "Dad, I was huge. I think I was a man. I was tall and had large muscles."

"I thought you said you were a monster?"

"I think I was both."

"Why?"

"I noticed I was holding a sword. It was long and had a smooth black handle. Then I saw my hands. They were hideous. They were large, hairy and it looked like I had claws. I remember thinking, 'These aren't my hands, are they?' "

"Dad, I stabbed him."

"What, why?"

"I don't know why. I couldn't control myself. He started chanting something in a language I didn't understand as I walked closer to him. That's when I saw my reflection. The guy stopped whatever he was doing. I looked into his eyes and saw myself. My eyes were red. I had a protruding mouth like a dog with pointed upper and lower teeth and some kinda rippled bone structure that went from my eyebrows over my temples and behind my ears."

"Julie, that sounds terrible."

"I know. I said to myself, 'No, I'm definitely not a man. I'm not even human.' That's when he said 'It-it is you!' like he was talking right to me."

"Right to you? I don't understand?"

"I mean it seemed like he looked right through the ugly monster and saw me and said it to me."

"That's strange. What did you do?"

"I stabbed him with the sword." Julie burst into tears and buried her head into her father's chest. "Dad, it was horrible."

He patted her head. "You've had quite a day, young lady. Try to get some rest and hopefully you'll forget all about these nightmares."

Chapter One

Two years after the naked guy in the woods and the nightmare of the man in the stairwell, the annoying clatter of an alarm clock broke the silence of Julie's sleep. "Ugh!" She slid out of bed, pulled her hair in a ponytail and shuffled down the stairs to the kitchen and the smell of bacon and eggs filling the house.

"Good morning, sunshine," her father said cheerfully.

"Hey," was Julie's short, unenthusiastic reply as she kissed him on the cheek.

"Do you want me to make you some eggs?" He smiled, waving a spatula, while putting the finishing touch on his scrambled eggs.

"No. Gross."

"You like eggs."

"Not at six o'clock in the morning," she grumbled.

"I just thought you might like to start the first day off right."

"No, thanks." Even though she had been waiting for this moment all summer, the thought of waking up early disgusted her.

"Okay," Phillip surrendered, putting his plate on the table and picking up his glasses. "What would my little girl like for her first day of high school?"

"Is there cake left?" she asked as she got herself a bowl from the cabinet and a box of cereal from the pantry closet.

"Honey, that's not…"

"Dad!"

"In the fridge," he said, swatting her playfully on the rear of her long cotton pajama bottoms with his spatula.

"Where's mom?" Julie took out a foil-wrapped plate of cake from the refrigerator.

"She's sleeping in this morning," her father frowned.

She cut a slice of chocolate cake and placed it in the middle of her cereal bowl. "Why?" she continued, while sprinkling the box of cereal over her cake. Julie finished her masterpiece by adding two scoops of sugar and filling the bowl with milk.

"Because she stayed up late last night."

"Don't tell me." Julie knew the reason why. It was easy to see the stacks of genealogy books and papers spread across the living room floor.

"You know how your mother is."

She took a seat at one end of the kitchen table, away from her father, pulled her legs up on the chair and ate the soggy cake covered in raisin bran and sugar.

"Well?" Julie interrupted the brief silence between bites, wiping milk from her chin.

"Well, what?" Phillip pushed his glasses back in place.

"Did she find anything?"

"I doubt it," he answered, taking a drink of orange juice.

"Why?"

"She would've woke me up."

"Yeah, probably." The two shared a glance in agreement.

Their quiet breakfast ended when Julie's mother came into the room. "Morning, mommy." Suddenly she sounded eight, instead of fifteen. Julie put her bowl in the sink, walked over to her mother and kissed her on the cheek.

"Hi honey," Michelle Ayers sighed with what Julie could guess as a case of early morning weariness.

Phillip turned to his wife. "What time did you come to bed?"

"Three."

"Crazy," he said.

Julie ignored her parents and went to the front door to check the weather. The sky was a crystal clear blue, the benefit of starting school in August. She closed the door and bounded upstairs to change clothes and brush her teeth.

She threw her white long sleeve shirt across the floor of her messy roomy and began looking for the perfect outfit to wear.

After settling on her outfit, Julie bolted out the room only to quickly return. "How could I forget?" She paused to kiss each of the three large posters on her bedroom walls of good looking men flexing their arms and showing off their torsos, then she was back downstairs.

"Love ya," she said, giving her parents a final kiss on the cheek. Julie skipped to the doorway where she pulled on her running shoes.

"Julie!" Phillip yelled to her. She froze playfully in motion like a statue and slowly twisted to her father.

"Have a great day," he called out, deliberately aggravating his daughter with a smile.

"Bye," Julie shouted, wrinkling her nose. She scurried out the door; not turning back, to catch the bus.

~ * ~

Once Julie was safely down the long driveway, Phillip Ayers turned to his wife. She looked like an older version of her daughter, with a more serious demeanor.

"I know," she apologized before he could get a word out. "But it feels like I am so close."

"You've been saying that for years."

"Phil, she is the first girl born in your family since God knows when. You aren't even a little curious?"

"Have I ever been?"

"No," she said.

"Don't start. I've let you drag me around the country researching her like she is some kind of circus freak."

"That's not fair."

"No, what's not fair is that you haven't enjoyed a single moment with her since she was born. We go to amusement parks. You go to libraries. We go sightseeing. You go to courthouses to check out their archive office. You nearly missed her first day of high school, Michelle."

"Phil."

"I know you're obsessed with this, but Patrick just left for college and Julie is only four years away. You have to let it go."

"I can't."

"I know, but I wish you could."

~ * ~

Julie watched her driveway disappear from the backseat of the school bus.

"Earth to Julie."

"Huh?" she snapped out of her daze to face her best friend, Claire. The two of them had been friends since third grade.

"Dude, you zoned out a little."

"Sorry about that," Julie apologized. "I just can't believe we're in high school."

"Me neither."

The bus ride was slow and tedious.

"Who starts school on a Wednesday?" Julie asked.

"Eh, is there ever a good time to start school?"

"No, probably not."

Julie looked out the window as they passed through the heart of the town, which was lined with brick streets on all four sides of the main square.

Sunset, Ohio was a traditional sleepy community, not yet big enough to be considered a town, though many called it such. A large colonial brick building sat in the center of the square and served as the public library.

A white gazebo anchored the corner nearest the police station. The police department was a four man force. Their duties consisted of writing speeding tickets, the occasional broken window, and blocking the streets during parades. "They never did find that naked guy," she mumbled.

"Huh?" Claire asked.

"I was just wondering if they ever found that guy?"

"Ha! Yeah, right." Claire joined her friend looking out the window.

On the south lawn a large water fountain cooled people off from the scorching hot days. Well groomed trees were lined every ten or fifteen meters across the plush green grass.

The corner opposite the gazebo was dedicated to war veterans. An American flag was centered between the flag of the state of Ohio, and a Prisoners of War flag. A white marble slab listed the names of former residents lost to wars long ago.

Antique shops, flea markets and the local newspaper, "The Sunset Gazette," anchored the store line of pizza parlors, insurance companies, flower shops, a small diner, and a tavern.

Doyle's Hardware took up most of one side of the street parallel from the fountain. It was the place where everyone from do-it-yourselfers to construction workers in Sunset went to get their building supplies.

"Here we go," Julie said as the bus bounced over the speed bumps placed along the winding hill to her new school building. "Are you ready?"

"Heck yea," Claire answered. "We've been waiting for this day for forever."

Julie laughed. "True!" Then her attention shifted to the school building. Cedar Creek High School looked like a castle; three stories of modern brick architecture with a stylish glass atrium at the main entrance. "Oh my goodness." She and Claire got off the bus. "Why does it look so much bigger?"

"It does, doesn't it?"

The school was clean, almost sparkling. The interior of the atrium was inviting, with marble floor tile which spelled out "Welcome to Cedar Creek" in the center.

"Welcome to Cedar Creek High School." A voice bellowed through the atrium. "I need all of you to make your way to the auditorium." Mr. Frye, the school's principal greeted them.

He and a host of teachers, councilors, and district administrators were waiting in the hallway for the new students.

Mr. Frye was of medium height with a thick head of brown hair and matching mustache. "While today is technically your first day of school, we will spend the morning talking to you about what to expect." He spoke to the students in a kind, warm voice. "The rest of the students will join us in a few hours as you take a tour of the building and get use to your new surroundings. After that, you will have shortened classes and meet your new teachers." He continued to explain the proceedings of the school year.

After the tour, the first bell rang right on schedule. Julie and Claire walked much slower than the others as they talked and made their way down the hallway. "I'm so glad our lockers are beside each other."

"Me too."

"What class do you have first?" Julie asked.

"Spanish. You?"

"History with Langston." Then the girls began to go their separate ways. "Hey."

"Yeah."

"We're freshmen!" Julie squealed.

"I know! Oh my gosh! Love you!"

"Love you too. See you at lunch."

By the time lunch came around, the other three classes had entered the building to start their day. Julie walked into the cafeteria. "*Thank God. I need a break.*" It was a large open space painted in bright pastel colors with four counters and cash registers.

"Pizza and a salad?" Claire quizzed her.

"Duh, what better way to christen a new year?"

"Well done."

"I thought so." Julie smiled and sat next to her best friend. They joined a group of three other girls. The cafeteria was filled with one-third of students from all four grades based on their schedule. "I like how we have lunch with all of the other classes."

"I'm not sure I do," Claire responded.

"Why? This is much better than middle school where we only had lunch with people in our grade."

"It's kinda scary."

"I think it's cool."

"You would."

"Okay, change of subject. Trotter is just as creepy as everybody says he is," Julie said.

"What did he do?"

"Nothing, but he wouldn't stop staring at me or Abby."

"Really?"

"Yes! And he stood way too close to all the girls."

"Why do you want to play basketball for him?"

"Because I love basketball."

"I think you're crazy."

Julie sighed. It wasn't the first time that she had been called that for wanting to play for the balding, skinny, cynical Science teacher who happened to be the girls' basketball coach. "What was Spanish like?" Julie changed the subject.

"Horrible," Claire answered.

"Great," she said sarcastically. "Why?"

"Mr. Vincent is a freaking Nazi. He came in speaking nothing but Spanish, then got mad because nobody understood him."

"Crap!"

"How was history?"

"He was cool. You'll like him."

"Isn't that him?" Claire pointed out the Social Studies teacher.

Norman Langston was in his mid-fifties with silver hair, a mustache, and glasses. He always proudly wore Ohio State University attire; today it was a scarlet polo shirt with gray etching of the word "Buckeyes" on the left breast.

"Yeah, so is Miss Slovarsky," Julie said, nodding toward a pretty, young teacher with a slight build and long straight black hair.

"Good. I have her sixth period."

Claire looked around. "Wonder why she and Langston are sitting in here?"

Julie shrugged. "They are sitting by the new teacher."

"Mr. Campbell."

"Yeah, well, we'll see what he's like eighth period."

"I was kinda looking forward to Mr. Christian—" Claire did not finish her sentence.

The entire cafeteria stopped what they were doing to check out the commotion. Two boys, both senior football players, began arguing over a girl. They got louder and started pushing each other.

Mr. Langston and the new teacher, Mr. Campbell, were the only male teachers in the cafeteria. They rapidly moved to break up the fight. Mr. Langston stepped in front one of them, a tall thick-muscled boy, and Mr. Campbell restrained the other, who was shorter and rounder.

The tall senior who was being blocked by Mr. Langston, shoved the older teacher out of the way and quickly approached the boy being calmed by Mr. Campbell. Frustrated, the boy took aim and prepared to punch the teacher. Mr. Campbell turned to face the angry teen.

In one swift motion Mr. Campbell bent his right leg to catch the bottom of a chair behind him with the heel of his foot, popping the chair in the air. He caught the chair at chest height, and rotated it towards the boy who had his fist clinched and was driving it towards Mr. Campbell's face.

The senior's knuckles struck the bottom of the hard plastic seat. A loud cracking noise filled the room. Everyone in the cafeteria watched as the boy held his right hand while screaming and crying from the pain.

"Did you see that?" Julie practically shrieked in amazement as Mr.

Langston and Mr. Campbell escorted the two boys towards the office. The tall boy did not want to go willingly, especially as Mr. Campbell tried to help him through the crowd by taking him by the arm.

"How in the world did he do that?" Claire asked, turning to her shorter friend, though neither she nor anyone else could answer the question.

Julie's schedule ended with Mr. Campbell's Freshman Composition class. "How was Science?" she started.

"You were right about Trotter. How was Spanish?"

"Terrible. I was kind of distracted though. I can't wait to hear about the lunch room fight."

"I've heard he hasn't mentioned it," a boy sitting behind them said.

"Do you blame him? He'll probably get in trouble for it," Julie answered.

"I did hear that he was called into the office," Claire mentioned.

"But he's still here," Julie said.

"He's not in here now," the boy said.

"I'm not going to ask him about it,"

"Me neither."

"I wonder what happened to Mr. Christian," Claire asked.

"I heard he got sick," Julie answered.

"I heard he lost his mind," another boy said.

"Shut up! That isn't nice," Julie responded.

"Well, it's true. He was fine one day and then, bam! He's gone," the same boy added.

Mr. Campbell walked through the door. He was a tall, athletic looking man with brown hair. He wore a royal blue dress shirt and matching tie which Julie noticed brought out the color of his blue eyes. "Hello, class. My name is Mr. Campbell."

"He seems distracted," Julie noticed.

"I guess breaking up a fight would do that."

"More like he's looking for somebody."

The two girls listened as Mr. Campbell sputtered through the class guidelines, expectations, and syllabus. When the school period bell sounded for the final time, the students filed out and Mr. Campbell began cleaning up his room from his first day on the job.

Julie made it a point to stop by the teacher, who was erasing one of the white boards in front of the classroom. "Tomorrow will be better," she assured the new instructor.

"Thank you. I certainly hope so…"

"Julie," she helped him out with her name.

"Thank you," he tried again. "I certainly hope so, Julie." He smiled.

"Okay, bye. See ya tomorrow." She skipped down the carpeted stairwell to her locker and a short time later arrived at cheerleading practice wearing shorts and a tank top.

"Okay, was it me or did it seem to be a thousand degrees out there today?" Claire asked in the locker room after practice.

"No, it wasn't just you. I thought I was going to melt."

"And of course drill sergeant wouldn't let up."

"I know, how many times can we go over the 'Hello' cheer? Seriously."

"Thank God we're not varsity. They're still out there," Julie said.

"No doubt. I really thought I wanted to be varsity until now."

"Me too."

"You should've been," Claire said.

"Not without you."

"Yeah, but you can do all the tumbling. I can't do any."

"You will. Then we can suffer together," Julie laughed.

"Hey, did you guys have Campbell after lunch?" one of the junior varsity cheerleaders asked.

"Yep!" Julie answered.

"How in the world did he do that with that chair?"

"I dunno."

"It was freaking awesome, I mean come on," another cheerleader added.

"I know." Julie animated the movement Mr. Campbell did with his leg, causing her to lose balance and tumble into Claire which caused the locker room to burst into laughter.

"It was a good thing he was in there. I think poor Mr. Langston would've gotten punched in the nose."

"Yeah, that guy was pissed."

"Do you think he's cute?" asked Claire, wiping away tears of laughter.

"Who, that senior guy?"

"No, Mr. Campbell?"

"He's like eighty years old——," Julie said, raising an eye brow to her friend.

"And?"

"Well, he's not too bad for an older guy," one girl listening in answered honestly.

"I think so too," Claire agreed. She looked at Julie, waiting for her response.

"Yeah, a little," she admitted with a grin.

"Thought so," Claire said, and with that the two walked out to meet their mothers who were waiting to pick them up alongside the curb of the locker room.

Julie climbed into her mother's minivan.

"Hi, Mommy."

"Hi, honey. How was your day?"

"It was good." Before she could continue, her mother gave her a look that Julie recognized as a signal that she wanted her daughter to put on her seatbelt. Julie quickly fastened herself in.

"So, why was it good?"

"Oh my goodness. There was a fight in the cafeteria."

"That's not good. That's awful!" Michelle exclaimed.

"I know, but the new teacher, Mr. Campbell, took care of it."

"It's a good thing he was in there."

"Yeah, it was. I think I'm gonna like him," Julie told her mother.

~ * ~

That night Julie dreamt of a raging battle.

She saw a hulking citadel soaring above rolling hills which flanked both sides of the main gate. The sound of drums echoed through the valley. Scattered within the surrounding area of the fort were deserted houses, gardens, and cattle fences. It appeared as if the residents had long abandoned their homes and farms to seek safety inside the walls of the fort.

Five large towers protruded over each of the corners of its hexagon shape. Two wooden gates resided below the tallest tower in the middle. Julie saw from a distance a steady line of archers posted high above the walls facing each open field leading to the stronghold.

At the bottom of the tall, thick gate a leather-bound man bellowed "Heave!" as seven similarly large men thrust a freshly cut tree into the frame of the fortress gate.

"Heave!" the bulky, leathered man called, again.

Splinters of timber from the battered wooden door materialized after the mighty strike. Before he could repeat his command a third time, he and his men were showered by a hailstorm of arrows which ripped through their flesh. They fell to the ground dead; their leader dropped over with a shaft through his skull.

Like in her dream two years ago, Julie could tell the body she was observing these strange sights in was not her own. *"I'm a man again."*

She was dressed in some type of black attire with black boots and form-fitting gloves which sprouted three dorsal fins from the backside of the forearm. Her long black cloak had a royal blue under cloak, and there was an outlined form of a forward-facing ram with mighty curled horns in the same royal blue on her breastplate. *"Well, at least I'm not a monster."*

Julie realized that she was riding a horse toward a solitary figure who was watching motionlessly as the surrounding army continued to try to gain entrance to the well guarded castle.

A pale white horse with crimson eyes grazed on a patch of grass several feet away.

The lone man's momentary reflection was interrupted when Julie, atop her horse, approached. He did not move or turn to greet her. She felt the weight of her body slide effortlessly from the large horse.

The man had features which looked of Asian influence with raven black hair that spread across his shoulders and halfway down the hood of his ebony cloak. He was dressed head to toe in a similar colored uniform.

However, the shroud which covered his outfit had a majestic purple under cloak instead of the blue; and an outline of a front facing bull with long protruding horns was adorned in purple on his breastplate.

Julie could hear the man talking, but she could not make out the words. The stranger turned to face her. His coal-black eyes were fierce and clever and glimmered in the sunlight as he overlooked the carnage in front of them. Then, through a venomous smile, he said something to her and laughed.

Other books by the Author
at Rogue Phoenix Press

The Elders
The Heart of Seras: Book Two

Julie Ayer's freshman year of high school ended horribly. Now Marcus Campbell must try to convince her to return to Seras to learn the secrets of Seras from the mysterious immortal, Redderick Bobo. Going back to Seras is the last thing on Julie's mind. She wants no part of Seras, or her teacher. What secrets does Redderick Bobo have to tell? Who were the Elders known as "The Five Lions of God"? Why is Julie Ayers the chosen savior of Seras?

Only returning to the dreaded dimension will answer these questions and more for Julie. Can she bring herself to forgive Marcus, and return to Seras? The future of Seras and Earth depends on it.

Revelation
The Heart of Seras: Book Three

The first half of Julie Ayers' junior year is going horribly wrong. Balancing life between Earth and Seras is taking its toll on her. She doesn't know who she can trust; her best friends are fighting, her basketball coach is harassing her, and things are about to get a lot worse. As the forces of evil in Seras strengthen their resolve against those that oppose them, Queen Pallanex moves to secure aid from distant supporters, and launches an attack on those that Marcus feels necessary to protect. William's plan begins to take shape to destroy Allon and give Pallanex power beyond Seras or Earth. As Julie already struggles to figure out the meaning behind Redderick Bobo calling her the "Betrothed", a much deadly secret is suddenly revealed that will shake her to the core.

About the Author

Joe Evener lives in Central Ohio with his wife, Bronwen. He is a graduate of The Ohio State University and Mount Vernon Nazarene University. He is a history teacher and girls' track and field coach in his hometown of Sunbury, Ohio. When Joe is not teaching, coaching, or writing he enjoys traveling and hanging out with his family, particularly his two grown sons and two grandsons.

VISIT OUR WEBSITE
FOR THE FULL INVENTORY
OF QUALITY BOOKS:
http://www.roguephoenixpress.com

Rogue Phoenix Press
Representing Excellence in Publishing

Quality trade paperbacks and downloads
in multiple formats,
in genres ranging from historical to contemporary romance, mystery
and science fiction.
Visit the website then bookmark it.
We add new titles each month!